DESCENDANT

A Starling Novel

DESCENDANT

A Starling Novel

LESLEY LIVINGSTON

HARPER TEEN

An Imprint of HarperCollins*Publishers*

HarperTeen is an imprint of HarperCollins Publishers.

Library of Congress Cataloging-in-Publication Data

Livingston, Lesley.

Descendant : a Starling novel / by Lesley Livingston. — First edition.

pages cm

Summary: After Mason crosses over into the realm of the Norse gods, Fenn descends into the underworld and races against fate to find Mason and bring her home before she can be transformed into a Valkyrie, which would set the end of the world in motion.

ISBN 978-0-06-206310-6 (hardcover bdg.)

[1. Supernatural—Fiction. 2. Mythology, Norse—Fiction. 3. End of the world—Fiction.] I. Title.

PZ7.L7613De 2013   2013000029

[Fic]—dc23   CIP

                                                                                AC

Typography by Jane Archer

13 14 15 16 17   CG/RRDH   10 9 8 7 6 5 4 3 2 1

First Edition

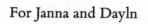

For Janna and Dayln

I

M ason . . .

The Fennrys Wolf stared up into the night as smoke and flaming debris drifted down around him, burning embers falling through the dark sky above the shattered remains of the bridge that had been called Hell Gate.

That night, the bridge had lived up to its name, in more ways than one.

Gone. She's gone. . . .

The breath heaved raggedly in and out of Fennrys's lungs, and the front of his shirt was painted crimson from the bullet wound in his shoulder. His head was beginning to fill with white noise. But all he could do was stand there, looking up. Searching in vain for the raven-haired girl who had disappeared into the night . . . across the bridge and out of the mortal realm.

It felt like she'd torn his heart out and taken it with her.

Mason . . .

The Hell Gate's entire middle section, which had once spanned New York's East River from Manhattan to Queens, was missing—the result of the massive explosion. Acrid smoke still billowed into the sky, and chunks of burning bridge lay scattered all over Wards Island. Fennrys and Rafe had only just made it down one of the Hell Gate's spindly maintenance ladders, and they could now hear the sirens screaming in the night.

In the sky overhead, lightning flashed from the dark underbellies of roiling thunderclouds. With any luck—and luck had been in drastically short supply for Fennrys so far that night—the lowering storm would at least keep the police helicopters out of the air. The last thing they needed was for a chopper searchlight to pick them out of the gloom and send NYPD SWAT teams to investigate.

As he slumped against a concrete buttress, Fennrys's gaze drifted over to where Rafe now stood hunched, breathing heavily, his hands on his knees. The ancient Egyptian god of the dead had half carried, half dragged the wounded Fennrys down off the Hell Gate, south along the shore of Wards Island, and into concealing shadows beneath the Triborough Bridge. He was justifiably winded. But at least that was the extent of *his* physical distress. Rafe walked over and knelt beside Fenn to examine his shoulder.

"Man . . ." He shook his head as he pulled the blood-soaked material to the side. "Remember when I said you looked like nine miles of bad road? You're into double digits now."

Under the circumstances, Fennrys wasn't about to argue

with him. All things considered, this night had already gone from bad to catastrophic in just a few short minutes.

What comes after catastrophic? he wondered distantly.

Not that the sensation was necessarily unfamiliar to him. He ignored it and focused, instead, on the next task. If he stopped for even a second to think about what had just happened . . . about what he'd just *lost* . . .

"The bullet is lodged in your shoulder. You know we're going to have to find a way to get that out, right?" Rafe's voice sounded very far away. "And soon. Or you'll be dead before dawn."

Somehow, Fennrys managed to force the shadow of a grin onto his face. "You're forgetting something," he said in a voice that sounded like gravel and broken glass in his own ears. "I'm already dead."

"You'll be *deader*," Rafe snapped, clearly unmoved by his companion's grim bravado. "I should know." Rafe left him there to walk the few steps to the waterline, where he peered out over the black expanse of the river. "Where *is* that damned boat?"

Boat? What boat?

Then suddenly, something shot out of the middle of the dark waters. Round and glossy black, it landed at their feet with a dull, hollow thud, scattering gravel. Rafe bent down to pick it up.

It was a motorcycle helmet.

The very same helmet Calum Aristarchos had been wearing when he and Fennrys had chased down a train on the Hell Gate Bridge. The clear plastic face shield was spiderwebbed

3

with cracks, and the left side of the helmet was broken open and streaked with rust-colored paint that looked like blood. Rafe turned it over. The nylon chin strap had been torn away on one side. His dark eyes narrowed, and he swore under his breath.

Out in the river, the ink-black water rippled and frothed. Poison-green streaks of light shimmered and writhed beneath the surface, moving toward them—fast—and a creature of nightmare rose up out of the waves.

Fenn squinted into the darkness at the monstrosity heaving its way up the rocky strip of shoreline toward them. From the waist up, the impossible creature was a naked, beautiful woman. Beautiful until the moment she smiled. As she clawed her way up out of the river, her crimson lips peeled back to reveal a mouth full of teeth like knives. From the waist down, two serpent's tails—sprouting from where her legs should have been—whipsawed across the rocks, scattering pebbles in their scaly wake. A trio of hideous creatures—Fennrys could only think of them as dog-sharks—were tethered on leashes, attached to an ornate, heavy belt that girdled her waist. They swam through the air as if it was the ocean depths, snapping their massive, malformed jaws.

Rafe stepped in front of Fennrys, putting out a hand to steady him. "Back off, Scylla," he said, his voice lowering almost to a subsonic growl. The air shuddered with the thunder of it.

Scylla? Fennrys thought. *Is that* the *Scylla? You've got to be kidding me. . . .*

He knew that the jut of land where they now stood was

part of a park called Scylla Point, named by some overly clever parks commissioner in the eighties to correspond with a children's playground in Astoria Park, directly across on the other side of the East River, named Charybdis. Fenn had always thought naming a place where kids played after a pair of hideous, man-eating monsters out of Greek mythology was in poor taste. He never figured it might also be prophetic.

New York, New York . . . it's a helluva town.

More and more lately, it seemed.

But it was his town. And Mason's. And Fennrys didn't have time for this. He needed to find her—wherever she'd gone—and get her back. That was what Rafe had promised him they would do.

"Look. We don't want any trouble," Rafe said, handing Fennrys the broken helmet and stepping between him and Scylla. "We just—"

"You've been naughty boys," the monstrosity purred, nodding at Cal's helmet. "The daughters of Nereus are very angry. You broke their favorite plaything. They sent me to punish you."

"What in hell is she talking about?" Fennrys looked down at the cracked plastic face shield. "Does she mean Calum?"

"That wasn't our fault," Rafe said, ignoring Fenn for the moment. "And the Nereids shouldn't have been messing around with that Aristarchos kid in the first place. You know that as well as I do."

"Fair game, I say. Just like your friend there." She nodded at Fennrys. "Your soon-to-be-dead friend."

Fennrys couldn't take his eyes off the battered helmet. Cal

must have ditched the bike after Fenn had made his leap from the passenger seat onto the train where Mason was being held by her brother. Fenn hadn't seen what had happened to Cal after he'd jumped. He'd assumed that the kid had been fine.

A fresh wave of pain washed over Fennrys that had nothing to do with his injuries. He hadn't wanted this. Nothing even close. Sure the kid was annoying. Arrogant, hot-tempered, way too good-looking and clearly achingly in love with Mason Starling. A rival for her affections? Sure, maybe . . . But Fenn hadn't wanted Cal hurt. Or worse.

"What happened?" he asked Rafe.

Rafe lifted a shoulder, not taking his eyes off Scylla as she circled around to block their path. "I don't know. He lost control. Not sure why. Bike pitched him into one of the girders like he'd been shot from a catapult, and he dropped like a stone into the river. Then the bridge blew all to hell."

Scylla tsk-tsked and shook a taloned finger at them.

"Naughty," she said again, and licked her lips. "I've been sent to make you pay. Blood for blood."

"I said back *off*, Scylla," Rafe snarled. "Or this won't end well."

Scylla hissed. "You may be a god, Dead Dog, but this one is merely mortal. I see how he bleeds. I can smell it. And I *will* taste his flesh."

"Only when I punch you in the mouth," Fennrys said.

Scylla's hideous grin stretched wide in anticipation.

The dog-sharks snapped viciously and strained at their spiked collars, teeth gnashing. Through a haze of pain and anger, Fennrys decided enough was enough. He stepped forward and bashed one of the slavering things over the head with Cal's helmet. He seized another by the throat and, wrapping his good arm around its head, snapped its thick, ugly neck. Scylla howled in fury as the second dog-shark dropped to the ground.

"Really not one for diplomacy, are you?" Rafe muttered. "You're gonna have to fight a sea monster now. You know that, right?"

"I was counting on it."

Enraged, Scylla dug her taloned fingers into the rock-strewn ground and dragged herself farther up the shore. She was gnashing her teeth now so violently that she drew blood from her own lips, and foaming crimson spit flew in a circle as she furiously shook her head.

Fennrys felt a familiar, savage joy welling up inside of him. *This is what I was born for.*

The fight, the kill . . . *this* was his destiny. He realized that now, beyond the shadows of unknowing that had clouded his mind for weeks. Ever since he'd returned to the mortal realm without his memories. But now that he had those back, and understood where—and from what—he had come, he felt no hesitation giving in to the red, ravaging surge of terrible, storm-bright battle madness that boiled deep within him. As he faced the monster, Fennrys's rage rose to sweep every other sensation aside except the driving need to kill.

The pain of his wounds, the pain of losing Mason Starling—the girl who had become so very precious to him in such a short time—only served to feed his fury.

"The only thing that's going to make this day any better is

ridding the world of something as ugly as you," he snarled at Scylla, and lunged for the last of her hideous pets.

He seized the thing's jaws, top and bottom, and wrenched them apart with a sickening, tearing sound. But Fennrys wasn't quite so lucky this time. The venomous spines of the thing's dorsal fins whipped around as it writhed in its death throes and slashed him across the rib cage, tearing his shirt into bloody strips. He barely felt the toxin's searing kiss. The acid-sweet seduction of his Viking rage lowered like a thick, crimson fog and he reached around to the small of his back, to where he kept a large, keenly honed dagger concealed in a sheath beneath his shirt.

He darted and feinted, but with the bullet lodged in his left shoulder, Fenn had only one fully functioning arm. His thrusts were slow and off target. Scylla's long, ropy limbs scythed through the air, and her serpent's tails carried her with ungainly swiftness. One misstep and Scylla could wrap him in her coils and pull him in tight.

Well, Fennrys thought, *why not?*

He ducked in low, darting past her grasping, claw-tipped hands . . . and stopped. Instantly, the monstrous tails whipped up and wrapped around him, drawing him close in a deadly embrace. The vise of her serpentine limbs constricted and she smiled her ghastly smile, jaws opened wide. As she did, Fennrys lunged, and—as he'd promised—punched Scylla right in the mouth, with the fist that held his dagger.

Fennrys drove the knife blade straight past her teeth, smashed through the roof of her mouth, and buried it to the hilt in the creature's vile brain. In her final convulsions, Scylla's teeth clamped down on Fenn's arm. The monster went stiff and toppled over backward, taking Fennrys with her, and the two combatants collapsed on the ground in a tangle of blood and body parts. Fennrys lay there gasping, his fist still firmly wedged inside the sea monster's mouth. After Scylla finally stopped twitching, Rafe walked over to stand by Fennrys's head, looking down.

"You killed a sea monster," Rafe said. "Now that . . . is fairly damn impressive."

Fennrys turned his head so he could look up at the ancient Egyptian werewolf death god. "*Some*thing good had to come out of this night," he said in a voice scraped thin by exhaustion.

"It was also disgusting," Rafe continued. "And brave . . . and kinda stupid."

"Uh-huh," Fenn grunted, his chest heaving.

"And you're stuck." Rafe gestured at where Fenn's limb was trapped. Scylla's teeth were angled backward like barbs. If Fennrys tried to pull his arm free, he would shred every inch of flesh from his bones. "What, exactly, are you gonna do now?"

"Dunno. Little help, maybe?"

Fenn's vision was beginning to tunnel. He hadn't, he supposed, really thought this one through completely. Rafe smiled grimly and flicked his wrist, conjuring a long, coppery-colored blade out of thin air, and raised it over Fennrys's arm.

"Right," he said, a gleam in his eye. "I guess *that's* gotta come off."

The blade slashed down and Fennrys shouted a ragged protest, bracing himself for the searing explosion of pain that would come as Rafe hacked through his arm. But the blade hit its mark less than a quarter of an inch below Fenn's trapped limb, slicing neatly through the dead Scylla's neck. Her spinal column severed, Rafe reached around behind her head and jammed his fingers into a divot beneath the skull. The creature's jaws popped open like the trunk of a car and Fennrys pulled his arm free, leaving his blade buried deep in Scylla's brain.

He staggered to his feet, right arm stinging, left arm utterly useless from the bullet wound. Funny. He'd been so busy fighting an immortal sea monster of ancient legend, he'd almost forgotten about the mere mortal who'd tried to kill him earlier that evening. He glared at the horrifying creature who now lay dead at his feet, knowing that Rory Starling was still alive.

"Immortality isn't what it used to be," Fenn muttered as his legs threatened to give out.

"It really isn't," Rafe agreed, propping Fennrys up.

In the distance, Fennrys heard the quiet coughing of a small outboard motor. He looked up to see an old, aluminum-sided fishing boat gliding out of the darkness, piloted by a spare, hunched man with coffee-brown skin and a long silver goatee, dressed in a tattered gray rain slicker. The ember on his cigarette glowed like a tiny red beacon in the gloom.

The boat bumped and grated to a halt on the rocky shingle of the beach, and with Rafe's help, Fennrys dragged himself out knee-deep into the cold, oily water.

"He's not quite dead yet," said the sailor as Fenn half fell into the boat.

"No, he's not dead—at least not *this* time—and he's not going to die, either," Rafe said irritably. "Not if I have anything to say about it."

"Goin' soft, boss?" the man asked, taking a drag on his smoke.

"Shut up, Aken." Rafe grabbed onto the prow of the little craft and heaved it back toward deeper water before throwing a leg over the side and climbing in. "This is just a cab ride tonight. Not a final journey."

"Highly irregular." The boatman shook his head, regarding Fennrys skeptically. "Can he pay?"

"This one's on me." Rafe grinned coldly. "Get us to where we're going before he dies and I'll knock a week's worth off your bar tab."

Aken brightened considerably at the offer and revved the little engine.

His bar tab, Fenn thought distantly, must have been significant.

Wonder what I'll *wind up owing when all this is over.* . . .

"Where to, boss?" Aken asked.

And then a dense, shimmering fog descended, and Fennrys's last coherent thought was a memory—the image of Mason, standing on top of the train car, her black hair spread out like wings, her sword hanging at her side, both hands reaching out to him as the brightness of the Bifrost bridge portal swallowed her in light.

Gone . . .

She was gone.

Across the bridge . . .

II

"You can't go across the bridge. Bad things will hap-
pen. Do you understand?" The words echoed in
Mason's head. Where had she heard that? When?
Bad things . . .

"Hello, Mason. Welcome to Hel."

Nightmare. I have nightmares all the time. This is just another one
of those.

Wake up, Mase. Wake the hell up!

"I'm your mother and I've been waiting for you."

And in that moment, Mason knew it was no dream.

My mother . . . ?

The dark-haired woman reached toward Mason but
stopped short of embracing her. Instead, she plucked up the
iron medallion that hung on a braided leather cord around
Mason's neck. Fenn's medallion. A talisman that he'd promised would keep her safe. Bring her luck.

Fennrys . . .

"So. He failed . . . and now you are here."

"I don't know where here is," Mason said.

I don't know who you are. . . .

"It doesn't matter. You have to leave," the woman said. "At once."

"You just said you've been waiting for me—"

"And I would have been content to wait an eternity." A humorless smile bent the corners of the woman's mouth. "Perhaps it would have been more accurate to say I have been *dreading* this moment, not waiting for it. . . ."

She dropped the medallion back onto Mason's chest. It hurt when the iron disk hit her skin—as if it weighed far more than it should have. Mason tried, unsuccessfully, not to flinch.

She felt a moaning breeze begin to stir, bringing with it a chill, dreary dampness. Stray wisps of fog rose up out of the ground and swirled all around her. As the mists thickened, Mason thought she could make out shapes, rising up out of the ground with the veil of fog. People—or the shades of them—hunched or stretched thin, they looked like ghosts. On every side, wherever Mason turned, there was nothing but a bleak, wide-open plain as far as the eye could see. She looked down at the ground beneath her and saw faces. Twisted bodies, reaching hands . . . the endless plain upon which she stood seemed as if it was composed of an infinite number of bodies all jammed together into a solid mass. The eyes of the face Mason looked at, numb with horror, seemed in that moment to look back. The ground felt to her as if it writhed ever so slightly. She felt her stomach heave.

Her left hand convulsively gripped the collar of the black

leather scabbard that hung at her side, home to her silver, swept-hilt rapier. Her right hand gripped the sword's hilt. Both her hands were slick with blood. Mason had torn the ends of her fingertips to shreds, ripping away most of her nails, escaping the confines of the trunk of her brother's car, trying to flee from him.

She still didn't even know why he'd done that.

And now she didn't know where she was.

She didn't, at that moment, care.

One moment, Mason had been standing on top of the transport compartment of her father's private train as it crossed over the Hell Gate Bridge in New York City. The next, she was standing here. In a twilight-tinged wasteland, a vast empty vista ringed with thunderclouds. It was an eerie, alien place that Mason knew instinctively was very, *very* far from home. She heard her own voice cry out, and she squeezed her eyes shut.

The brightness had swallowed Mason whole, then darkness.

Then . . . here.

"Mason! Did you hear what I said?" The words, sharp and commanding, broke her reverie. "For your own good—for the good of *all*—you must leave this place."

"I don't know how to get back," Mason answered, her voice sounding very small.

She turned to face the tall, beautiful woman cloaked in darkness who stood in front of her. Her mother. At least . . . that was who she'd said she was. Mason felt her throat closing against a hot surge of tears.

"I don't even know how I *got* here. . . ."

"*I* know how to get you home," the woman said. "I rule

here in this place, and I can help you. But you must come with me. Now."

Wait. You're my mother . . . and a queen . . . and . . .

"You want me to leave?" Mason asked. It wasn't the question she wanted to ask. But the other one stuck in her throat. *Are you my mother?*

"Your presence here is an anomaly."

An anomaly . . . that's not a very maternal thing to say to the daughter you've just met for the first time. . . .

"I don't say that to be cruel." The woman's face softened, as if she sensed Mason's thoughts. "But your presence in the Beyond Realms creates an . . . imbalance. Something that could, if you stay, cascade into something much worse. I'm sorry, but you must go back."

Her mother reached out for her arm, as if she would drag her forcibly away, and Mason stepped back. Her hand convulsed, sticky with blood, on the hilt of her sword and she almost drew the weapon Fennrys had given her as a gift.

Wait.

Fennrys . . .

He'd been there.

On . . . on the train.

The train . . .

Fennrys had been on the same train that had brought her to this place. Hadn't he? Mason squeezed her eyes shut and tried to think about exactly what had happened. But it was all so jumbled—images of blinding light and rainbows that set the sky on fire . . . a massive, eight-legged horse pulling the train . . . and a sleek black wolf that chased them across the bridge . . . and Rory, her brother.

Rory, his arm twisted, the bones shattered in a brutal fight with Fennrys.

Rory . . . with a gun. Not just *with* a gun . . . but aiming it. Pulling the trigger.

No!

Mason could see him, his face purple and distorted with rage, spittle flying from his lips and his mouth stretched wide as he howled at her and pointed the weapon.

Blood . . . oh god!

He shot Fennrys.

Mason remembered the bright-dark burst of crimson, blooming out from Fenn's shoulder. Fenn falling . . . tumbling through the air, off the back of the train . . . gone.

"NO!"

Her cry shook the air and was answered by an echoing howl of anguish that sounded as if it came from far away. All of a sudden, as if triggered by the sound, the ground beneath Mason's feet buckled and surged upward, throwing her backward and away from the dark, stern woman who stood before her. And who added her own cry of denial as a fissure opened up in the ground directly under Mason's feet and she felt herself tumbling, falling into darkness.

She skidded and bounced down a steep incline, and as she fell, she could feel arms and hands thrusting out from the rock face, fingers reaching to clasp at her hair and clothing, snatching at her limbs. It was horrifying, a nightmare, and yet Mason almost felt the urge to grab hold of those hands to keep herself from falling farther.

She could hear her own voice screaming; a sharp, shrill sound ricocheting off the side of the rocky crevasse, and—high above—she heard the frantic calls of the woman who'd called herself her mother.

Suddenly, the incline leveled sharply and Mason's feet jarred painfully against what seemed to be the rocky floor of the cavern. Shock waves rippled up her shins, and she grunted in pain as she catapulted forward, instinctively tucking into a shoulder roll to protect her head and face as she tumbled through the darkness to come, finally, to a stop against what felt like the base of a jutting outcrop of jagged stone. She lay there, panting, for a long few minutes after the sounds of her own screams and the roaring of her pulse in her ears had faded to silence.

"You can't go across the bridge. Bad things will happen. Do you understand?"

Fennrys.

He'd been the one who'd warned her with those words. Back in New York, on the train as it had thundered toward the Hell Gate Bridge. He had been trying to help her. Trying to save her—again—and all she'd been able to do was stand there, frozen in shock, as he'd gotten himself shot for his troubles. She'd just stood there, dumb. And her father's train had crossed the bridge with her on it. She'd realized in that moment that it hadn't been just any old bridge.

Bifrost.

The rainbow bridge of Norse myth. The causeway between the mortal world and the realm of the gods.

"Bad things will happen . . ."

Had she, then, crossed over to somewhere where just her

very existence spelled disaster? Squinting in the almost total darkness, Mason looked down at the ruined fencing jacket she wore. The once-bright white fabric was stained with her own blood and striped with grease from when she'd forced her way out of the trunk of her brother's Aston Martin, trying to escape both from it and from the train that had carried the sports car over the bridge. Her hands were a red disaster and her leggings were torn, more blood trickling down from a deep gash in her calf, pooling in her sneaker.

She ignored it and struggled to stretch out with her senses. At first, she thought the red-tinged glow that seemed to diffuse in the gloom was just the afterimage of blood vessels in her own eyes. But the harder she peered into the dark, the brighter the ruddy light grew until she could make out the jagged contours of the cave in which she'd found herself. Slowly, steadily, her eyes began to adjust, and the glow resolved itself into flickering torchlight. Mason could smell the thick, smoky burn of pitch, and she could hear the whisper-quiet crackle of flames. She thought she heard the rustle of movement from somewhere, and she held her breath. But the only other sound that she could positively identify was a slow, steady drip—like water from a leaky tap.

Feeling her way in the darkness, Mason stood and made tentative progress across the uneven rock floor in the direction of the sound. Water might mean a stream or a river—the possibility of a way out. But as she rounded a striated pillar of red and gray rock, she drew a breath in horror. It wasn't the dripping of *water* she'd heard.

Flanked by guttering torches set in heavy iron sconces

bolted to the rock walls, Mason saw a serpent, massive and coiled on a wide ledge, its muscled body undulating like a wave, scales rustling and shimmering with the movement. Its tail flicked restlessly back and forth as it slithered forward on the rock shelf, its evil-looking mouth opening wide. Sickly yellow venom dripped from its fangs, each droplet shattering the black-glassy surface of a dark pool below.

That was the sound Mason had heard.

What was worse . . . the next sound she heard was a soft, anguished groan.

Half-hidden by rocks that thrust up out of the ground like stout prison bars, Mason could just make out the shape of a man, lying on a bed of stone beneath the serpent's ledge, surrounded by the pool. The snake's body convulsed and propelled it forward until its head hovered directly over the place where the man lay. A single, viscous drop of poison gathered at the needle tip of one of the great snake's fangs—the one positioned above the man's face—and clung there for an infinite, torturous moment . . . before dropping, glittering like a tiny shard of broken yellow crystal, through the blood-dark air.

Mason couldn't see the man's face from where she stood, but she could certainly hear his cry of pure, piercing agony as the poison hit what was probably his cheek or forehead and he writhed and bucked, straining at the chains that bound him, wrists and ankles, to the slab. The howl of agony turned to a roaring bellow of rage, and the entire cavern shook. Yawning cracks shot up the walls on all sides, and bits of rock and dust rattled down all around Mason. It must have been the same ear-shattering cries that had caused the ground to open up beneath her feet moments earlier, sending her plunging into this horrible place.

After what seemed like forever, the wails faded once again to low moans. A last rattle of rocks cascaded down, landing right beside Mason, and she yelped and covered her head. At the noise she made, the man's groans stopped abruptly, and she could almost sense him straining to hear if there was someone there. She held her breath.

"You'd think I would have grown used to it by now." The man sighed raggedly, the breath panting in and out of his lungs.

Mason wasn't sure if he was talking to her, but then it became apparent he was.

"Here," he murmured gently, as if coaxing a frightened animal out of hiding. "Come here, child. I won't hurt you."

Mason froze.

"I promise." His hand twitched weakly, indicating the chains. "I couldn't, in any case. Even if I wanted to . . . and I assure you, I don't."

That much was obvious. The chains gave him just enough mobility to arch painfully when the poison hit his flesh. Still, Mason hesitated.

"Please." There was a note of quiet desperation in the word.

Mason frowned. He was chained. Hurt. There was nothing he could do to her in the state he was in. If he even existed at all, which she sincerely doubted.

Well . . . what the hell.

Nothing about this could possibly be real, anyway. Since the moment Rory had stuffed her into the trunk of his car, nothing Mason had experienced had made sense. It sure as hell didn't now. So either she was drugged, or dreaming—it was entirely possible she was just experiencing the most vivid night terrors she'd ever had, or she was deep in the throes of a profound psychotic episode—the kind the therapists had warned her father she might experience someday if she didn't continue on with the treatments that she'd summarily rejected at the age of ten—and it had most likely been triggered by Rory's act of unfathomable cruelty.

Or maybe, she thought, trying to muster charitable feelings toward her brother, he hadn't really meant to hurt her like that. Maybe it had all been some kind of joke that had just gotten out of hand. A stupid frat-boy stunt the jocks he'd been hanging out with lately had put him up to. She remembered that Taggert Overlea, star quarterback and egregious meathead, had been with Rory. She remembered hearing Tag make lewd comments about Heather Palmerston—Heather, who'd shown up out of nowhere to warn Mason that something bad was about to go down. Mason hoped Heather was okay.

She's probably fine, you know. None of this is actually happening.

Sure. You just keep telling yourself that.

In truth, Mason really *was* hard-pressed to delineate where reality had ended for her and unreality had swallowed her whole. Maybe the last few weeks had just finally gotten to her and she'd snapped. Maybe the whole damn day was really all one long, lavish nightmare and she hadn't even entered the fencing competition yet—and failed miserably. For a moment, she felt a bright spark of hope flare in her chest. Was it possible that there was still hope for her fencing career? Hope for her and Fennrys? Hope for her in the real world?

That's assuming he's *even real . . .*

The bright spark sputtered and threatened to go out. Mason shook her head sharply. Either way, there was *clearly* nothing the least bit real about the situation she found herself in at that very moment.

So what does it matter if you talk to this guy or not?

Mason stepped out from around the pillar that hid her from the bound man's view, and the snake hovering above his head hissed and withdrew with whiplash speed into a dark seam in the rock behind its shelf, disappearing from sight.

With the snake gone, utter stillness descended on the cavern. A fine, shimmering haze of powdery dust hung like a veil in the air, and an acrid tang drifted, foglike, stinging Mason's eyes and burning the sensitive skin of her nostrils.

The man chained to the rock was richly dressed—at least, he had been, once—but his gold-and-green tunic, edged with a wide band of elaborate, knot-work embroidery, was torn and stained with ages of filth. His breeches were tattered, his feet bare and coated with blood, dried and fresh, from having fought against his cruel restraints. His dark-blond hair had grown long, and his beard was unkempt. And yet, somehow, he still looked princely.

Mason edged toward him, between the rock pillars and across a narrow stone bridge that spanned the dark pool. Slowly, wearily, the man rolled his head in Mason's direction, just enough so that she could see one of his eyes. Sky-blue and bright in the ashen gloom, it almost seemed to glow, as if lit from within. He stared at her, unblinking, and his gaze, beneath a sheen of excruciating pain, held warmth and wisdom and—Mason got the distinct impression—a wicked sense of humor.

"Who are you?" she asked, a tremor in her voice.

"Me?" the man answered. "Oh . . . no one of consequence . . ."

"Wow," Mason said, swallowing her fear. "You must have done something pretty shitty to merit this kind of punishment, in that case."

She waited for a moment, expecting to see anger or denial or bitterness fill the stranger's expression at what she'd said. But he just continued to smile through the pain and shifted his shoulder in an approximation of a shrug. The one blue eye she could see remained fixed placidly upon her.

"Looks can be terribly deceiving," he said.

The muscles of his cheek and jaw spasmed in pain.

"Right. So . . . what *did* you do then?" she asked.

"Something pretty shitty." He chuckled. "Obviously. At least . . . there are those who clearly seem to think so."

"But *you* just said looks are deceiving."

"I said they *can* be—" His mirth collapsed into a racking coughing fit, the breath rattling in his lungs, and Mason winced in sympathy. He must have been terribly parched, lying there like that, chained in that smoky, dusty cavern for who knew how long.

When the hacking subsided and he turned his head farther to look at her, Mason had to swallow hard to keep the bile from rising in her throat. Half of the man's handsome face had been seared to a raw, blackened mess by the snake's corrosive drool. His hair and beard were singed, and she thought she could see the pale gleam of his cheekbone through the ruined flesh.

He shrugged again, seeing her reaction. "I'm sure it probably looks far worse than it feels. *Looks*, remember?"

"Deceiving," Mason said through clenched teeth. "Yeah. Right . . ."

She swallowed hard again and forced her gaze not to shift, like it had every time she'd looked at Cal. This, after all, was much, *much* worse. Mason might have unintentionally shamed Cal by the way she'd reacted to him after the attack on the school gym, when his handsome face had been slashed open by the claws of a draugr, but she wouldn't shame this man—whoever he was—by doing the same thing. She'd learned her lesson, and there would be no looking away this time. No matter how horrifying it was.

But then he did her the favor of shifting again anyway, so Mason could no longer see the terrible wound. She closed her eyes for a moment, and when she opened them again, she saw that the rich blue orb of his undamaged eye was fastened on the iron medallion around her neck.

"What's your name, child?" he asked again, in that same gentle tone.

"Mason. Mason Starling," she said, even though he still hadn't told her who he was.

"Starling . . ." He smiled as if in recollection of a pleasant memory. "Pretty birdie."

Mason snorted. "Most people think starlings are pests," she said. "They're considered an invasive species in some parts of the world."

"Ha!" The man laughed again. "I've had the very same accusations leveled at me. I prefer to think of such creatures as . . . adventurous. Survivors. Conquerors."

"Is that what you are?" Mason asked, intrigued in spite of herself. She put a hand out, gingerly touching the rusted shackle that circled around the man's wrist. The skin beneath it was raw and scored with the iron's bite. He must have torn the skin every time the serpent dripped its poison. She wondered how often that happened. It reminded her of the scars that Fennrys carried. "Is that why you're here?"

"Because I was invasive? Or because I survived? Both, I suppose." He sighed, and it was a sound that carried bone-deep, age-old weariness in it. "Why are *you* here, Mason?"

She felt a frown creasing her forehead. "I keep telling people, I don't even know where 'here' is."

"Oh. I see." The blue eye filled with understanding. Sympathy. "They really don't like to play fair."

"Who?"

"The Powers That Be." The shoulder lifted again in a shrug. "All of which is to say that isn't saying much of anything definite. The board shifts and the players come and go. All of which means, *I* don't know why you're here either, Mason. Not exactly. But I *do* know you should probably be careful while you are."

"Careful of what?"

"Everything," he said wearily. "And everyone."

"Even you?"

"Especially me. For I am the God of Lies."

III

"Y**ou're a liar and a thief."

Heather Palmerston had never heard a voice so cold sound so angry.

"Get up."

She shrank back into the farthest corner of the leather banquette seat in the opulent confines of the train car. She'd been huddled there, numb, her head hidden in the crook of her arm ever since she'd seen Calum slam into the Hell Gate Bridge and plummet over the side.

"I said . . . get *up*."

The command, issued in tones laden with heavy rage, wasn't directed at her, and Heather had never been so glad to *not* be the center of attention in her entire life. Instead, the words were aimed at Rory Starling, who lay crumpled on the expensive Persian rug, his body folded protectively around his right arm, which was bloodied and bent at an awkward angle . . . in at least *two* places. Heather could see a jagged end of bone showing through his skin, and the sight made her stomach clench. Rory's face was ashen where it wasn't mottled with red splotches or bruising. He was wild-eyed, and there was a web of pinkish foam at the corners of his open, gasping mouth. He struggled to force himself up into a sitting position, in response to the man who'd spoken.

Heather knew, even without having seen his face when he'd entered the train car, that it was Rory's father—Gunnar Starling—one of the most powerful men in New York City. Maybe even the world. With his lion's mane of silver hair and the cloaklike overcoat hanging from his broad muscled shoulders, he was unmistakable.

Outside the windows, everything was dark. Much darker than it would be if they were still outside. They were in a tunnel. Somewhere beneath Queens, she figured, from the direction they'd been traveling. She still wasn't sure exactly what had happened, beyond the fact that she had been kidnapped, along with Mason Starling—a fellow student at Gosforth who had recently become a friend—by Mason's complete jerk-ass tool of a brother, Rory, and a meathead quarterback from the Columbia U football team named Taggert Overlea.

Heather still had no idea *why* she and Mason had been kidnapped. At the moment, all she cared about was getting out of the train car alive. Because she'd gotten the distinct impression over the last hour or so that whatever it was that was going on, it went way beyond college fraternity prank territory and had crossed into deadly serious. The danger had been obvious even before Cal had . . . before he . . .

Heather covered her mouth in silent agony.

Cal's gone.

The thought made her feel like she'd been punched in the stomach. Mason, too, was gone, although whether she was alive or dead, Heather had no clue. She hoped like hell that she was okay at least. Far away from this madness and okay.

She tried to think logically through the series of events as they had happened. Heather hadn't been competing that night in the Nationals fencing trials and hadn't really felt like going. She knew Cal would be there to watch Mason compete, and every time she saw Cal those days, the experience invariably left her feeling drained and just plain weary. He seemed to actually get off on torturing himself over Mason, and now that Mason and Heather had become friends, Heather couldn't stand the drama.

So she'd actually been studying that night in the dorm common lounge, curled up in an easy chair and reading through her biology notes. The academy had felt strangely deserted, but Heather had also felt a kind of electricity in the air—like another thunderstorm was on its way. It had made her restless.

And then Gwen had shown up.

A few years older than Heather, Gwendolyn Littlefield was slight and almost elfin, a girl with spiky purple hair and a startlingly pretty face. She'd stepped furtively into the common room, her eyes wide and her pupils so dilated that Heather had wondered aloud if she was stoned or something.

Gwen assured her she was not.

Then she'd told Heather her name.

Gwen Littlefield was a notorious figure around campus. The first student—the *only* one—to ever be kicked out of Gosforth. She'd been a few years ahead of Heather, who, even though she'd heard the stories at the time, hadn't paid much attention and so would have been hard-pressed to pick Gwen out of a police lineup—even without the bright purple dye job.

The academy administration had tried to keep the matter quiet at the time, but it had been a little hard to—especially when the subject in question had run howling like a maniac through the halls of the school one day, frantically predicting the demise of the captain of the rowing team . . . who'd then drowned in an apparent tragic accident.

The very next day.

Last night, Gwen had told Heather that the rowing incident hadn't been a coincidence. Gwen could *actually* glimpse into the future. And what she'd seen . . . had been terrible.

"Why are you telling me this?" Heather had asked her. "What does this have to do with me?"

"It has very little to do with *you*," Gwen had answered. "It has everything to do with your friend Mason."

She then proceeded to tell Heather that Mason was in a world of trouble. She had wanted to warn Mason directly, but apparently, Gwen's precognitive abilities were occasionally a little hazy on details—she had no idea where to even begin to look for her. But Heather did. After a moment, the girls had decided that it would be far better, and require much less explanation as to why Gwen had suddenly reappeared, if Heather was the one to relay the warning to Mason.

And so that's what she'd done.

Heather had gone to find Mason Starling and warn her that she was in grave, possibly mortal, danger. As a by-product of Gwen Littlefield's grim prediction, Heather now found herself in that *exact* same situation. She wondered if Gwen hadn't just managed to turn her into some kind of instrument of a self-fulfilling prophecy in an attempt to avoid the very same fate: if Heather hadn't delayed Mason when she was leaving the Columbia U gym, maybe Rory and Tag wouldn't have caught up with her.

Well, it's pretty useless to speculate on that now, isn't it?

Heather *had* found Mason. She'd delayed Mason's departure by those precious few moments. And one of the end results was that the next thing Heather knew, she was waking up with a sore jaw in a cargo transport compartment, with Taggert Overlea half carrying her through to the passenger car of an opulent, obviously privately owned train. . . .

And she hadn't seen Mason again.

She'd gathered, from ensuing events, that somehow Mason had ended up on the top of one of the train cars—presumably in an attempt to escape the cruel trap her horrible brother had snared her in—and then that the guy who called himself the Fennrys Wolf and Calum Aristarchos had appeared out of nowhere on Harleys, doing their damnedest to ride to Mason's rescue. With, it became apparent, limited success. From inside the train, Heather had watched Fennrys climb from the back of the bike Cal was driving onto the train. She'd been a helpless observer, trapped behind a pane of glass as Cal's bike had wobbled treacherously and then pitched him off.

She closed her eyes at the memory of him cartwheeling

into the air . . . falling down toward the unforgiving waters of the East River far below. Just like that, in a flash, Calum was gone. And with him, Heather's broken heart.

In the wake of Cal's plunge into darkness had come a sudden, blinding brightness. It had lit up the interior of the train car like a blazing sun, rainbow colors building to coruscating whiteness. The air in the cabin had crackled with lightning-storm energy, and time had seemed to slow and stretch. . . .

Then everything went dark.

Once Heather had been able to see again, the world had returned to normalcy. The train chugged across to Long Island and down the ramp that curved away to the south. Framed by the lounge car's picture window, the elegant, sweeping bow curve of the Hell Gate Bridge grew smaller behind them.

And then, Heather recalled, *the bridge exploded.*

When the center section of the massive iron span blew apart, the train had been far enough away not to derail. The tracks had shuddered and bucked, and Heather had screamed and fallen to the floor, jarred by the shock-wave impact.

Moments later, Rory had come staggering back into the passenger compartment, beaten and bloodied, his arm a twisted wreck and his face pummeled. He'd collapsed on the floor across from Heather, whimpering in agony, as the train had shunted off a main track and entered the mouth of a tunnel, slowing to a stop in a dimly lit, rock-walled cavern somewhere beneath Queens. And only a few moments after that, the door had slid open once again, and Gunnar Starling had stepped inside.

Now Heather Palmerston—rich, privileged, beautiful,

never one to back down from anything or anybody—cowered in a corner, afraid for her life. She watched, scarcely daring to breathe, as Rory climbed awkwardly to his feet and stood swaying, his arm hanging useless, bloodied, bent in places where arms don't bend.

"What happened?" Gunnar asked, all his attention focused, for the moment, on his son. "Where is Rothgar?"

Heather wondered fleetingly what Mason's hottie older brother Roth had to do with this whole situation. As far as she knew, he wasn't on the train. She hadn't seen him anywhere and hoped, just for the sake of her own opinion of him, that he wasn't involved in this insanity.

"And where is the Fennrys Wolf?" Gunnar continued. "*Not* in Asgard, I take it."

Asgard? Heather thought, her thoughts a tangle of disbelief. *He's not serious. That's gotta be a code word or something. Or, like, the name of a nightclub. Or a high-tech business park. Or . . .*

Or was it?

Maybe when Gunnar Starling said "Asgard," he actually meant . . . Asgard.

Every year, one of the mandatory humanities courses for all students at Gosforth Academy was a comparative history of world mythologies. The faculty had always taken it seriously, which was why Heather had to repeat it in summer school when she'd blown it off in her junior year. But suddenly she was grateful that she *knew* her gods and goddesses—and the places they called home. Places like Asgard. The faint hope that Gunnar Starling was employing some kind of weird metaphor began to dissolve in her mind.

He's not. You know he's not.

But that was crazy. Wasn't it?

Crazier than storm zombies? Fighting naked guys with swords? Or any of the other bizarro stuff Mason has told you about? Maybe not so much.

She shook her head and tried to concentrate on what was being said.

"What went wrong?" Gunnar continued to pepper his battered son with questions.

"I did what *I* was supposed to," Rory sputtered in protest. "I got Mason and I brought her to the bridge. But . . . I dunno."

He shook his head, sweat beading on his brow. In the opposite corner from where Heather crouched, Tag Overlea was shifting back and forth from one foot to the other. He looked like he was just barely resisting the urge to bolt for the door.

"Roth must have screwed up," Rory mumbled. "He never showed. But that son of a bitch Fennrys turned up all on his own and"—his eyes shifted back and forth—"and he had a gun. He was going to *shoot* Mason, Dad."

Heather almost protested out loud about what a load of BS that was. According to what Mason had told Heather, and according to what Heather herself knew of the mysterious Fennrys Wolf, that was a highly unlikely possibility. Only a few days earlier, Mason had confided in Heather that she and Fennrys had been seeing each other secretly. And to say that it was going well between the two of them would have been, from what Heather had gathered, a vast understatement. It was funny, because Mason was the only person Heather had never been able to read. She'd always been able to tell when people were in love, if they'd ever been in love, if they ever would be in love, and with whom, if they'd already met. She'd never gotten a read on Mason. Or, for that matter, Fennrys. And yet, her instincts screamed to her that they *were*, 100 percent, falling in love. Fenn would never have tried to hurt her. He was the kind of guy who would have died trying to save Mason rather than see her hurt.

Died like Calum did. A jolt of pain stabbed at Heather's heart.

"The Wolf had a gun?" the elder Starling asked quietly.

Rory glanced at Tag, who was ash-gray in complexion and sweating profusely. His fists were jammed in the pockets of his letterman jacket, and he looked like he wanted to sink into the floor.

"Yeah." Rory nodded. "He did. I mean . . . I *wish* I'd had one."

"But you didn't."

"Of course not. Where would I get a gun, y'know?"

Over by the polished brass-and-mahogany bar, Tag suddenly went so shifty-eyed he looked like he might pop a vein in his forehead. *What a jackass,* Heather thought. He'd been more than happy to lob not-so-veiled threats at her—in between ogling her chest and pilfering cigars and chugging brandy straight from the bottle—less than an hour earlier. But now his bravado seemed to have evaporated into the ether. And judging from his reaction to what had just been said, Heather figured he was the one who'd supplied Rory with a firearm. She wondered what Rory had offered him in return.

"So, yeah. He had a gun, and he was threatening Mason. He would have killed her if I hadn't fought him and"—here a note of *real* pain and horror crept into Rory's voice—"look what he did to my *arm*, Dad. . . ."

Gunnar stared impassively down at the injury. Which even Heather had to admit was pretty horrific, the bones of his forearm piercing through the skin like that.

There was a feverish look in Rory's eyes as he looked from his mangled limb to his father. "But I got the gun away from him. I saved Mason, Dad. *I* saved her. Only . . . I had to knock Fennrys off the train to do it. And by that time, it was too late and the bridge was all lit up. I know you wanted him to cross over. I know. But . . . I had to save my *sister*." His voice broke plaintively on that last word.

Suddenly, the front door to the train car opened, and Heather was shocked to see Toby Fortier step through. At first she felt an initial surge of hope. Toby was one of the good guys. He was the fencing master at the academy, and even if he was kind of a drill sergeant when it came to practices, he was okay. But then she saw Toby's eyes flick in her direction . . . and slide away without even acknowledging her.

His expression was cold. Hard. Mercenary.

He turned his attention entirely on Gunnar Starling, and his attitude was almost that of a foot soldier facing a four-star general. He stood, feet apart, hands clasped behind his back, head up and shoulders back.

"Tobias?" Gunnar asked without taking his eyes off Rory, where he had sunk back down on the carpet in pain. Heather almost felt sorry for him, but then she remembered how he had come staggering back into the car after the blinding flash outside, gloating through the pain about how he'd just shot the guy who, only a few weeks earlier, had saved a handful of Gosforth students—Rory among them—from a bunch of monsters.

"Tell me, Tobias," Gunnar said. "Is that what happened?"

"How the hell would *he* know?" Rory asked.

"Because he's been on the train the entire time. In the locomotive cab."

Rory started to make strange, strangled noises. "Toby— jeezus—*you* were driving the train?"

"Toby is a trusted member of my staff," Gunnar said. "When I made arrangements for the train to be waiting for you tonight, I didn't think I needed to provide an employee manifest for you as well."

Rory lowered his eyes, only to have his gaze slide sideways. He glared in venomous trepidation at the man he'd obviously known only as the fencing master at Gosforth up until that very moment.

"Tobias," Gunnar said again. "You heard what he said about the altercation on top of the train. Is my son telling the truth?"

Toby hesitated, but it was only for a fraction of a second. Almost imperceptible. "I don't know. Sir. I was occupied with monitoring the engine as we crossed the bridge. There were . . . some strange spikes in pressure readings in some of the hydraulics systems."

Gunnar inclined his head slightly toward the other man and regarded him silently.

"I can review the digital files from the surveillance cameras mounted on the train cars if you wish."

"Do it."

"Yes, sir."

Gunnar's shoulders shifted beneath the mantle of his overcoat, and he turned back to his son. "Where's Mason now?"

"I—I don't know," Rory whimpered.

Gunnar's knuckles popped as his hands knotted into fists, and he took a step forward.

"Dude!" Tag Overlea blurted suddenly, overcome by the tension of the situation.

The football jock lurched forward, stepping half in front of Rory as if he would protect him against his father's wrath. It was, Heather thought, the single most asinine thing he could have done. But also sort of brave in the most tragically stupid kind of way. Toby's facial expression confirmed Heather's feelings about that.

"You gotta chill, man," Tag blundered on in Rory's defense. "He's totally being straight with you. I'll vouch, man. It was all that crazy Viking biker dude."

"And who are you?" Gunnar asked in a deceptively mild tone.

Tag faltered to silence, seeming to sense the perilous attention he'd just drawn down upon himself. Heather watched, stone still and not even daring to breathe, as Gunnar raised a hand and held it up, palm-out toward Tag, as if trying to sense a temperature or pressure change in the air surrounding the star quarterback. The elder Starling's gaze fastened, unblinking, on Tag's face. It seemed to Heather in that moment that Gunnar's left eye reflected the light strangely. Almost like a cat in the darkness—there was a flash of greenish-gold light that flared in a circle, and then was gone.

Gunnar's upper lip lifted in the shadow of a disgusted sneer. "Tobias," he said, "check my son's pockets, please. I'd like to know if he carries any rune gold that he might have unwisely gifted to this . . . this walking knuckle."

Without a moment's hesitation, Toby did as he was instructed, hauling Rory to his feet and patting him down. He turned out his pockets with brisk efficiency, not stopping until he got to an inner pocket of Rory's jacket, where he paused. A long moment passed, and when Toby turned around, Heather saw that he held five tiny golden objects, acorn-shaped, in the palm of his hand. They gleamed with what seemed to be their own inner light in the dim confines of the train car.

Toby stood, tense and unblinking, while Gunnar Starling plucked one of the acorns from the fencing master's palm and lifted the little golden orb up in front of his face. It seemed a bit dimmer than the others, but as he moved it closer to Tag, it seemed to flicker feebly and grow a tiny bit brighter. Tag put a hand up to his neck, where the collar of his jacket stood up, as if hiding something. Gunnar's glance flicked from the acorn, to his son, to the hapless quarterback.

"Defiled," Gunnar said in a low growl. "Debased . . ."

Heather saw the tips of his fingers grow white as he began to squeeze the acorn.

"As I suspected. You *are* a liar, my son. And a thief," Gunnar said in a chill, dead-calm voice. "And a careless one at that."

"Rory, man . . . ," Tag started to splutter. "What the hell—"

"Dad, stop. Please!"

"You need a lesson in good judgment."

The acorn glowed with a sullen, saturated light that turned bloodred.

And then it burst.

Tag clutched frantically at his neck—and then at his chest, as if his heart was suddenly about to explode from his rib cage. His mouth went wide in a silent scream, and his face turned a shade of deep purple. Heather whimpered as the blood vessels burst in the whites of his bulging eyes.

"Dad—NO!"

Rory staggered forward a step and then lurched awkwardly out of the way to avoid being crushed as Tag Overlea toppled stiffly forward, hitting the floor of the train car face-first without twitching a muscle to save himself. He bounced once and rolled over onto one side, his crimson eyes wide and staring.

He wasn't breathing.

Silence spun out from where Tag lay on the carpet, as if a kind of void was opening all around him. An emptiness that, only a moment earlier, had been filled with a life.

"Jeezus, Dad!" Rory choked out finally, through teeth clenched in pain. "What in *hell*? I poured a lot of power into that gorilla just to make him useful. Now it's gone. Wasted!"

Heather couldn't believe her ears. But then she also suspected that Rory was deathly terrified. Gunnar stared impassively down at Tag's body. His fury seemed to have dissipated, vanishing in the wake of Tag's departed life force.

"A weak, flawed tool is a reflection of the one who uses it," he said, his words void of emotion. "Remember that and we can avoid any such unpleasantness going forward." He looked back down at the fragments of golden acorn in his palm, then held out his hand for Toby to give him the rest of Rory's stolen stash. He did, and Gunnar closed his fist, shoving them into the pocket of his coat. "And I'll thank you, in the future, to leave the locked places in my study *locked* . . . for now, it is important for us to remember that we must be both united and committed beyond all other concerns to our nobler cause in this endeavor. I've placed a great deal of faith in you, Rory. And I will continue to do so, so long as you give me reason. What we are trying to do—right here, right *now*—is the most important, the highest cause you can dedicate your life to. This is something outside yourself. Do you understand?"

Rory swallowed noisily and nodded, his relief almost palpable. Heather felt the bitter taste of disgust in her mouth as she watched his gaze slide away from Tag's prone form.

"Good." Gunnar sighed gustily and ran a hand through the thick silver waves of his hair. "Maybe Rothgar can shed some light on just exactly how badly this plan of yours went awry. And who was responsible for blowing up the bridge. While we wait, I suppose I'll have to make arrangements for that to be fixed." He gestured to Rory's broken arm. "But the problem remains this: even if we can circumnavigate the destruction of the Bifrost, without the Fennrys Wolf, we still have no available means of retrieving the Odin spear."

"Which might be a moot point anyway," Toby said quietly, "without Mason to give it to."

When a spark of anger at the mention of his missing

daughter flared in Gunnar's eyes, Toby lowered his own gaze to the floor between his feet. But he didn't back off. Heather had to admire him for that. In the same position, she would have been running for the hills. She wished she was now. It had occurred to her, as Gunnar spoke, that she shouldn't be there. She shouldn't have seen Tag die. She shouldn't be hearing any of what was being discussed—even though she had less than no idea what the hell they were all talking about. She shouldn't be there. Not if Mason's father had any worries about her blabbing her story to anyone.

The logical conclusion was that Gunnar Starling wasn't worried . . . because he'd already decided Heather wouldn't be given the opportunity to blab. Just like Taggert Overlea, she wasn't going to leave that train car alive.

IV

The God of Lies closed his one good eye, and his head rolled in exhaustion on the rock slab beneath his head. "Tell me a story," he murmured.

Mason shook her head, not sure she'd heard him correctly. "I'm sorry?"

"It's been an age since I've had anyone talk to me. Just . . . talk to me, Mason Starling. Tell me a story."

"You just told me not to trust you."

"I didn't say you couldn't *talk* to me. And if I'm not the one talking, you really don't have to worry about believing anything I say, now, do you?"

She could hardly argue with that logic. And, in truth, now that the shock of finding herself where she did was wearing off, Mason was curious. If the "God of Lies" really was what he claimed to be, then she also knew *who* he was. And she thought that maybe he could help her understand what was going on. If only she could draw the truth from him.

If earning his trust—or just plain entertaining him for a few moments—could help her find out what was going on, she judged it worth a try.

"What kind of story do you want to hear?" she asked.

"Oh, anything. Tell me about . . ." He paused, his bright eye rolling as if he searched the empty air for an interesting topic. Then his gaze fell on Mason again and he continued, saying, "Tell me about the medallion you wear. Is it yours? It's a very interesting design. Unique . . ."

Mason's hand drifted up to the iron disk, and she ran her fingertips over the raised, knotted designs on its surface. "It's not mine," she said. "At least it shouldn't be. It might be . . . now." Her throat tightened. She couldn't bring herself to think of what had happened to Fennrys after Rory had shot him. Wounded him. *Just* wounded . . . it had to be. Any other possibility—she couldn't bear to even contemplate. Mason realized that she'd fallen silent and the chained man was watching her.

"Who gave it to you?" he asked.

"His name is Fenn."

The blue eye drifted closed again, and the lines of his face softened as he turned his head away from the torch burning nearest Mason. "And what kind of a person is this . . . Fenn?"

"He's perfect," Mason blurted out the word without thinking. But then she stopped, startled by her own sudden proclamation and a little embarrassed. She was pretty sure she hadn't meant to say that. At least, not out loud.

The man on the stone slab laughed softly. "Surely not."

No, he was *far* from perfect. He was damaged and fragile

and, at the same time, too strong and stubborn for his own good. He was reckless and hard-edged and quick to anger. But never at her. He had done terrible things and tried to make amends and just wound up in even worse situations because of it. He didn't play nice with others. He'd said to her on more than one occasion that he wasn't good for anything . . . except her. For Mason, he *was* perfect.

"Well, no." She could feel her cheeks warming at the thought of every imperfect thing she loved about him. "I mean . . . of *course* he's not perfect. He's just . . . Fennrys."

"Interesting name," the man said softly, his gaze drifting from her face.

"Yeah . . ." Mason cocked her head and regarded the man steadily. "He was named after a god. Well, more like a monster. You know . . . the *Fenris Wolf* . . ."

"Why would anyone name their child after a monster?"

"I don't know. Maybe because they wanted him to be strong. Protected. Maybe they didn't want anyone to mess with him. I mean . . . you tell me." She crossed her arms and waited for his response to that. When he stayed silent, she leaned forward so that he was looking up at her again. "*You* should know, right? I mean—whoever named him, they named him after one of *your* mythical monstrous brood . . . Loki."

"Ah." The corner of his mouth bent upward. "So you know me."

"I know *of* you," Mason said, doing her damnedest to keep her tone conversational. "I've read the stories. When I was little, I had them read *to* me." She shrugged. "And—in my current psychosis or dream state or pharmaceutically induced episode or whatever *this* is—I sort of recognize the trappings. The chains, the serpent . . . the super-charming demeanor."

"You flatter me," said Loki, the trickster god of the Norse, opening his eye and grinning up at her. The prank-playing, charming—yes, he was definitely that, even with only half a face—chief engineer of the eventual end of the world. The architect of Ragnarok. At least according to the myths.

"Also? The whole 'for I am the God of Lies' thing? That was kind of a tell. Although I suppose you could have been . . . y'know, *lying* about that. At any rate, whatever. It's fine. I don't believe you're real anyway," Mason said.

"Why not?" Loki asked. "Because if I was—real and here and in this place—then that would mean you're really here, too? In this place?"

"That's the thing, though—I don't think I *am*," Mason said. "I think something has happened to me. Something bad. I think . . . maybe I'm coping."

Loki laughed, and it was a warm, inviting sound. "Coping is such a passive response, Mason. If I were you, I'd take that sword you wear so well and use it to start fighting my way out of here."

Mason smiled back at him—she couldn't help herself—but she shook her head and loosened her grip on the rapier's hilt. She'd been unaware that she was holding it so tightly. "Right. Okay," she said. "And because *you've* just suggested I do that, it's highly unlikely that I will."

Loki pouted comically. "You really don't trust me."

Mason snorted. "Should I?"

"Oh, I shouldn't think so!" He rolled his head back and forth on the rough-hewn stone slab. It seemed as if the pain of his venom wounds was easing. In fact, it almost seemed as if he was healing slightly, before her eyes. "I *am* the master of lies. According to Odin's press agent, at least. Arrogant bastard, may the winds of Jotunheim frost his pasty arse and tear his soul to pieces for his infernal ravens to feast on! *My* eye grows back, you bastard!" he shouted at no one. "You hear that?"

"Wow . . ." Mason blinked at the sudden burst of cheerful acrimony. "Pissed much?"

"Have I not reason?" The chains clanked.

"I guess you do." Mason levered herself up to sit on the edge of the stone on which Loki was bound. If she was going to stay where she was, chatting amiably with a nefarious, chaos-loving ballbuster of a god, she might as well make herself comfortable.

It was funny, but something about the whole situation reminded her of the first few—entirely surreal—conversations she'd had with Fennrys. That thought, in fact *any* thought of Fenn, warmed her. Anyway, there was something about Loki she just kind of . . . liked. Found appealing. And Mason couldn't really think of anything else to do in that particular moment.

"Where's the real wolf?" she asked, a bit worried that the gigantic, god-devouring wolf—the one that, according to the myth, was supposed to be bound by unbreakable chains until Ragnarok started to roll—that Fenn had been named after might be imprisoned somewhere nearby.

"My terrible, monstrous pup?" Loki asked with a bit of a chuckle. "I can honestly say, I do not know. There was a time when I did. When I could hear his cries and whimpers as he fought against his chains and I would try to whisper soothing things for him to hear. Poor pup. I could feel his anguish in my bones. Not anymore. Perhaps I've just been here too long." He looked at Mason, his gaze piercing. "What do you think, Mason?"

"I think if you're trying to convince me to help you escape, you're the one barking up the wrong tree."

Loki laughed. "Why's that?"

Mason shook her head in bemusement. "Aren't you here because you want to destroy the world?"

"Is that what they're saying?"

"You know it is. And from where I sit, I'm guessing they're right . . . and that's still somehow on your agenda. I mean, you're pretty sanguine for a guy who's getting his face melted off on a regular basis." She noticed that, in fact, his other eye seemed to have repaired itself somewhat. It was still a milky blue and there was no pupil that she could see yet, but at least there was an eye in the socket. "Your attitude is pretty telling."

"What does it tell you?"

"That you know something." Mason shrugged. "That it's not always going to be like this for you. That you have some kind of an endgame in mind."

"Perhaps I'm just resigned to my fate."

"I don't buy that."

"Do you know that I used to have a wife—one of them,

at least—who would sit and catch the viper's poison in a bowl rather than let it drip onto my face?"

Mason let the subject change slide and went with it. She was pretty sure she wasn't going to get anything out of Loki that he didn't want to tell her. "What happened to her?"

Again the shrug. "She left. They all left. I haven't seen a single one of the Aesir in . . . oh, a while. Not really sure how long. I know that there are some who still hold on, still hang about waiting for destiny to get off its arse and get Ragnarok moving. Heimdall, for one. He's such a self-righteous . . . oh, what's the word?"

"Prick?"

"Ha!" Loki's laughter rang off the cavern walls. "I like that. I like *you*, Mason Starling."

Mason ducked her head. She didn't know how to react to a compliment from a god. It was a little awkward. Especially considering the fact that Loki was, ostensibly, evil.

"I like you too," she said, surprising herself a little with the admission. "You seem like someone who hasn't . . . uh . . ."

"Hasn't what?"

Mason's throat constricted with emotion. "Someone who hasn't given up."

He reached out with his shackled hand, and his fingers lightly circled hers. "I haven't," he said, and gently squeezed her hand.

"Then why would you count on one day breaking free of one nightmare, just so you could then go and whip up an even bigger one? What's the sense in that?"

Loki sighed and shifted. The cold stone beneath his back

must have been torturously uncomfortable. She didn't know how he could stand it. But she also stood by her observation. He didn't seem like someone who wanted to see a whole world go up in flames, just because it was supposed to happen according to some stupid prophecy.

"Mason," he said, "I bore me. Let's talk about something else."

"Okay." It was pretty clear he either couldn't or wouldn't talk about the grand mythic prophecy of Ragnarok. So she decided to change tack. She drew back her hand and hopped off the stone slab. "Can we talk about how I can get out of here?"

"Sadly, I'm of little help in that department," Loki said ruefully. "For one thing, I don't know the way. No one ever saw fit to point out the exit signs. I suppose they figured that I'm never going to get around to using them, or if I did, they didn't want to make it any easier for me."

"I guess I can kind of understand that." Mason nodded. "From their perspective, I mean."

Loki shifted his head so he was looking at her again—this time with two piercing sky-blue eyes, glittering and gemlike. Beautiful. And there was a fierce, surprising honesty in them when he said, "I didn't write the stories, Mason. I've never even *read* them. Can you believe that? I don't know what people say about me. About what I've done. What I *will* do. So I really can't say that I believe a word of it."

"What . . ." Mason was a bit speechless at his admission. She gathered her thoughts and tried again. "You don't believe that you're the reason the whole world's going to one day end in a cataclysm of ice and fire? That armies of undead and frost giants and fire demons and all kinds of other monsters— especially your 'pup,' as you call him—will wreak havoc and destruction on mankind? And that you'll do it just . . . just because it's in your nature? Because *that's* pretty much what they say about you."

Loki didn't say anything to refute that.

"Really?" Mason sighed and looked at him sideways when he remained silent. "Ya got nothin'?"

"If you already think I'm a liar and you ask me if it's the truth, are you going to believe me when I say no?" He smiled sadly. "Better to say nothing than to speak a truth that will never be believed."

There was a sudden sound, like loose pebbles rattling in the moments before a rock slide. It came from somewhere above Mason's head, and she glanced up just in time to see the cold, gleaming eyes of the snake glaring like twin spotlights down on her. And on the helpless figure of Loki, whose expression wavered between resignation and fear.

Suddenly, a surge of rage washed over Mason. The same kind of red fog that had taken hold of her when she and Fennrys had fought the draugr in a riverside café in Manhattan. Without stopping to think, she drew her rapier from its sheath and vaulted up onto the stone slab beside Loki. She shouted angrily, incoherently, at the vile creature and— attacking in the way that Fennrys had taught her to—lunged for the serpent, burying the tip of her sword in one of its hideous eyes. The snake made a furious squealing shriek—a sound like claws dragging down a chalkboard—and snapped its head back, thrashed madly as it retreated into its crevasse.

When Mason stopped screaming at the top of her lungs, she realized that Loki was laughing, the rich, delighted rolling sound that made her smile through her own blind panic and rage. She jumped back down and leaned shakily on the edge of the stone bed. Her rapier blade was sticky with greenish blood, and she used the tattered edge of Loki's cloak to carefully wipe it clean. As his laughter subsided, she shook her head, pushing the black hair from her face with one arm, and gazed down at the bound god.

"Sorry," she said, ruefully. "You'll probably have to pay for that."

"Don't apologize. That?" He nodded in the direction of the snake's hasty retreat. "That was worth the extra drop of venom she will bestow upon me next time around."

"You know . . . you're wrong about being the only one here."

"Really? Have you been making the social rounds since you arrived?"

"I met a woman."

"That sounds promising. I like women," Loki said with a lazy grin.

"She said she was my mother. Yelena Starling."

"Ah." The grin faded. "Did you believe her?"

"She also said . . . she was a queen here."

"Well. Yelena Starling is both those things. She is your mother by nature . . . and she is Hel, dark and terrible goddess, queen of Helheim, also called Hel, by *my* hand. She is very dear to me." His voice was soft and his gaze gentle as he looked at Mason. Then he looked away and said, "You have her eyes and her beauty."

"I don't understand. The myth says that Hel is your daughter."

"I told you. I haven't read the stories. Mostly because they tend to get everything wrong." He sighed, and it was a frustrated sound. "I transformed Yelena, granting her the power of Hel not long after she first came to this place. So in a way, I suppose, she is my creation. A daughter in *spirit*, if you will." He turned his grin on her. "Don't worry, Mason. I'm not your grandfather."

Mason didn't know whether to be relieved or disappointed. She wondered what it would be like to have the blood of a god running through her veins and was suddenly filled with questions. And with a longing to know just what Loki was talking about when he spoke of her mother. The woman he'd described . . . *that* sounded like the mother she would've wanted to meet. She craved to know what had transpired between them.

But suddenly, the ground began to shudder again, like it had in the moments before the crevasse had opened up and swallowed her. Loki turned his full gaze on her again, crystalline and bright blue and full of urgency. "You'll have to go now, pretty Starling. Remember everything that I have said to you."

Mason gripped the edges of the rock ledge as it heaved. "You know you haven't really said all that much, right?"

"Then it shouldn't be that hard to remember, should it?" he snapped, suddenly brusque.

Mason blinked at him, but then a lightning-like fissure appeared in the rock face opposite them—a jagged, branching crack that split the stone open and sent sharp, flinty shards flying. The stone blew apart and a gaping hole appeared. And the tall, dark-haired woman stepped through.

"Mason!" She thrust out her hand, a frantic look of panic turning the planes of her face sharp. "Daughter—come to me! You are in terrible danger!"

"Are you referring to me?" Loki drawled. "You wound me—"

"Be *silent*, deceiver!"

Mason glanced wildly back and forth between the two of them. She couldn't wrap her head around the situation—not after what Loki had just said about how much he cared for Yelena. Clearly, if the feeling had ever been mutual, it certainly wasn't now.

"Mason," her mother said again. "He is a liar. Whatever he has told you, do not believe him. He cannot help you. I can take you home. Together we can make everything right again."

"Well, if you put it that way . . ." Loki's voice was rich with casual disdain. "*Looks* like you might want to do what *she* says, pretty Starling."

Mason frowned down at the so-called trickster god and took a step back. She couldn't be at all certain, but she thought that Loki had added a strange, pointed inflection to the words "looks" and "she" that made her think he was trying to say something to her. Something else. Of course . . . did it really matter what he said to her? After all was said and done, Loki was a liar. Wasn't he?

And he wanted to destroy the world. Didn't he?

The woman lifted her hand, beckoning urgently to Mason.

No. Not "the woman," Mason chastised herself. *She's your mother. . . .*

She is Hel.

Mason glanced over her shoulder at the bound god one last time as she made her way toward where her mother stood at the foot of a path that led up into a narrow, dark-shadowed canyon. Mason hadn't even noticed the path when she'd been sitting talking to Loki—even though she'd probably been staring right at it. She got the distinct impression that nothing in this place revealed itself willingly or without reason.

The trickster god's gaze was unblinking, placid, and laser-beam focused on Mason's mother. Like a blazing blue searchlight, it raked over her from head to toe. Loki opened his mouth and looked as if he was on the verge of saying something. Mason hesitated, wondering if she should stay and hear what it was.

Yelena—Hel—saw her hesitate, and in a low voice murmured, "He lies. I'm your mother, and he lies."

Loki's gaze sharpened, and Mason knew he'd heard. But his mouth drifted closed and he lay his head back down on the stone slab, turning his face away.

Better to say nothing than to speak a truth that will never be believed.

Mason felt a sympathetic twinge, but she still turned away, back to where her mother stood, waiting. The dark stuff of Hel's cloak draped from her outstretched arm like a raven's wing, and Mason saw that beneath it she wore a long gown of sapphire blue, the color of her eyes. Hers—and her daughter's. A pouch hung from the broad, ornate belt that girdled her slender waist, and it looked as though it was made of silvery-furred sealskin. She also wore a heavy golden rope crossways over her torso, and from it a curved horn, bone-pale and chased with more gold—ornately wrought, gleaming golden filigree—hung at her hip. She looked like a queen.

And she was waiting for her only daughter to step forward into an embrace that Mason had dreamed about, but known all her life she would never experience. Her mother Yelena, beloved wife of Gunnar Starling, had died giving birth to Mason, and she'd always carried that small, secret guilt deep in her heart. She'd yearned to know the woman that her father had spoken of with such tenderness and devotion. And now, here she was, waiting for Mason to step into the circle of her arms. And so Mason left Loki behind and walked forward, determined not to look back as her mother stepped toward her and wrapped her cloak around Mason's shoulders.

She turned her back on the chained god and, following in her mother's footsteps, left him lying there alone.

V

"How long do you think he's gonna lie there feeling sorry for himself?" a voice in the darkness asked. The familiar voice was male, full of candor and a wry amusement that held hints of both concern and exasperation.

Fennrys tried to ignore it, except he couldn't. Music, coming from another room, kept him awake. Singing—a throaty, smoke-and-whiskey kind of voice—curled around Fennrys's mind and beckoned him back from the edge of the abyss. He struggled against the lure of that sound, wanting nothing more than to sink back into nothingness, where every molecule of his body didn't pulse with the kind of dull, fiery ache that seemed to eat away at his very core. More than that, he wanted to escape the pain in his head—and in his heart—that was born from the knowledge that he had failed, again. Failed to protect Mason. Failed to save her.

His facial muscles must have twitched, because the voice spoke again.

"Right, then," it said. "C'mon, Sleeping Ugly. Wakey wakey . . ."

Fennrys could feel someone nudging his foot. And he suddenly placed both of the voices he'd heard. The singer was a girl—a Siren, actually—named Chloe. The other voice, the one irritating Fennrys out from his blissful insensibility, belonged to an ex-coworker, for lack of a better term. Fennrys cracked open one eye and gazed blearily up at the young man, whose name was Maddox Whytehall, and who used to be one of Fenn's fellow Janus Guards. There had been thirteen of them once, guardians of the gateway between the mortal realm and the Kingdoms of Faerie. Fennrys saw that Maddox still wore the iron medallion—the Janus Guard badge of office, similar to Fenn's own but with symbols unique to him—around his neck.

Fennrys's medallion had disappeared along with Mason Starling when he'd lost her on the Bifrost. He heard himself groan in pain at the thought.

"There he is!" Maddox said cheerfully. "Just in time for the finale . . ."

He waved a hand, and Fennrys opened his other eye to see someone else standing beside him where he lay, shirtless, on what seemed to be a banquet table in a low-lit room— apparently the unused back room of a club or a restaurant or something, judging from the stacked chairs and table linens and shelves lined with red glass candleholders and columns of dinner plates. The person standing there, tall and rather homely featured, was one of the Fair Folk. Fennrys recognized him instantly.

Webber was one of the *Ghillie Dhu*, a race of Fae with certain uncanny abilities. "Webber" wasn't his real name. Rather, he was nicknamed for the iridescent membranes that stretched between the long fingers of his hands. Hands that, at that very moment, he had pressed to the wound on Fennrys's shoulder. The blood flow had slowed to a dark, sullen trickle thanks to Webber's healing magick.

Fennrys rolled his head to the side and watched with detached fascination, as a small crumpled ball of dull gray metal rose up out of his shoulder, with a small, sucking *pop* sound. It passed between the tips of Webber's fingers, hovered in the air for a moment, and then, with a disdainful glance from him, it vaporized with a flash and a tiny puff of acrid smoke.

"Ta-da!" Maddox enthused with a grin.

"Humans and their nasty little toys," Webber muttered, his goatish face drawn with disgust. "Barbaric. That's the last of the damage taken care of. Couldn't do much about Scylla's sea-dog venom, but that'll probably just give him a taste like cilantro in his mouth for a few hours. Horrible, sure, but no real danger of expiring from it."

He glanced down at Fennrys and smiled. Fenn noticed that there was a hint of wariness—or perhaps, worry—in the expression. But the healer-Fae just nodded briskly, and with another pass of those long, webbed hands, a wave of numbness washed over Fennrys's wounds, dulling the pain enough for him to try to sit up.

"Oh, good," Rafe said drily from where he stood over by a red velvet curtain that hung in a doorway. "I'd hate for you to be the first person to ever actually expire in my club."

Fennrys glanced around the room. "This is your place?" he asked.

Rafe nodded. "Welcome to the Obelisk." He raised an eyebrow and looked over at the healer Fae. "You sure he's not going to die? He sure looks like he is."

"No, no," Webber said, dusting his palms together. "Everything should be right as rain now. Or near enough, at least, for him to go out and try to get himself killed again . . ."

"What happened?" Fennrys sat up slowly and swung his legs over the side of the table he'd been lying on. He ran a hand over his face. His brain felt cottony, his thoughts unfocused. And, yeah—his mouth tasted like he'd been eating at a cheap Mexican restaurant.

"You got shot and fell off a train," Maddox cheerfully enlightened him as he held out a hand to help Fennrys stand. "Then the bridge you were on exploded. Then you fought a sea monster. As far as I understand it, that is."

"Right . . ." Fennrys nodded stiffly. That account seemed to correlate with his own impressions of the night's events. And with his various aches and pains. He groaned and rolled his uninjured shoulder. He still wore his jeans and boots, but they'd obviously had to cut the shirt off him so that Webber could do his work.

"Where's Roth Starling?" he asked, remembering suddenly that he hadn't seen Mason's older brother since the moments before the bridge explosion. He wondered what had happened to him—whether he was okay, or had suffered a fate similar to Cal Aristarchos. He hoped it was the former. He knew how dearly Mason loved Roth.

Rafe put his glass back down on the bar. "After the Hell Gate exploded, he took off to go see if he could find his father and do damage control. The old man is going to be wanting to know just exactly what happened to his little girl, and why his bridge to Asgard suddenly vaporized."

"So I'm guessing we have no idea who would've wanted the bridge destroyed."

"Not a clue." The ancient god shook his head. "Well . . . aside from everyone who knew that it was actually a secret gateway to another realm—and who didn't necessarily want anyone else using it to go there. I guess."

"Wouldn't it have made more sense, in that case, to blow it up *before* anyone decided to use it as Bifrost?"

Maddox and Rafe exchanged shrugs.

"Right." Fennrys eased himself off the edge of the table and stood.

"Where are you going?"

"I have to find Mason."

Rafe just raised an eyebrow at him as he wavered a bit on his feet.

"Wait . . ." Maddox reached behind him and retrieved something from a sideboard that he handed to Fennrys. It was a knife. More like a short sword, really. The hilt was plain but with a good strong grip and, knowing Maddox, the blade was doubtless sharp enough to shave with. It was housed in a sturdy leather sheath that the wearer could attach to a belt

and tie down to their leg for ease of movement if necessary—
which Fennrys proceeded to do. "Thought you might need a
loaner. Rafe told me you left your standby buried hilt-deep in
monster brains."

"Yeah. I did," Fennrys grunted as he tied the thong securely
above his knee. "I liked that knife, too." He checked the hang
of the sheath, making sure the knife was secure but ready to
draw. "What are you doing here, Maddox?"

"Kind of a lucky coincidence, really." The other Janus
Guard shrugged. "Chloe's been singing in the club, and I
come to listen. When Rafe dragged your sorry carcass in
tonight, he asked if I could find someone to get you fixed up.
So I went down to the reservoir—the Faerie sanctuary in the
park—and found Webber."

"Thanks." Fennrys nodded, grateful and a little surprised.
He and Maddox had never been close. But then, Fennrys had
never been close with any of the Janus Guards. "Nice to see
you again, Madd."

"Yeah . . . you, too." The tall, sandy-haired young man
with the open, trustworthy face grinned. "Um. *Surprising*,
y'know . . . what with you being dead an' all. But nice."

Fennrys noticed that Maddox was staring at the rapidly
healing, but still bright-pink scar that marked the bullet's
point of entry into Fenn's shoulder. He stood still as Madd's
professionally appraising gaze traveled over the puncture
marks from Scylla's teeth. Then over the bruises and various
abrasions mapping Fenn's torso, most acquired from his fall
off the train car. Maddox winced a bit with the noting of each
injury, but his eyes narrowed and his brows drew together

when he noticed the scars, both reasonably fresh and time-worn, that circled his wrists.

"So, boyo . . ." The Janus Guard shook his head. "Had a few adventures in your time away, I see."

"Could say that, I suppose," Fennrys muttered.

"You've never done anything by half measures, have you?"

Fennrys sighed and offered up a weary, watery grin. "If I'd ever been given the opportunity to? I might have. But I sort of doubt it."

"True enough." Maddox laughed.

A moment of silence stretched out between the two, and then Fennrys asked, "How is . . . everyone?"

Maddox gazed at him steadily and said, "Everyone is fine. Happy. Busy. Most of them are back in the Otherworld at the moment. Strengthening defenses."

Fennrys frowned. "Why would they need to do that?"

"Because of the rift that's opened up between the realms. There've been . . . incursions." Maddox shrugged. "Remember North Brother Island?"

How could Fennrys forget? It was the place he'd died. A forsaken lump of rock that had once jutted out of the East River—in plain sight of the Hell Gate Bridge, in fact—but had been transformed into a portal, a gateway between realms, by a mad Faerie king. A king Fennrys had helped . . . and then helped kill. "I thought we left a hole where that island used to be."

"We did," Maddox said drily. "It grew back. And it's proving to be a nexus of dangerous magick."

Fennrys raised an eyebrow at him.

"Aw, hell. Don't ask me for specifics." Maddox put up a hand. "That's all I know. Me and a few of the others, we've stayed Hereside. But Faerie is shutting itself off from the mortal realm for the time being. Just in case."

"In case of what?"

"In case the mortal realm . . . ends."

"Oh, come *on*." Fennrys snorted. "How likely do you think that is?"

"You tell me."

Fennrys didn't really have anything to say to that. For all he knew, yeah—it was pretty likely. He didn't really care. Even if the sky fell or the seas boiled, there was only one thing on his mind. And that was finding Mason and bringing her home.

"Now that I have a weapon," Fenn said, grimacing, "anybody got an extra shirt? I don't want to catch my death. Again."

Rafe snorted and left his position by the curtained doorway. He walked over to a cabinet in the wall that held an assortment of what looked like promotional T-shirts for various brands of beer and jazz bands. He pulled out a black one with a Blue Moon beer logo on the back side and tossed it over to Fennrys. Fenn remembered how Mason had once posited a theory that he was a werewolf—and how her theory was based partly on the fact that he had expressed a fondness for that particular brand of beverage. That was in the days before they had met Rafe, who was really Anubis, and *really* a werewolf. It seemed like a lifetime ago. It had only been a few days.

Fennrys nodded his thanks to the Egyptian deity and pulled the shirt on over his head. His shoulder pained him only slightly as he tugged the shirt down. Webber had done good work.

Suddenly, there was a low, sonorous rumbling that came from somewhere deep beneath them. Deeper than the subway tunnels. *Much* deeper. The overhead light fixtures in the club began to sway, and an entire stack of plates began to clatter and shimmy, rattling toward the edge of the shelf, where they toppled off and smashed on the floor with an earsplitting crash. The floor of the restaurant felt as if it was alive—a bucking, writhing, broad-backed creature trying to shake them off. From out in the main room of the jazz club, the sounds of the band tangled madly, stuttering to a discordant halt, and some of the patrons began to scream and shout in alarm.

The dim overhead lights winked out completely, and aside from the candles on the tables, the whole club was plunged into darkness. It lasted for only a moment, and then the rumbling stopped and the lights sputtered reluctantly back to life. In the glow from the wall sconces, Fennrys noticed that Webber wore a deeply worried expression on his long face. His too-large eyes stared, unblinking, at Fennrys.

"You're a pre-cog," Fenn said. "I remember you telling me that long ago. You can see the future. What do you see?"

Webber held up one long hand. "I catch . . . glimpses. Mostly by accident. At least, I used to, but everything is so in flux right now that even if I wanted to I sincerely doubt I'd be able to tell you much of anything about what's going to happen."

"Really? Then why is it that every time you think I'm not looking, you're staring at me like I'm a rabid dog that should've been put down?" Fennrys asked. "Rather than patched up and let back out of his cage."

"Hey . . . I have nothing personal against you," Webber said. "In fact, I happen to think that what you did—with the Valkyrie and all, saving Herne's life and sacrificing your own—that was commendable."

"But now you're wishing I'd just stayed dead after the fact, right?"

Webber sighed and his tangled brows knit together in a fierce frown. "I hate prophecy. *Hate* it. Prophecies never come true in the way people expect they will, and the minute anyone hears one, they start running around like idiots, doing whatever they can to either make something happen or keep it from happening. And it invariably has exactly the opposite effect from what they're trying to achieve. It's terribly frustrating. That's why I try so hard *not* to see the future. Any of it. And I don't tell people what I see about them when I do."

"No exceptions?"

Webber was quiet for a long moment. Then he shook his head. "I don't have to make an exception for you, Fennrys Wolf. I don't *see* you in the future."

VI

The cloak her mother wrapped her in was heavy and thick, but Mason still couldn't stop shivering. There was no warmth emanating from Hel as she led Mason in a direction only she could discern. There was a horrifying sameness to the landscape, but it seemed as if her mother knew exactly which way to go, and so Mason stumbled blindly along at her side for what seemed like hours.

Eventually, Mason noticed that the underground landscape had begun to alter. Subtly at first—almost in the way a scene in one of her dreams would shift—and then seemingly all at once. The craggy, jagged rocks had given way, abruptly, to a winding, unencumbered path and a vast, starry blackness that stretched above their heads—although Mason was positive they had never left the cavern. Sheer, mountainous cliffs rose on one side of the path and dropped off into endless chasms on the other. Mason's footsteps began to falter as weariness threatened to finally overtake her, but her mother urged her on with a tightened grip on her aching shoulders. Deep purple shadows seamed the soaring rock faces, and Mason was almost certain she could feel eyes on her, peering out from the dark fissures.

She halted in her tracks, tired of not knowing what was going on. Mother or no mother, she was not going to meekly follow this stern, dark woman up a mountain without knowing what was waiting for her once they got to the top. Her mother's cloak fell from her shoulders as she kept moving past Mason up the path.

"Tell me where we're going," Mason said.

Her mother turned and cast her an unblinking stare.

"Asgard," Hel said finally, after a long pause. "To the great hall of Valhalla. There we will find the spear of Odin."

"Why?"

"Because the Bifrost has been shattered, and you need a way to get home."

"And . . . a *spear* can do that?"

"A magick spear, yes," Hel answered drily in the face of Mason's skepticism. "The Odin spear can do a lot of things. Traveling between the realms is one of them. Now. Do you want to go home?"

More than anything, Mason thought, and was almost shocked by how desperately she wanted to leave the dark woman at her side behind. What was wrong with her? She'd wanted all her life to meet her mother. So why did she react to her now as if she was a complete stranger—and a dangerous one at that?

You should be ashamed of yourself, she thought.

Her mother was dead. Because of her. Who knew what

kinds of torments she'd endured in this place? Mason took a deep breath and tried to find a spark of compassion somewhere inside herself. After a long moment, she found it. But that was only because she'd thought fleetingly of her father. Suddenly, she could imagine what the look on Gunnar Starling's face would be if she could somehow manage to find a way to bring his beloved Yelena back to him.

"Will . . . you be coming with me?" Mason asked haltingly, a pang of hopeful longing in her chest. But it was a faint hope—instantly quashed by her mother's flat response.

"I cannot," she said. "I am Hel. My place is here."

"Right." Mason turned away, brutally shoving aside thoughts of her father's happiness. Her mother wasn't her mother anymore. Her mother was Hel, and a goddess. That was what Loki had said, too. But Mason still didn't understand it. "And that happened . . . *how* exactly?"

Hel sighed. "My daughter is full of questions, I see. I was not always as I am now. Not even here. There was a time when I was nothing but a shade in this place. Like all the rest. But I grew stronger." She turned and placed one cool, long-fingered hand on Mason's cheek. "Oh, Mason. How can I make you understand this? Everything I've done, I've done for the best. I only wanted to find a way, somehow, to make *you* safe in the world."

"You sound as if you made a choice to leave me there."

"A choice. A sacrifice . . ." Hel seemed disinclined to elaborate and turned back to the path. She increased her pace up the winding way that led to the steep side of the craggy rock face in front of them. "When Loki offered power, I took it—took up the mantle of the goddess Hel—for *you*."

"And why, then, are you in such a rush to get me out of here again?"

"Because you shouldn't be here. You are a disruption. An imbalance. Anything that introduces an element of chaos into the delicate matrix of the realms of the gods is the province of those like Loki." She frowned, as if disturbed by the very thought. "You could become an unwitting tool that he could use to bring about a terrible fate. It's not that I *don't* want you here, Mason. It's that I *can't* allow you to stay. Do you understand?"

She did. And she was trying desperately not to take it personally. "Okay . . ." She shrugged. "So we get to Valhalla and find this spear. And then you can get rid of me and carry on being a goddess. That's great."

"It's not like—"

"Whatever." Mason ignored her mother's protest. "Look. I'm not stupid, and I've read enough to know that it's never that easy. You don't just walk into a magickal land and fetch a mystical object and walk back out again unchallenged. There's always something standing by that wants to eat your face or rip your arms off or turn you into a newt." Mason's hand dropped to rest on the hilt of her sword. "So what's it going to be? Because I'm not going anywhere until I know what's waiting there to greet me with a big ugly hug."

Hel's spine was stiff with disapproval. It was abundantly clear that she wasn't used to being challenged. Her deep sapphire eyes flashed dangerously for an instant. But then she seemed to pause, to take a breath—although Mason hadn't

been able to discern whether her mother actually *did* that—
and her mouth bent into a soft, gentle smile. The expression
changed her, and Mason felt suddenly as if the sun had broken through the bleak, ashen clouds overhead and poured
its warmth down upon her. For a moment, she wavered and
almost gave in to the desire to follow her mother anywhere.
But she wrapped her hand tightly around the hilt of her
rapier—so tightly that the coiled silver wire bit into her palm,
and the pain brought a fresh welling of tears to her eyes and
kept her focused. She saw her mother's glance flick down to
the sword. She stared at the elegant, silvery weapon for a long
moment, and then her eyes shifted back up to Mason's face.

"I'm sorry," she said, and her voice was actually soothing
for the first time. "My dear girl. I know this isn't easy for you.
The truth of the matter is this: You are right. It never is easy.
And there was a time when you would have had to fight your
way through hordes of draugr just to even set foot on the path
that leads to Asgard."

The word "draugr" sent a cold wave of fear washing over
Mason. Those were the gray-skinned monstrosities that had
attacked her and Fennrys twice in New York City. And she
could wave her bravado flag all she wanted, but if it came to
facing down those things again, Mason knew she couldn't
do it.

Her mother must have seen the fear in her eyes. She put
a hand on Mason's shoulder. "That isn't going to happen.
Valhalla is . . . not the same as it once was. The great sadness of
it is that it's just not a place worth fighting to get to anymore.
You'll see what I mean."

"Oh."

"I'm sorry to disappoint."

"That's okay." Mason looked down at her tattered fencing whites and then back up at her mother, trying her hardest to muster a smile. "I'm not really dressed for a great hall, anyway. . . ."

Hel reached out with her other hand so that she held Mason by both shoulders. Her grip was firm, but surprisingly gentle, and Mason felt an electric tingling running all over her body. Dark, sparkling energy engulfed her in a wave. After a moment, the sensation faded and her mother lifted away her hands, her fingers combing through Mason's suddenly shining, tangle-free hair as she did. It fell in a silken curtain that Mason could see in her peripheral vision on either side of her face. In the weird, stormy light, it looked almost as if the dark fall of strands was shot through with indigo highlights. When Mason looked down, she saw that her destroyed fencing whites were gone. Instead, she found herself wearing her favorite pair of dark jeans and boots and the sleek, shimmery top that she'd been wearing the last time she'd gone over to Fennrys's for an evening of surreptitious swordplay and moonlit strolling through the after-hours High Line park in Manhattan.

Thinking about that moment now, Mason understood why her mother had chosen those clothes. Because what she'd been wearing when Fennrys had looked at her the way he had that night really had made her feel like a princess. "Dressed for a great hall," like she'd said . . . Her black tooled-leather baldric—the gift Fenn had given her to go with the silver, swept-hilt rapier—still hung across her body, the blue jewel in the silver buckle winking at her. She lifted a hand to the buckle and saw that her hands, torn and bloodied from escaping Rory's car, were whole again; her long, pale fingers clean and unmarked, her nails unbroken.

Mason felt the tightness in her chest loosen a little.

"Now," Hel said quietly. "Will you come with me?" She gestured back toward the path.

Mason nodded, and they began to climb once more, up toward Valhalla, the home of her ancestors' gods.

They reached another bend in the path, and the ground beneath Mason's feet shuddered—the movement coinciding with another now-familiar distant wail of pain. Loki. Mason remembered reading in her myth classes that the ancient Norse had used the bound god's convulsions deep below the earth as an explanation for the cause of earthquakes. It didn't seem like such a far-fetched theory to her anymore.

"Just how often does he get subjected to the snake spit?" she asked her mother as they stepped out of the mouth of the cavern they'd been traveling up through.

The ghost of a frown swept over Hel's face. Shadows stirred in her deep blue gaze, and Mason tried to read what she was thinking. It was impossible. "I know it's hard for you to understand what goes on here, Mason. It was hard, at first, for me too. But there is a very good reason that monster is kept in the state he's in."

"Imprisoned and tortured? You're okay with that?"

"Imprisoned, yes. Absolutely." Hel's voice was firm. "And as for what you call torture . . . I know it seems cruel, but it keeps Loki weak. Distracted. The pain directs his energies elsewhere, energies that otherwise would be wholly dedicated to finding an avenue of escape. That cannot happen." Hel turned and lifted a hand, laying it gently on Mason's cheek. "I so loved the world when I walked upon it. I would do anything to preserve it. Even if it means keeping that treacherous beast chained and hurting in the darkness. Even if it means sending you back into the world . . . when all I want to do is keep you by my side and never let you go again."

The warmth of her mother's sad smile almost made up for the fact that her hand, where it lay along Mason's cheek, was ice-cold.

"But," she said, "here we are."

She turned and led Mason around a last sharp bend of the cavern path that led to where an arching hole in the mountain opened up onto a wide rock shelf. Hel gestured Mason forward and she stepped through into the open air and marveled at the vista that spread before her. It was the most breathtaking landscape she had ever seen. In the far distance, a range of high, sharp-peaked mountains rose, purple in the fading light of what seemed to Mason like late afternoon, although she couldn't see the sun and didn't know exactly where the light was coming from. Snowcaps shimmered silvery white on top while below, situated at the center of a lush green vale several miles wide, the golden roofs of a cluster of buildings surrounded by a high, palisaded wall sparked blinding fire. The largest structure of all was a huge, long hall, with a roof tiled with what looked like thousands of gold and silver scales—warriors' shields—and its gables curved upward like the fore and aft of a great dragon-prowed ship. Mason knew, instinctively, what this place was. Asgard.

Valhalla.

Home . . .

She shook her head to dispel the subtle voice that whispered that last word inside her head. It had sounded a little bit like Loki, but she knew that it had to be just her imagination playing tricks on her.

The cave they had just come out of was a little ways up one of the lesser mountains that ringed the valley plain. Mason took another step forward so she could better take in the view. She walked to the very edge of a steep descending staircase cut into the side of the mountain and peered over a rocky outcropping to look straight down. Directly below where she stood, she could see the green plain that stretched out toward the Asgardian halls. . . . At least, Mason imagined it *would* be a green plain, when it wasn't covered in fighting men and blood and body parts.

"I thought you said I wouldn't have to fight anyone!" she said, drawing back from the edge of the rock shelf, horrified. There were so many men fighting, and it wasn't just on one front. The fighting actually completely encircled the cluster of buildings that was their destination. They didn't have a hope of reaching it . . .

Beside her, Mason heard her mother laugh for the first time.

"What?"

"Those are Odin's Einherjar. The Lone Warriors."

"None of those guys is *alone*," Mason said. "There are a

bazillion of them. And *they* are what's standing between us and the hall." She couldn't even tell if there were two sides to the battle. It just seemed to her that, once a warrior had dispatched the man in front of him, he just turned to the next nearest and repeated the process. Friend and foe seemed utterly indistinguishable to her. It was chaos.

"They will not lift a hand against you," her mother said, and started forth. "You must trust me."

Mason didn't, but she didn't say so out loud. She was admittedly running out of options. As her mother began their descent down the steeply sloping path that led down to the battlefield and Asgard beyond, Mason fell in beside her.

"Why are they fighting?" she asked as they got closer and closer to the edge of the terrible melee.

Her mother answered, "Because they are fighters. It is simply what they do. They are Odin's personal war band, chosen in ages past by his Valkyries to die glorious deaths and join him here to await the ending of days. Ragnarok."

"Right. The thing we're all trying to avoid have happen by maintaining the status quo. Get me out of here, keep Loki bound and snaked . . . And hey, I'm all for the world *not* ending. It just makes me wonder"—she waved a hand at the Einherjar—"what's in it for *these* guys if it doesn't?"

"This is the honored Viking's promised reward. A glorious death, followed by endless days filled with battle, endless nights replete with mead and meat. The possibility, one day, of something even greater." Hel gazed at the spectacle, her expression hard to read. Mason wasn't sure whether she was actually endorsing the idea of Ragnarok, or just offering the

Norse perspective on it, but she sincerely hoped it was the latter.

"Sounds like it'd be an excruciating bore after about three days," Mason said.

At least, she thought, it would be the way *they* were doing it. The closer they got to the warriors, the more it seemed to Mason that they were kind of just . . . going through the motions. But of course, she wasn't blind to the irony of her offhand dismissal of their pastime. Especially where she herself was concerned. After all, she'd done very little else *but* fight and practice for the last several years—and with a similar kind of mindless determination. She had approached fencing with a kind of zealous tunnel vision. And yet, in all the time she had fought and practiced to be the best, honing her skills, her strength, her speed, she had never even approached the kind of finesse as she had over the last few weeks working with Fennrys. He'd instilled in her a kind of genius instinct with a blade. Made her one with her weapon.

She was no longer just a product of technique and grim determination. When she fought with Fenn, she fought with *joy*. Mason felt a brief surge of panicked despair at the thought of never experiencing that sensation again.

No. She slammed the door on that thought with all her mental might. *I'm going home.*

And Fenn is fine. He *had* to be.

Yes, she'd seen him hurt, terribly. A hole torn in his shoulder. But it wasn't as if she hadn't done the very same thing to him herself—accidentally stabbed him in the very same shoulder—only a few days earlier, and he'd recovered from *that* just fine. Fennrys was tougher than anyone she'd ever met. A bullet hole and a tumble off a train? That was like most people getting a hangnail.

Mason took a few deep breaths to calm herself down and shake her panic.

Her footsteps slowed as they approached the leading edge of the battle.

"You must go first," her mother said, nudging her forward.

Right. Of course I must.

Mason thought of Fennrys—of his fearlessness in the face of a fight—and clamped down on the urge to turn and fly as a wall of noise and the stench of blood and spilled viscera washed violently over her. The thunderous sounds of war were a physical assault on her ears and the surface of her skin. They beat on her like hammers on drums, and she knew that at any second, those hacking, slashing berserkers would turn and charge at her and she would be dead and in pieces before she'd even drawn her elegant little blade, which seemed like a toy sword in comparison. Her hand tightened on the hilt. . . .

No. Don't give them a reason to attack.

Her mother promised her she'd be fine.

Trust her. . . .

Suddenly, the two warriors fighting closest to her abruptly disengaged. They lowered their weapons and stepped back, making a space in the chaos for Mason to step into. Then so did the men beyond them, and the ones beyond them. Mason held her breath and strode purposefully forward into the breach, her eyes fixed unblinking on the glittering eaves of Valhalla in the distance. As the path continued to open up in front of her, she could sense that, as soon as she and her mother had passed, the men behind them would close ranks and start fighting again, as if nothing had interrupted them.

Once she was halfway across the battlefield, Mason relaxed enough to glance surreptitiously at the men fighting on either side of her. Some of them were great hulking beasts and some were lean and lithe, skirmishers and melee bruisers and all sorts in-between—there was no one distinct "type." And yet, they all seemed the same. It was strange. *Wrong.* Mason had sensed it from a distance, but in close quarters it was even more apparent. They hacked and slashed away at each other, but it was without individual flourishes of technique. It reminded her of the draugr. They fought like zombies.

Mason thought of her bouts with Fennrys—the kind of fighting where every blow, every block, attack and riposte and feint, felt like a move in an intricate, fiercely intimate dance—and felt sorry for the Einherjar. If *this* was their supposed reward for a life of service to the Aesir, the ultimate prize granted to the brave and the bold and the best . . . then they must not have read the fine print in the contract. They were all essentially robotic dummies, who were just going through the same motions they had been since the dawn of time—each face, each opponent, striped of its individuality . . . its humanity. Each death exactly the same. Because, beyond the different weapons and the different wounds, that's what they were—the same.

All except for *one* of them.

As Mason and her mother passed, untouched, across the battlefield, winding their way between the combatants,

Mason suddenly noticed a lone figure out of the corner of her eye that did not move the way all the other Einherjar did. She twisted her head to get a better glimpse between bodies . . .

. . . and was shocked to see Tag Overlea stumble out of the sea of warriors.

VII

Gunnar Starling pretty much confirmed Heather's fears that—just like Taggert Overlea—she wasn't going to leave his train alive. She'd watched enough crime dramas to know what it meant when his glance flicked first over Tag, where he lay stretched out on the floor, then over to where Heather still cowered in the corner.

"I'll deal with my sons and find my daughter," he said to Toby. "You clean this mess up."

Toby nodded and stepped aside as Gunnar swept out of the car, and Heather felt her heart sink into her stomach. She was part of the "mess." And there was really only one way to "clean" it up.

Rory trailed behind his father to the door, hesitating for a moment before stepping through. He cast a glance over his shoulder at Heather, his forehead knotted in a deep frown. He looked for a moment as if he wanted to say something to her. Apologize maybe? Try to explain? *Stop* what was about to happen to her? He did none of that, of course. Just stood there.

Heather took the opportunity to give Rory the finger.

He blinked at her, startled. Then his mouth twisted in a sneer and he shook his head, disappearing out the door in his father's wake.

Toby stood for a long few moments, staring at the door that had just closed behind Rory and his boss. Even in the depth of her near-panic despair, Heather was still trying to wrap her head around what, *exactly*, Toby Fortier did for Gunnar Starling other than drive his train. But then there was no more time for her to give the matter further thought.

Toby's head snapped around and he stared at Heather, every line of muscle in his fighter's physique taut as steel cabling. Heather tried her best not to shrink away from his piercing stare, to little avail. She could feel the leather of the banquette creaking behind her as her shoulder blades pressed into it when Toby reached into a back pocket of his jeans and pulled out a switchblade. The blade was flat black, nonreflective, and looked military issue. It was also instantly apparent that Toby was an expert in its use. The way he spun it around in his hand as he approached Heather actually made her feel the tiniest bit better. Like whatever way he decided to dispatch her would be quick and—hopefully—relatively painless. She tried to keep her lip from quivering and stared defiantly up into his eyes.

She almost burst into tears when Toby *didn't* slit her throat ear to ear.

Instead, the fencing master opened up his fist not holding

the knife, revealing one of Gunnar's acorns. With the point of the carbon-bladed knife, he hastily scratched a symbol into the gleaming golden surface and then held it up in front of Heather's face.

"Take this," he said, glancing over his shoulder at the compartment door. "It's marked with a protection rune. It should keep them from being able to find you while you're in possession of it. At least, for a while. *Don't* lose it."

Heather reached out a shaky hand. Outside the train, they heard a car start up, the engine loud and echoing in the tunnel. Then the sound moved off into the distance, and all was deathly silent again.

"Keep your wits, Heather. I know you've got 'em," Toby said, his eyes like burning coals in his head. "I can't help you any further from here on—and I'm a dead man if he finds out about this."

"Why are you doing this?" Heather asked.

He didn't answer her. Just grabbed her shaking fingers and wrapped them tightly around the rune-inscribed gold acorn. "Listen to me: go back to Gosforth. The school is neutral ground, *protected*. They can't touch you there. Be strong, be smart . . . and pray that someone finds a way to stop Gunnar Starling before it's too late. Now go. Run like hell!"

She nodded. He didn't need to tell her twice.

Blindly, instinctively, until the breath seared in her lungs and her pounding feet ached, Heather ran, heading west when she could, keeping her head down in the darkness and hoping she wasn't being followed. When the stitch in her side made it impossible to keep running, Heather slowed to a stumbling jog and massaged the muscles over her ribs, glancing nervously over her shoulder every few seconds at the virtually empty street behind her. Eventually, blind panic ebbed and she stopped at an intersection to get her bearings. Twenty-Eighth Avenue and Thirty-First. Okay. She knew where she was now. If she turned south, in a few blocks she'd hit the aboveground station where the N train stopped. She'd taken it a couple of times with Cal when they'd come over to Queens for one reason or another when they'd been dating. The N train would get her back into Manhattan. In Manhattan she would be safe.

Heather wasn't used to taking the subway, but she'd done it often enough that she knew her way around. She rifled through the pockets of her jeans and found a crumpled five-dollar bill—enough to get her a ticket card that would get her on the train. She had no idea where her cell phone was, and she hadn't been carrying her wallet when she'd run to find Mason at the academy.

Up ahead in the darkness, she saw the elevated station platform floating above the street, and her heart started to flutter. She almost sprinted the last hundred yards and up the stairs. Her fingers shook as she stabbed at the touch-screen buttons on the ticket machine, and then she was through the turnstile, getting on a brightly lit, empty train car. She almost wept with relief when the train started to move. She slumped down onto a seat and slowly began to relax. For the first four stops, the train car remained unoccupied, and Heather closed her eyes and dropped her head wearily into her hands for a moment.

"Hi."

Heather nearly jumped out of her skin. She lifted her head and turned a shaky attempt at her best withering glare on the stranger who sat opposite her, a slight grin curving his mouth.

"Sorry?" she said coldly.

It was just some teenage guy she didn't know, but it still freaked her out. The last stop had been Queensboro Plaza, and Heather was positive that no one had gotten on the train. There wasn't another stop until Lexington Avenue, once the train had crossed over the river into Manhattan.

"It's a typical North American greeting," the stranger said. "*Hi.*"

He wore a black leather jacket, faded jeans, and a pair of Ray-Bans, darker than the sky outside the train window, that completely hid his eyes.

"Right," Heather muttered. "Whatever."

Her fingers gripped the golden acorn tightly, and she found herself slightly reassured by the gentle, tingling warmth that seemed to emanate from it. Toby said the thing would protect her. She wondered if that applied to random strangers on trains. She turned away from the guy and stared determinedly at a poster on the wall of the train car. It advertised an upcoming heritage festival taking place in Queens.

The boy twisted his head, following Heather's eye line, and waved a hand at the poster. "Ah, yon Lady of War, Wisdom, and the Home Arts," he said, referring to a picture of Athena on the poster. "Frankly, I could never imagine the ol ' girl donning a frilly apron and churning out a batch of muffins in the kitchen. Could you?"

"No," Heather said flatly, wondering why the hell this guy wasn't going away. "But then I never really bothered to speculate on the hobbies of some moldy old Roman goddess, thanks."

"Oh. Ouch." His expression turned pained, and he waggled a finger at her. "*That* moldy old goddess there is *Greek*."

Heather shrugged. She knew that. She just didn't care. "Same diff," she muttered, silently willing the train to go faster.

Above the rim of his sunglasses, one dark eyebrow arched sharply. "Okay," he sighed. "You've obviously had a seriously shitty night so far, so I'm gonna let that one slide. But just for the record—even though I'm pretty sure you're smart enough to know this—the Greek and Roman gods are *so* not the same thing."

Heather could only stare at the guy in dull astonishment. This was one of the weirder conversations she'd had recently—and that was saying something—but there wasn't a whole lot she could do about it. She was trapped. There was no easy escape until the next station. And even then, what was to stop the guy from following her off the train? At least he hadn't tried to shift over onto the seat next to her. And strangely, when she thought about it, she realized she also wasn't getting go-for-the-mace warning vibes from him. *Yet . . .*

So Heather just sat there, staring at her own reflection in his shades, as he went on about the differences between the two pantheons of gods like he was the class nerd in her Comp Myth class at Gosforth. Maybe he was an ex-student. Except that couldn't be. He looked like he was around the same age as

Heather, and that would have meant they'd have shared some classes. And she was sure she'd never seen him before in her life. Although . . . the more she looked at him, the more she was struck with a sense of familiarity.

He didn't seem to notice her scrutiny. Or if he did, he didn't mind. "I mean, seriously," he was saying, "I dare you to just try telling Cupid he's the same guy as Eros." He flashed a grin at Heather that was only half a tooth shy of maniacal. "You'd likely wake up the next morning strapped to the underside of an amorous goat while a handsome young man uses you for target practice at the local archery range."

Heather figured he probably wasn't *actually* crazy. . . . Just some Queens rocker wannabe who saw a sad, pretty girl alone on the train in the middle of the night and thought maybe he could cheer her up. And maybe get some play if he was successful. Under other circumstances, she might have even indulged him a bit. Not tonight.

"Look." She sighed. "I'm sorry. I'm really not in the mood, okay?"

"Why?"

He leaned forward, elbows resting on his knees, expression earnest.

"Why?" she asked warily. "What do you mean, 'why'?"

"I mean, why aren't you in the mood? And what mood would that be, anyway?" He tilted his head and regarded her across the space between them. Heather got the impression that, behind the shades, he wasn't blinking. "A good one? 'Cause if that's what you meant, then you're absolutely right. You're *not*. But if you meant you're not in the mood to talk to me, then . . . I think you might be wrong. You sure look like you could use *some*one to talk to. Even if it is just some incredibly handsome random guy on a train at three in the morning."

Heather rolled her eyes. She also, on second thought, realized that he was right about two things. One: he *was* incredibly handsome. Almost unrealistically so. To the point that, when he smiled at her, she wanted to reach across the space between them, take off his shades, and gaze into what she was sure must be the most mesmerizing pair of eyes on the planet Earth. And two: she really *did* need to talk to someone.

Calum . . .

"What was his name?" he asked gently.

Heather glared at him, startled by the question.

"The guy you loved. The one you lost. He had a name, didn't he?"

She opened her mouth and closed it again, almost afraid to say it. "What makes you think I lost a guy?"

Ray-Bans shrugged. "Okay. Girl then. Whatever. All I know is you definitely lost someone. Someone you loved more than anyone else in the whole world. There's no other reason for you to be out here at this time of night, looking the way you do and feeling the way you feel."

"How do you know how I feel?"

His grin returned, but it was less maniacal this time. "Let's just say I'm pretty perceptive when it comes to matters of the heart. Years and years of practice."

"You're kidding. You look like you're—what—my age."

He shrugged again. "I try to stay out of the sun. Eat right. Moisturize . . ."

Heather felt herself almost cracking a smile. She shook her head and gazed down at the floor between her feet.

"But I'd also have had to be blind, deaf, dumb, and chained to a rock somewhere half a world away not to hear your heart breaking, Heather. It was louder than the bridge blowing."

Heather's head whipped back up at the sound of her name coming from the stranger's lips. She hadn't told him her name. And the bridge . . . how did he know she'd been there when the Hell Gate had blown?

Who the hell is this guy?

She stared at him, speechless, wary.

He stared back and took off his sunglasses.

Heather's breath caught in her chest. She'd been wrong about his eyes. They *weren't* beautiful. They were bloodshot and smudged with shadows. A shade of brown so deep they were almost black—like his pupils were overlarge. Eyes that had seen way too much. There were the beginnings of creases fanning out at their corners. In fact, his eyes made it look as if he'd been weeping bitterly for a thousand days straight. Eyes like that, set into a face with bone structure and pure perfect symmetry like *that* . . . Heather blinked when she realized that those eyes, world-weary, sorrow-laden, wrung dry of tears by unimaginable heartache, just made him even more incredible.

"Who *are* you?" she whispered.

"Call me Valen," he said, the grin sliding back into place. It put a hint of sparkle back into the darkness of his gaze.

"How do you know me?" she asked, fear creeping up her spine. "Did Gunnar Starling send you to find me?"

Valen's expression clouded, and he put his Ray-Bans back on. "No. But I'm pretty sure he's one of the *reasons* I found you. Not that I haven't been looking, Heather, but . . . well, it's not as easy as it was in the old days. And *they've* kept you all pretty safe from us. I'd like to keep you even safer."

She wondered who he meant by "they" and "us," but she didn't have a chance to ask before he reached inside his jacket and pulled out what looked like a compact crossbow.

A . . . crossbow. Okay then.

It was tiny, shiny, and sleek. It was also preloaded with two miniature bolts—a golden one and a dull, gray leaden-looking one. The golden arrow was needle sharp. The gray one was blunt and looked as though it would bounce off the hide of any intended target.

"Yeah . . ." Valen chuckled, seeing the way Heather was looking at the drab projectile. "Appearances. Deceiving. *That* one? Hurts like every hell there is." He handed over the strange little weapon.

"What am I supposed to do with this?"

"Use it." Valen stood, looking pleased with himself.

Heather rolled her eyes. "For what?"

He laughed. "You're smart enough to know that things are happening, Heather. Strange things."

That was a colossal understatement, Heather thought. *Yeah. "Things" are definitely happening.*

"And this is supposed to help me somehow?" She brandished the delicate weapon.

"Maybe. You'll figure it out eventually. And when you do, use it however you see fit. I don't need it anymore. Not since I upgraded." He reached into another pocket of his jacket and withdrew what looked like some kind of souped-up remote control for a high-tech video gaming system, with two short, spiky metallic nodes on the front end of it. He pulled a trigger, and bright golden sparks arced between the nodes. Then he adjusted a control and pulled the trigger again, and sullen purple sparks arced. "I have *you* to thank for this, Heather. I just wanted to return the favor." He glanced over and smiled his dazzling smile at her.

Heather felt herself grow almost dizzy in response.

He wasn't handsome. He was *beautiful*.

"Take care of yourself," he said. "For me."

And then the doors of the train opened. They'd reached the station at Lexington and Fifty-Ninth Street, and before she could stop him—before she could even open her mouth to ask him the thousand questions that were tumbling through her brain—he stood and stepped off onto the platform, and the doors slid shut behind him.

As the train pulled away, Heather saw that on the back of the leather jacket he wore, there was a cracked and faded image of a bleeding heart, shot through with an arrow and sporting a pair of fluffy, white-feathered wings. She wasn't sure whether it was meant to represent agony or ecstasy. Or maybe both.

She glanced back down at the little weapon in her hand and, after a moment, tucked it into the pocket of her jacket with a sigh.

As the train rumbled on, Heather recognized that she was probably in a state of shock. Inside, she was still numb with horror—with fear and exhaustion and hollowed out from the sudden loss of Cal—but somehow, with her hands shoved in her pockets, one curled around the compact crossbow stock, finger resting lightly on the trigger . . . the other wrapped around the little golden acorn, she felt stronger than she ever had before.

All her life, Heather had always been acutely aware that her family wasn't one of the power-broker families in their circle. They were rich, certainly. But not influential. Her father had sat on the board at Gosforth, but he'd never had any real say in how the affairs of the academy were run. He'd just sort of been a yes-man to Calum Aristarchos's mother (who'd hated Heather with an almost pathological fervor the entire time she and Cal had dated). So even when Heather had hit the top of the popularity charts at the academy, she'd always known it had been mostly due to Cal. And the fact that she'd been blessed with pretty phenomenal good looks. Looks that, if she was honest with herself, had never kept her from feeling massively insecure. Especially when she'd realized—a gut-deep feeling—that Cal was never going to be in love with her. It had made her feel weak. Exposed. Vulnerable.

But in that moment, sitting on an empty subway train winding its way through the middle of late-night Manhattan, she felt strong. And if Gunnar Starling, or Daria Aristarchos, or Toby, or even that psycho little rat bastard Rory came looking for her . . . well, let them come. She was going back to Gosforth, just like the fencing master had told her to. And if they came looking for her, they'd be the ones who'd wish they hadn't.

VIII

"Don't get me wrong," Maddox was saying, as he grabbed a bit desperately for his seat belt and yanked it across his body. "It's a nice car! I just thought you would have gone for something a little flashier, what with being a god an' all. . . ."

"I try to fly under the radar *and* remain stylish all at the same time." Rafe cranked the wheel of the vintage Jaguar, narrowly avoiding a police car that drifted across two lanes of Columbus Avenue traffic so it could slow to a stop curbside just above West Sixtieth Street. The tires screamed, and Rafe flung an obscene gesture out the window at the cops.

"And I'd rather not get arrested on the way to hell," Fennrys muttered grimly, trying not to clutch too obviously at the door handle as the car's momentum slung him from one side of the backseat to the other.

"Relax. There's not a cop car in existence that could catch

me, and those flatfoots didn't even see us go past." He grinned rakishly.

Fennrys stifled his impatience as best he could and followed Maddox's lead, reaching for his own seatbelt. He needed Rafe. And he needed Madd, although he was reluctant to drag the other Janus Guard into a situation that had nothing to do with his gate-guarding duties. Not that it would have made much difference. Back in the Obelisk, once the tremors had stopped and power had flickered back on and everything had returned to normal—with the help of a free round of drinks on the house, courtesy of Rafe—Fennrys had reiterated his intention to find Mason. And Maddox had offered to ride shotgun on the venture and then preempted any objection Fenn might have made by saying that if Manhattan sank into the Atlantic as a result of whatever the hell was going on with Mason Starling, then guarding a gate in the middle of it became something of a moot point. So wherever Fennrys had in mind to go rescue his girl, Maddox was going to help him get there.

End of discussion.

Fennrys had wisely shut up, and just accepted the backup he knew he'd probably need anyway once they got to where they were going. Wherever *that* was. He hadn't had a clue. For that, he'd needed Rafe.

"Relax," the ancient god said, glancing over to look at his two passengers as he cornered so sharply the Jag was almost riding on two wheels. "You're gonna need to be nice and loose once we get to the library."

"The what?"

"New York Public Library. Main branch on Forty-Second Street."

Fennrys huffed in frustration and ran a hand through his hair. "I thought you said you *knew* where we were going."

"I do."

"They why do you need a bunch of books?"

"I don't." Rafe leaned on the horn as they passed a city bus. "We don't have a Bifrost anymore, so the direct approach is out of the question. The rift on North Brother Island is unstable on the other end—no telling where it'll come out—so that's not an option. We're going to need to take the scenic route into Valhalla."

"And how do we do that?"

"The borders between the Beyond Realms are blurring—have been for ages now—and in places they overlap. That's how *you* were able to get out of Asgard in the first place. Through a back door from Helheim into Hades, and out across the River Lethe."

Fennrys shuddered, remembering the dark woman who'd led him to the banks of that river. The river that had then stolen his memories—up until the moment when the ghost of a dead Janus Guard nicknamed, appropriately enough, "Ghost" had helped restore them. Painfully.

"Personally," Rafe continued, "I'm not willing to risk catastrophic amnesia—and I sincerely doubt you want to go through that again. We need another way, another underworld. *My* underworld."

"Which is?" Maddox asked.

"At the library," Rafe grunted. When Fennrys and Maddox

exchanged a confused glance, the ancient god sighed. "Oh, come on. You're Janus Guards, aren't you? And you've both been kicking around this town long enough to know that it's nothing but layers built on top of *other* layers."

Rafe's black eyes glittered, reflecting back at Fennrys from the car's rearview mirror. Okay, Fennrys thought. So they needed to go not just *to* the library but to . . . whatever was *underneath* it.

What's the library built on top of?

He cast back through his memories, sifting through all the years he'd made an annual pilgrimage to the great gray mortal city at the behest of the Faerie King in order to guard a gate that opened once a year in fall.

"The reservoir," he murmured.

Rafe just raised an eyebrow at him in the mirror as he turned left on West Fortieth Street.

"The old Croton Distributing Reservoir," Fennrys said to Maddox, who was still frowning with some puzzlement. "It used to stand on the same ground as the library, didn't it?"

"Yeah." Maddox nodded. "Yeah . . . I remember now. Took up that whole block and most of the one that's now Bryant Park."

Fennrys thought about that for a moment. The library and the park occupied two city blocks, right in the middle of Manhattan. He'd been to the library himself only a few days earlier, before he'd regained his memory, to use one of the public computer terminals there to search for clues to his identity. He'd found virtually nothing. Then he'd chatted with an old homeless guy and his teddy bear in Bryant Park, and found out almost *everything* . . . except he hadn't known it at the time.

But that wasn't what Rafe was getting at.

The structures that occupied that space now—the library and the park—were latecomers on the Manhattan landscape. A massive, man-made reservoir, part of the water delivery system for the island, had been there first. It had stood aboveground, with soaring fifty-foot walls, twenty-five feet thick, and topped with a wide promenade where the likes of Edgar Allan Poe used to take nightly strolls around the dark, star-reflecting pools. Fennrys had gone there once in the late 1800s, and he remembered how the place had seemed to have a strange, eerie quality to it. He remembered it had been built with a very distinctive style. It had, in fact, been designed to resemble . . .

"An Egyptian temple!" Maddox blurted out suddenly. "I remember now! The thing looked like a bloody great hulking Karnak." He turned and looked at Rafe, his eyes narrowing.

"What?" The man-god shrugged with extreme nonchalance. "You think that was *my* idea? Egyptian Revival style was very big back then." Rafe pulled the Jag over and parked illegally in the shadow of the library's South Court. "Here we are."

The three of them piled out of the car, and Fennrys and Maddox followed Rafe as he headed for the wide sweep of stone steps where normally, on any given night, New Yorkers and tourists would still be hanging about, sitting on the steps or strolling or taking pictures. But on that night, the place was deserted. Almost. A handful of individuals stood scattered about the perimeter of the terrace. At a glance, they looked as if they had absolutely nothing to do with one another . . . but every one of them watched Rafe and the two Janus Guards approach with the same focused intensity.

Rafe glanced over his shoulder to see that Fennrys and Maddox had slowed and were eyeing the group warily. In the deep shadows behind one of the library's massive pillars, Fennrys saw one woman with dark hair, wearing a tailored suit, suddenly blur like smoke, and a sleek black wolf appeared in her place. Maddox saw it too and stopped in his tracks, one hand going to the leather pouch he wore on his belt.

"Relax," Rafe said. "They're my pack. I thought we could use some backup. They'll stay here and make sure nothing unexpected follows us."

Fennrys remembered the wolves from his first encounter with Rafe in Central Park and figured that they must have some kind of psychic bond with the Egyptian god. He looked over at Maddox, who still stood, frowning with uncertainty.

"What?" Fennrys said. "He's the god of werewolves. You didn't know that?"

Maddox blinked in surprise. "Well, of course I—"

Fennrys just grinned and followed Rafe up the shallow stairs. The wide stone terrace at the top was flanked majestically by twin marble lions, which led up toward the grand edifice of the main branch of the New York Public Library. For a moment, it seemed as though a shadow passed over the terrace—a cloud scudding over the moon maybe—and for that moment, the stone lions had resembled something else entirely.

Sphinxes . . .

From the way Maddox glanced between the statues, Fennrys knew he'd seen it, too. But Rafe just stalked on past them toward the main entrance. Fenn followed, noting warily that the massive lion statues on either side of him turned their regal stone heads to watch as the Egyptian god passed, the carved contours of their manes rippling and flowing in the exact way that chiseled rock . . . didn't. The one on the left was growling.

Maybe it's just purring.

The woman who'd transformed into a wolf whined uneasily.

Maybe not.

Fennrys turned and put a hand on Maddox's shoulder. "Look," he said. "Madd . . . I have to do this. You don't. I think maybe it would be best if you turned back. I don't want Chloe coming after me if something bad happens to you."

Maddox laughed. "No, you really don't!" He reached up and plucked Fennrys's hand from his shoulder. "On the other hand, *I'm* not about to go back and tell her that I abandoned my noble friend on his epic quest to rescue his one true love from the clutches of darkness. She'd never forgive me."

Fennrys snorted. "Don't tell me Chloe's turned into some kind of romantic. Jeezus, Madd. What have you done to the girl?"

"I know, right?" Maddox rolled his eyes, but Fennrys could see he was nothing short of blissfully happy in his relationship with the previously occasionally homicidal Siren. "She's gone all hearts 'n' flowers these days. And so she'd just tear the hide right off me and send me limping back here to help you anyway if I turned back now. True love an' all, yeah?"

True love.

Was *that* what this was? Did he really feel that way about Mason? He remembered what Rafe had said about the bind she was in; that if Mase somehow got her hands on the Odin spear, she would transform and become an agent of destruction, a harbinger of the End of Days, Ragnarok-style. That was the thing they were on their way to try and prevent. Rescuing Mason was, as far as Rafe was concerned, a fringe benefit. The unspoken agreement between Fennrys and the Egyptian god—Fennrys knew—was that their first priority was to make sure that Gunnar Starling's daughter never got the opportunity to get close enough to the spear to take it up. No matter how they had to go about it.

But . . .

Well, for one thing, what if that had already happened? What if they got to Asgard only to discover that she'd already turned Valkyrie? What if Fennrys had to leave her there . . . or worse? Would he do that? Could he?

Not even if the fate of the world depended on it.

Valkyrie or no—Fennrys wasn't going to leave Mase behind in the place where he himself had suffered so terribly. He was going to get her out of there.

And if bringing Mason Starling back into the mortal realm meant that the mortal realm burned, then the Fennrys Wolf would happily go down in flames with it. With *her.* So maybe it was true love. Or maybe it was just the fatalistic Viking in him. He was okay with that, either way.

The night was silent—eerily so, especially for midtown Manhattan—but Fennrys suddenly heard the gentle cooing of a bird. He looked around and saw a lone mourning dove, sitting at the base of one of the massive stone urns that stood between the lions and the library's arched portico. The bird stared at him with its obsidian-bead eye and cocked its head. Fennrys stepped past Maddox and approached the creature. He'd always had an affinity for birds, ever since he used to care for the Faerie King Auberon's hunting hawks in the Otherworld.

Maybe that's why you're so hung up on a girl with the last name of Starling, he thought with grim amusement.

Without thinking, Fennrys reached out toward the resting bird. It nuzzled his wrist with its beak as he ran his hand along its back, smoothing its sleek wings. One of the creature's tail feathers came loose in his fingers, and he expected the bird to flap away. But it just cooed at him again and tucked its head down between its shoulders, closing its eyes for sleep.

Fennrys smiled and gazed at the feather for a moment. It was a pale, pearly white, shading to silver at the end, tinted to blush near the base. It was beautiful. A marvel of simplicity and elegance; a thing of nature. The mourning dove was a pure creature. There was nothing strange or tainted or unnatural about it . . . and it had let him touch it. It had sensed nothing wrong about *him* either. Seeing as how he was now about to enter a place that would at some point only allow him admittance because he was already a dead man once over, he found that enormously comforting in that moment. Maddox, being mortal and wholly alive, would have to turn back eventually, before they reached the point of no return in this quest. They both knew that. But Fenn could walk between the worlds of the living and the dead with ease. *Relative* ease. That made him a serious freak. But the bird hadn't thought so. He tucked the loose feather in the inside breast pocket of his jacket. It wasn't a starling feather, but perhaps it was a lucky talisman for him nevertheless.

Overhead, there was a rumble of thunder, and Fennrys wondered if the storm was returning. He cast an eye skyward and realized that he had lost all track of the time in the hours since Mason's disastrous fencing competition when he'd made a grave mistake and let her walk away from him, distraught. She hadn't been thinking straight. Off her guard. An easy target for those who might seek to harm her . . . even if they were her own flesh and blood.

"Will you two please stop screwing around and come *on*?" Rafe poked his dreadlocked head back out of the solid wood-and-iron door through which he'd apparently walked, quite unimpeded, when Fennrys wasn't paying attention.

"I don't have to hold your hand or anything, do I?" Fennrys asked, eyeing the very solid-looking door skeptically.

"The door is 'open' because *they* opened it," Rafe said, gesturing to the stone lions. "They are the guardians of this place. You keep wasting time out here and they'll just shut it in your face. And then probably *eat* your face."

Fennrys and Maddox exchanged a glance.

"And *please*," Rafe continued. "I know that at this very moment you're eager to get your girl back, and probably tempted to say something like, 'They can try' . . ." He pegged

Fennrys with a stone-cold serious stare. "Don't."

Fenn nodded and uncurled his fingers—which had knotted into fists of their own accord.

Rafe stepped all the way back through the door. "Where we are now, the places we're going to . . . the things we're about to do," he said quietly, "they go beyond what you boys have fought against in the past. No disrespect to the Fair Folk—ever, and I *mean* that sincerely—but this is a whole different playing field, Fennrys Wolf. I hope you're ready, because this is going to be a very different kind of fight. There are things where we're going—powers—that can not only kill you . . . they can obliterate you. Wipe you from the universe, body *and* soul, as if you'd never been. Do you understand?"

Fenn glanced back at the stone guardians. One of the lions was sitting up now, head attentively cocked in their direction, as if waiting to hear what he said. The other one had relaxed into a recumbent pose, head resting on its massive stone paws. But Fennrys noticed it still kept one ear flicked in their direction, and the stone muscles sliding beneath the marble skin were coiled and ready to spring.

"I understand. And I'm not going anywhere but forward, Lord Anubis," he said quietly. "But I thank you for your concern. And for the gracious welcome of your guardians in letting me pass even so far as this."

Rafe raised a slow eyebrow at Fennrys, and one corner of his elegant mouth lifted in a half smile of approval. The subsonic thunder-rumble growl of the guardian turned into a definite purr—Fennrys could feel it through the soles of his boots—and so it seemed as if he had, somehow, passed some kind of a test. Probably the first of many. Rafe stepped aside and gestured to the solid-seeming door in front of them.

"After you, then," he said.

Behind him, Fennrys heard Maddox's whispered sigh of relief.

Inside the library, everything was dark. Quiet.

"Before the reservoir was built," Fenn mused quietly as they walked through the halls, footsteps echoing, "I seem to recall the land here was used for something else."

Rafe nodded. "It was a potter's field. A mass, unmarked grave for soldiers and the poor. Kind of set a precedent as an ideal place for an entrance into the underworld, wouldn't you say?"

Maddox glanced around, suddenly on edge, as if the ghosts of the dead were about to descend upon them.

Rafe grinned and said, "Don't look so nervous. There's nothing to fear here anymore. Well . . . not from those poor souls, anyway."

"They dug up the bodies before they built the reservoir foundation," Fennrys explained. "I remember it was a fairly massive undertaking, but they moved them all."

"They did," Rafe said. "Tens of thousands of them."

"Where did they move them *to*?" Fennrys asked.

Rafe shrugged. "Dunno. It was a long time ago."

Maddox frowned. "For a god?"

"For a god who has better things to remember, yes," Rafe said tartly.

"But you're a god of the dead," Fennrys pointed out. "That seems like rather a lot of dead to lose track of—"

"Listen. When I lost my kingdom, I made myself a part of the land of the living. I'm much more interested in that now, if it's all right with you two," Rafe rebuked them both with a sharp glare.

Maddox muttered an apology, and Fennrys gestured for Rafe to lead on.

The red eyes of closed-circuit cameras gazed unblinking at them from ceiling corners, and they passed through security checkpoints, but Rafe didn't pause or so much as bat an eyelash, and Fennrys knew that they were protected from such mundane, human precautions while in the presence of the man-god. The gloom of the after-hours Astor Hall was sepulchral. Veering left, Rafe walked swiftly toward a staircase that, according to signage, led down to some kind of lecture hall. It was roped off, and another standing sign declared it politely off-limits to the general public. Rafe unhooked the rope and stood aside to let Fennrys and Maddox pass.

Bouncing lightly on the balls of his feet, ready for a fight, Fennrys led the way down the staircase. The steps were made of frosted glass, suspended in a stairwell that seemed to have been built not of the same polished marble as the rest of the library building, but of rough-hewn blocks of grim, gray granite. As Fenn and Maddox reached the landing at the midpoint turning of the stairs, Rafe called for them to stop where they were and not go any farther. They did as they were told, waiting for the Jackal God to catch up.

Faint golden illumination seemed to be filtering upward from beneath them, making it appear as if they stood poised on a gently glowing square made of solid light. Rafe reached them and leaned out over the railing. He placed the palm of his hand on the rough contours of the granite and sighed.

"Home sweet home," he murmured. "It's been far too long. . . ."

Fennrys and Maddox stepped back as Rafe's appearance suddenly began to blur and the outlines of his face and body altered drastically, shifting into his intermediary form, between man and wolf. Fennrys was familiar with the transformation, but Maddox backpedaled almost off the edge of the landing in surprise.

"Whoa!" he exclaimed.

Fennrys thrust out a hand to keep him from tumbling all the way down to the museum's lower level.

"That's . . . wow." Maddox whistled low. "That's pretty cool, actually."

Rafe—Anubis—turned and raised one black-furred eyebrow at the Janus Guard. It was a bit disconcerting to see such a human expression on the canine visage. His nose and ears had lengthened and tapered into the finely pointed features of the figure universally recognized as the Egyptian god of the dead. His body was covered head to toe in a sleek black pelt, and a wide gold collar circled his neck, resting like wings on his broadly muscled shoulders. Gold beads shone throughout the helmet of dreadlocks he still wore in his transitional form, and gold rings pierced his ears. Aside from the winged collar and jeweled bands circling his wrists and ankles, the Jackal God was naked except for the crisply pleated, embroidered white linen loincloth that draped around his hips.

He was easily one of the most regal figures Fennrys and

Maddox had ever encountered. And for a couple of boys who were used to hanging out with Fae royalty on a regular basis, that was saying something. Rafe stalked past them, stepping to the edge of the platform, and placed a lapis-taloned hand on either railing. He began to speak in a language so old, it hadn't been properly heard by human ears for thousands and thousands of years. The words thrummed through the air, the railings glowed, shimmered, and then vanished. The glass stairs hung in space, now truly suspended but by what means, Fennrys couldn't perceive.

Like a king returning to his realm after a long absence, the Jackal God strode majestically down the stairs, head high, chest out. Challenger and conqueror, both. As Rafe's bare foot landed on the ground below the stairs, the darkness shimmered like a mirage. Suddenly, they found themselves standing in a vast, torch-lit hall. Massive columns, fluted to look like lotus flowers, soared into the vaulting, star-spattered darkness over their heads that was reflected in the gleaming, polished marble floor. Black granite statues of gods, alternating with massive translucent alabaster urns, appeared as if they were marching in rows off into the invisible distance. The whole place had an air of austere opulence.

It was the entryway to the home of a god.

Fennrys and Maddox stood there, uncertain as to what to do next. Then the air seemed to start to quiver all around them. It was as if someone had plucked a massive harp string somewhere and the vibrations were reaching them before the sound. And then the sound *did* reach them. . . .

But it was nothing musical like a harp.

This sounded more like one of those car-masher machines in a junkyard, chewing through the engine compartment of an SUV . . . only it was a distressingly *organic* sound. The horrible gnashing and roaring echoed off what sounded like cavern walls in the darkened distance. And it was getting closer.

"You know what this reminds me of?" Maddox asked.

"I dunno," Fennrys said, loosening the blade in the sheath he'd strapped to his leg. "The good ol' days?"

"Exactly! Especially that one time—when that Jack-in-Irons tried to get through the Samhain Gate. Remember that?"

"What was good about that?" Fennrys glared sideways at Maddox. "That pit-spawned monstrosity almost tore my arms off, and it put you in Auberon's infirmary for the better part of a mortal year."

"Good times . . ." Maddox sighed, pulling a stout length of silvery chain from a pouch at his belt. As he swung it in circles, the chain lengthened and grew spikes that whistled through the dank air.

Fennrys drew the loaner sword. "I miss my ax," he muttered.

And then the ground shook as the thing that would be the first test in their descent into the underworld came barreling out of the darkness in front of them. Armored with scales the size of pancakes, greenish-gray and wafting a swampy stench that was an assault on the senses, the crocodile was maybe thirty feet long. Its massive, cumbersome body was carried along on short, stumpy legs, but even with all its ungainly girth, the thing moved swiftly.

Seeing what was coming, Fennrys resheathed his blade.

It would do him no good. In the Lands of the Dead, *death* itself was something to be employed extremely judiciously.

Fennrys glanced over to see that Rafe stood off to one side, arms crossed over his broad, furred chest. His stare was impassive, and Fennrys understood in that moment that there would be no help coming to him or Maddox. They would have to pass this test—prove their worthiness—on their own. It was just one of those unwritten rules of quests, Fennrys supposed. His shifted his gaze to Maddox, who stood loose and ready, the enspelled chain dangling from his fingers, swinging gently back and forth, and a grim smile of anticipation bending the corners of his mouth. He had no doubt that they probably could, between the two of them, put an end to the beast. But Fennrys decided that a bit of nonlethal diplomacy would serve them better.

"Madd!" he called out. "Let's do this one up rodeo-style."

"Ha!" Maddox barked a laugh. "All right—I call clown-in-the-barrel."

Fennrys grinned and took a step back as Maddox stalked forward, positioning himself just to the right of one of the lotus columns—the mighty stone support was the circumference of a decent-sized giant redwood tree.

"Look sharp," Fenn said, ducking behind a statue.

"Yo, ugly!" Madd stepped out and waved his arms in a wide arc over his head. "Over here!"

Jaws snapping, legs churning, the croc swung its massive head from side to side as it thundered down the great hall, its tiny eyes narrowing to focus on the movement in its field of vision. Once it zeroed in on Maddox, the thing charged straight for him, moving with blinding speed. Maddox was a fraction of a second faster. He sprinted for the pillar, skidded into a hairpin turn, and disappeared around the other side.

The beast's momentum carried it past the lotus column as its claws scrabbled for purchase on the polished floor. Its powerful neck muscles contracted, whipping its head to one side, as its enormous tail scythed to the other, compensating for the centrifugal force that slewed the creature's massive bulk in a half circle. It gathered its flailing legs underneath it again and, aiming its snout in the direction Maddox had fled, launched itself forward again.

The two Janus had the beast right where they wanted it.

Its momentum squandered, and its back end pointing to where Fennrys crouched behind the base of a statue of Horus, the croc was entirely focused on running down Maddox, who jumped nimbly for the mouth of one of the huge alabaster jars—and disappeared down inside, clown-in-a-barrel rodeo-style. Fennrys took the opportunity to sprint after the creature as the thing's shoulder glanced off the urn, spinning it like a top.

Fennrys leaped, landing deftly on the croc's broad, scaly tail, and ran up the creature's back, toward its head. He was halfway there when a flick of the croc's tail sent him forward in a shoulder roll along the uneven surface of the armored hide.

As the croc scrambled to a second stop, Fenn grabbed for a ridge of dorsal spikes and desperately pulled himself up along the reptile's enormous body to lunge for its head. If he fell, he'd be dead before he hit the ground, snapped in half by those terrible jaws. Inching forward, he managed to loop one arm around the beast's sensitive snout and, with his other arm wrapped around the top, threw all his weight behind keeping the jagged-toothed mandibles shut tight. As the croc thrashed and snarled beneath him, he struggled to keep the massive creature from tearing off his arm.

In that instant, Maddox popped out of his jar with his magickally malleable chain weapon fashioned into a functional lasso. With a deft throw and a sharp snap of his wrist, Maddox snared the great beast's muzzle, pulling as tight as he could. The creature thrashed and roared deep in its throat, outraged. Fennrys reached down and grabbed first one stubby front leg and then the other, pulling them back like a calf roper as Maddox ducked in again and used the rest of the chain length to secure the scaly, taloned appendages, tying them off with all the showy aplomb of an experienced rodeo hand.

From where he stood, Rafe sauntered toward them, shaking his canine head, an amused sneer curling one side of his muzzle to reveal a sharply pointed fang, gleaming white in the gloom. Fennrys and Maddox made way as he circled around to the front of the crocodile and crouched on his haunches to stare the beast directly in its unblinking eyes.

"Sobek," Rafe tsk-tsked. "You are the lamest excuse for a watchdog I have ever had the misfortune of encountering. You realize you just embarrassed yourself in front of a couple of Janus Guards. Don't you have any professional pride? I mean, seriously."

The crocodile snarled gutturally around the chain snare

that clamped his jaws shut tight.

"That," he growled through his teeth, "was not a fair fight. I am bound to keep the *living* from crossing over. *That* one's already dead." He jerked his head in Fenn's direction.

Rafe snorted in derision. "Yeah, whatever. The Wolf is only *sort of* dead."

"Whatever he is . . . he's in the wrong afterlife!"

"Not the first time," Fennrys muttered.

"I was only trying to fulfill my mandate according to *your* rules, Anubis." Sobek writhed on the dusty ground, glaring at Rafe. "Let me up."

"So you can eat my friends?" Rafe barked a laugh. "I left my kingdom behind, Sobek. Not my brain." He stood and, hands on linen-draped hips, cast a surveying glance around the place. His lips curled back from his teeth in displeasure. "Where are my baboons? Why isn't anyone tending the Lake of Fire?"

Fennrys looked in the direction of Rafe's glance, but all was shadowy darkness to his eyes. He certainly couldn't see any flaming lake, although that was probably because it had extinguished through lack of tending, he supposed. Whatever the case, he wasn't going to complain about the absence of fiery obstacles.

Rafe shook his head and turned to glare back down at the giant croc. "I should have known my brother would let things fall to pieces once I left. . . ."

"Things have changed, lord. There just aren't any believers left to mistakenly wander this way. Nothing to keep us going." Sobek wriggled again, clearly uncomfortable, and for a moment, the facade of ponderous dignity cracked. "Let me up," he complained piteously. "I'm getting a cramp."

Rafe turned to the two Janus Guards and lifted a questioning eyebrow.

"I can help you," Sobek said.

Fennrys clenched a fist. He was rapidly running out of patience. He knew how these things went. You didn't rush a quest—if that's what this truly was—you ran the gauntlet, accepted all challenges, vanquished foes, answered riddles, jumped through the hoops, danced to the tunes. . . . In short, you played by the rules. Fennrys had never been very good at playing by the rules. But Mason was down there, somewhere, caught in an infernal realm, and that was the only thing that mattered. He needed to find her. And if a talking crocodile had any useful insights, he'd spare a minute and listen. But only a minute.

"Let him up," he said to Maddox. "We'll just take him out again if he gets frisky. In a less gentle fashion."

Once freed, Sobek's reptilian form began to shimmer and twist, and then, suddenly, a man—bald, stocky, with a craggy complexion and blunt features—stood before them, garbed in a somewhat shabbier version of Rafe's glittering, elegant accoutrements. Sobek brushed the dust from his loincloth and turned to Fennrys, his eyes narrowing.

"Why are you down here, not-quite-dead boy? No . . . wait." Sobek held up a hand. His tone shifted, dripping with weary sarcasm. "Let me guess. A *girl*."

"Isn't it always?" Rafe sighed.

"Hmph . . ." Sobek's expression turned pinched, sour.

"I dunno." Maddox shrugged. "Look how well it turned out for that Greek kid. Whatzisname. Orpheus."

Fennrys raised an eyebrow at his friend. "He lost the girl and was ultimately torn to pieces at an orgy."

"He was?"

"Even I know that."

"Huh."

Sobek had fixed his ancient, watery gaze on Fennrys and was staring silently at him. "Listen to me," he said finally. "You should just turn back. There is something about this— whatever you think is happening here, wherever you think you are going—I have lived long enough, seen enough to know that this quest you are on has 'Bad Idea' written all over it. I hate to say it, but you, lad, are followed by an evil star."

"I'm not exactly sure how you can tell that," Fennrys said, unwilling to acknowledge just how much that stung him. "Seeing as how we're underground and all . . ."

"This place isn't underground." Sobek snorted, Fenn's sarcasm having escaped him utterly. "This place isn't a *place!*" He turned to Rafe. "Did you not explain the way of things before you decided to lead him here?"

"Are you blind, Sobek?" Rafe scoffed. "There's more to this one than meets the eye, old man." Rafe pushed Fennrys forward. "Here. Smell him."

Caught off guard by Rafe's shove, Fennrys stumbled a few reluctant steps toward Sobek, who suddenly seemed to get a good whiff of Fenn's scent or aura or soul—whatever the hell it was he was sniffing out—and Sobek's beady eyes suddenly went wide. He reeled backward, bumping into Maddox, who shot out a hand to keep the demigod from falling on his rump.

"*Ra* . . . ," Sobek murmured, an oath—the name of the most powerful and revered of the Egyptian gods. And the most feared.

He's afraid, Fennrys thought. *Of me.*

"What *is* he?" Sobek asked Rafe.

"He's what he is," Rafe answered unhelpfully. "A linchpin, maybe. The single thing that holds everything together. Or a time bomb that'll blow everything apart. Too early to tell." He sighed. "Can we pass now?"

"You know he'll never make it through the Hall of Judgment," Sobek said darkly. "If *I* can smell the wrongs on him, then he doesn't stand a chance with the Soul Eater. *She* cannot be fooled."

"Soul . . . Eater?" Maddox went a bit pale.

"I was wrong. I can't help him," Sobek continued. "I don't think anyone can. And I'm sorry to say this"—Sobek turned a grim look on Fennrys—"but it's probably for the best if she just tears you into pieces too small to find afterward."

Fennrys could feel his forehead contracting in an angry frown. Where did everyone get off judging him like that? Were the things he'd done in his life so very wrong? What ever happened to second chances?

Aw, to hell with it.

They could think whatever they wanted. He was a changed person. Mason Starling had seen to that. Through an effort of will, Fenn forced the creases from his brow and said lightly, "Says you." Then he turned to Rafe and tapped his wrist with one finger. "Time's a-wasting. . . ."

"Don't do it, Anubis," Sobek said. "No good can come of this."

Rafe looked back and forth between the old, worn deity and Fennrys.

And then he grinned his jackal grin and echoed Fennrys: "Says you."

Maddox stifled a chuckle and stepped up to flank Fenn, and the three of them started off toward the deeper darkness that was waiting. They'd almost made it the rest of the way down the hall when suddenly, a flaming projectile soared over their heads, and a great wall of flame roared up in front of them. They turned to see Sobek sprinting down the hall toward them, chased by a dozen howling simian creatures, fangs bared, hurling fireballs that they conjured out of the air.

Fennrys glanced at Rafe and saw that he'd gone wide-eyed.

"Your missing baboons?" he asked drily.

The creatures were more like enormous, mutant, apelike monstrosities with dagger blades for fangs and fiery yellow eyes. Bulging with muscle and malevolence, they were terrifying to behold. And closing fast. Sobek, only barely out in front of them, issued a high-pitched wail of panic as he ran.

"My missing baboons." Rafe nodded and glanced over his shoulder at the roiling conflagration the fireball had ignited, which now barred their way. "And my Lake of Fire . . . yeah. It's really more like a Pond of Fire these days, but it gets the job done. Unfortunately." He dodged another ball of fire and muttered, "I'd forgotten how much I hate those freaking monkeys. . . ."

"What do we do?" Maddox asked, unfazed by the situation.

Rafe frowned. "I can carry one of you across the flames. But that's it."

Fennrys opened his mouth in protest, but Maddox nodded and said, "Right. Off you go, then. I'll hang here and give old Sobek a hand."

"Madd—no!"

"Shut up and don't be stupid." Maddox turned to him, his gaze placid. "Your girl is waiting for you, and *this* isn't your big trial to face. I'm pretty sure that'll come next. This is a distraction." He pulled the chain weapon out of his belt pouch again and began to swing it in a circle. He grinned at Fennrys. "I'll see you back in Manhattan, yeah?"

Fennrys knew that Maddox was right. He knew, instinctively, that he could stay and fight beside Maddox and win, but in doing so he would have lost. Wasted too much time . . . allowed a door that was open to close . . . something. Part of the real winning was knowing when *not* to fight. Knowing when to trust his friend enough to leave him behind.

Fennrys had never really had friends to trust. It was a new sensation.

He held out his hand, and the two young men clasped wrists.

"You die and I'll kill you," Fennrys said. "And only 'cause Chloe will have killed me first."

"Again." Maddox grinned and shooed him on his way.

The screams of the baboons were so loud that they were almost deafening. Sobek was screaming, too, and the fireballs flew thick and fast. Rafe transformed into his huge, sleek black wolf self, and Fennrys threw himself onto the god's back, gripping the thick fur tightly and burying his face in the pelt to protect himself from the flames as Anubis, Protector of the Dead, did his job and, backing up so he could take a good run at leaping over the flames, got Fennrys the hell out of his own hellish domain.

IX

"**S**-Starling . . . ?" Tag Overlea called out to Mason, his voice weird and querulous. His letterman jacket stood out like a wildly inflamed sore thumb among all the leather and iron of the Einherjar, and he moved as if he was caught in the throes of a nightmare.

Mason remembered hearing his voice when she was on the train—he'd been there when they'd crossed the Bifrost— but what was he doing in Asgard? she wondered. It was only when he got closer to her that Mason gasped in realization as she took in his appearance. *She* might have wound up in the Beyond Realms by accident, but from the looks of him, Tag had wound up there through more . . . *traditional* means.

Tag Overlea was dead.

The football star's skin was mottled gray and purple. And the whites of his eyes were crimson with burst blood vessels. As he shambled toward her, the glancing blow from a sword, swung by a nearby fighter, tore a gash in Tag's arm, right through the sleeve of his jacket, but he didn't even really seem to feel it.

He just staggered a bit and mumbled, "Watch it, man. . . ."

He kept moving toward Mason, and she couldn't help but recoil in horror.

"Starling," he said again, reaching for her. "What's going on? Where are we? I feel so . . . god, I feel terrible . . . you gotta help me, Mason . . . I gotta get outta here. There's a big game coming up. . . ."

Mason felt a chill run up her spine.

"Taggert," she said, her mouth dry as dust, "how did you get here?"

"I just told you. I don't know. I gotta find Rory. He's the one who can help me. I need a little of that stuff. . . ." There was a tremor in his dead hand as he lifted it to his neck, absently tugging at the collar of his jacket, and Mason saw something on his skin. Like a tattoo, only it looked as if it had been drawn on the side of his neck with dark, metallic ink. It glowed with a sullen, flickering light. "Just one more shot of that liquid gold, you know?"

"What's he talking about?" Mason asked her mother.

Hel glanced at Tag and frowned. "Someone must have filled him full of rune magick," she said. "So much so that it sent him here, to the ranks of the Einherjar, when he died. There's no other way one of his . . . caliber would have found their way to this place. He never would have been one of the Valkyries' Chosen. No doubt it's been something of a shock to his mind."

Mason had never thought Tag had been all that smart to

begin with. But as he turned his gaze on her, she could see him struggling just to form a coherent thought. Clearly he had no idea where he was. Or how he'd gotten there.

"I know that you . . ." He faltered to a stop and then tried again. "I mean, I get that Rory wasn't so nice to you, with the bag and all that. But he just wants what's best for you, y'know? He told me . . . all this—what's coming? He told me it's for your own good. It's gonna be awesome . . . you know?"

"No, Tag. I don't know."

Mason backed farther away from him to avoid his awkward, lurching grasp. It seemed as though he didn't know how to make his muscles work properly anymore. Suddenly, Tag stopped and looked around, blinking dumbly.

"Where am I?" he murmured.

He looked so horribly lost and alone that—what he'd done to her at Rory's behest notwithstanding—Mason felt a surge of pity for him.

"I . . . somebody please tell me what to do. . . ."

Mason swallowed painfully. She had an idea and, kneeling, picked up a discarded sword that lay on the ground at her feet. "You're at the game, Tag," she said. "It's . . . it's the championship. Only the rules are a little different, okay?"

He turned his wounded, crimson gaze on her, a spark of hope flaring in the depths of his dull eyes at the mention of a game.

"Those guys?" Mason pointed at the sea of battling warriors. "They're the other team. Understand?"

He nodded vacantly.

"And you use *this*"—she handed him the sword, pommel

first—"instead of a football to get through them to the goal line."

Tag reached out and gripped the weapon clumsily, fingers convulsively constricting on the leather-wrapped hilt. Gently Mason nudged his shoulder and turned him in the direction of the ongoing fray. "See what those guys are doing?" She pointed to a pair of dueling Einherjar. "You do the same."

Tag looked down at the sword, and then back up at Mason, and nodded.

He turned and took a few tentative swipes at the air with the blade. Mason gave him another little push, and he lumbered forward a few steps into the fringe of the battle. He swung his blade at a stocky man in a helmet, who responded with a clashing blow right back at him. Mason heard a dissonant battle roar issue from Taggert's throat as he launched himself into the heart of a six-warrior cluster, scattering them. Mason saw that a kind of weird, accepting smile had crept across his face, and then Tag was swallowed up by the melee.

Mason watched him for as long as she could see his red jacket and then turned away, back to the remote figure of her mother—who'd stood silently, impatiently by throughout the whole exchange—feeling strangely even more alone. The irony wasn't lost on her. She *missed* Tag Overlea. On the other hand, she had the distinct feeling that the only reason he was in Asgard was because of her. Because of what Rory had done to her, and because he'd used Tag to help . . .

Mason had done what she could. She couldn't do anything else for him.

So she turned and, with her mother beside her, walked

toward the hall of Valhalla. When they ascended the wide, shallow steps that led to the massive, carved-oak doors of the hall, Mason saw that there were two huge piles of weapons, stacked high on either side of the doorway, and she knew, instinctively, what that meant.

One did not enter the hall of a host armed.

Not if one wanted to be received in welcome.

Most of the weapons looked as though they had lain there for untold ages. The blades of the swords and pikes and axes were all darkened with tarnish and rust. Some of the handles and shafts of the gear near the bottom of the piles had begun to decay, the wood rotting to dust, leather wrappings falling to tatters, iron blades pitting with age. . . .

Hesitantly, Mason ran her thumb along the cool, smooth curve of the sweeping silver guard on her rapier. A deep ache of longing closed her throat. She knew she'd have to leave the blade behind if she was to enter Valhalla, and she hated the thought. But giving up the sword Fennrys had given her was infinitely less painful than never getting to see him again. *That* fear prompted her to reach for the leather baldric strap that hung from her right shoulder to her left hip. Swiftly and decisively, Mason lifted it over her head, wrapped the strap tightly around the scabbarded blade, and placed it gently on top of the pile of discarded and long-forgotten weaponry. She kissed her fingertips and placed the kiss on the blue jewel of the baldric's silver buckle, promising herself that the next thing she kissed wouldn't be Fenn's gift, but Fennrys himself.

Again, her mother stood by, watching silently. She waited as Mason discarded her only means of defending herself, a look of satisfaction on her lovely face, and Mason guessed that she'd made the right choice.

Hurray for me.

Mason turned to face the soaring oak-and-iron doors, and as she did so, they groaned like a giant beast waking from slumber, and a crack appeared between them. They swung inward, slowly, ponderously, and a waft of stale sour-sweet air assaulted Mason's nostrils.

Her mother stepped back and gestured for her to proceed. "You must—"

"Go first. Yeah, I figured."

"No. You must go *alone*." Her mother's face was drawn tight. "I will not enter Odin's Hall."

Mason wasn't about to argue, even though the thought of walking through those doors alone was a terrifying prospect. She clenched her trembling hands into fists at her sides and, faking a confidence she absolutely did not feel, strode through the doorway into the hall of a god.

The *empty* hall of a god.

The place was massive, gloomy, and shrouded in shadow. Mason heard the flapping of wings in the stillness, but she couldn't see anything moving. She could barely see anything at all. The only light in the place was the cold illumination that spilled in through the doorway she stood in, but it was enough to paint a bleak picture. Mason glanced up. She had seen all the gilded warriors' shields covering the outside of the roof and had wondered at the size of the army that had gone down in defeat to provide those building materials. But what she hadn't stopped to consider was that the *inside* of the roof would be similarly tiled. The entire place was a monument to the Fallen Viking on a massive scale.

Mason imagined that vaulting space stuffed to capacity with a full company of raucous Einherjar, lit with roaring fires in the dozens of massive fire pits down the center, aglow with torchlight from the hundreds of sconces lining the walls. She thought of all the details she remembered from the stories she'd learned when she was a kid. Of the host of Valkyrie maids in winged helmets, bearing jugs of mead and platters of roast venison and boar . . . of Odin sitting on his throne beside his beautiful wife, presiding over the whole crazy party . . .

This? Wasn't like that.

A thick layer of dust shrouded everything in gray, and cobwebs hung like curtains in the spaces between the rafters. The fire pits were long dead, as were the torches in the sconces on the walls, and the rows of tables were piled with the remains of roast carcasses and loaves of bread that had long since petrified. The place looked like it had been deserted for centuries—as if the mindless hordes of Einherjar outside had simply forgotten to refresh themselves after the battle. Or maybe it was because the fighting had never ended. Days full of fighting, nights full of feasts . . . and yet, Mason recalled how she hadn't been able to tell where the sun was in the sky when she'd been outside, and she really no idea how long a day lasted Asgard. But looking around, she certainly understood something of the so-called "twilight of the gods." In the intervening years since the Aesir had been a dominant force in human belief systems, things had pretty obviously gone downhill. The hall stank of death—and not the good, fresh, violent kind that the Vikings reveled in, but rather the slow decline into decrepitude and irrelevance.

It doesn't matter, Mason thought. All that mattered to her was getting the spear and getting home.

She took a lurching step forward. But as she crossed the threshold, the massive doors swung shut behind her with a muted boom like distant thunder. She gasped, and suddenly, the sound echoed and distorted in her mind, warping into a refrain composed of a myriad of sounds. A car trunk slamming . . . The bolt lock on a shed door sliding home . . . The rattle of the Gosforth gym doors that wouldn't open . . . The creaking hinges of the storage cellar trapdoor closing. A twisted soundtrack to accompany her claustrophobia.

She couldn't breathe.

Couldn't move.

Trapped . . .

It felt as though something was shriveling, deep inside her. Shrinking back into the darkness. Her breath felt hot in her lungs, and her windpipe felt like it was closing.

I can't do this. . . .

Her hands reached up, clawing at her throat, and her fingers brushed the iron medallion she wore. Fennrys's medallion.

Yes. She heard his voice in her head. Calm and steady and cool as water on a burn. *You can.*

X

The measure of a man's worth is in the weight of his heart.

That was, according to Rafe, how the hieroglyphics on the lintel stone over the entrance to the Hall of Judgment translated. Fennrys had been hoping that the whole heart-weighing thing was a metaphor. Would that have been too much to ask for at this stage?

As he stepped into the torch-lit, vaulted stone chamber, his attention was entirely occupied by an elegant set of slender scales, standing on a raised stone platform in the middle of the space. Two small, shallow dishes—each just big enough to hold a human heart—hung suspended by slender golden chains. Fennrys felt his own heart thud painfully in his chest. His familiarity with Egyptian mythology was hazy, but even he had seen enough references to the Trial of the Soul to know what came next. If he wanted to pass through the Hall of Judgment and out the other side into the place that Rafe had told him was called Aaru—where the Egyptian underworld borders brushed against those of the Norse Helheim—then he would have to have his heart weighed.

The only catch, of course, was that Fennrys was—as Rafe had earlier told Sobek—only *sort of* dead. That might put a crimp in the proceedings, Fenn thought as he wondered just exactly how they would get the heart out of his chest, and how badly it would hurt. But it wasn't the idea of pain that terrified him. It was the judgment itself.

It was the fact that he knew, deep in his bones, that he was not a pure soul. There were petty crimes and misdemeanors, certainly. But more than that, there were the things he'd done that had forever tainted him. Marked him as a bad person. Fennrys had killed. In his capacity as a guardian of the Samhain Gate, the portal between the mortal realm and the kingdoms of Faerie that stood hidden in New York's Central Park, he had killed a *lot*. A lot of Fae that is, and in the service of protecting the mortal realm, certainly, but still. He'd done it, and with a kind of savage, red joy. He was good at it. In fact, he'd always been proud of his skills as a warrior. Always begrudged the Fae for having taken him away from a destiny that would have seen him kill *men*.

Fennrys was, in his heart of hearts, a killer. And a betrayer.

Rafe caught his eye in that moment and must have guessed what Fennrys was thinking. "Hey," he said quietly. "I've seen souls pass through this hall that I never thought would make it. Thieves, liars . . . murderers, even. The judgment isn't cut-and-dried. It's complicated. Just . . . I'm not going to say 'relax'—because that would be stupid—but . . . stay cool."

"Sure," Fenn said. "I'm a Viking. I'm damn near an icicle."

Rafe shook his head and slapped Fennrys gently on the shoulder, pushing him forward a step into the hall. But in spite of Rafe's reassurances, Fennrys felt himself nearing a panic state. Okay, maybe you didn't have to be spotless to make it through. But if the consistent reactions of every semidivine being he encountered these days were anything to go by, Fennrys was more than flawed. Much more. Much worse.

He didn't even know what that could be. But it suddenly occurred to him that maybe it would be for the best if he *didn't* make it all the way through the hall. Maybe it should all just end here.

Then he saw *her.*

Ammit. The Soul Eater.

Hunched and coiled, ready to spring, the creature crouched in a deep pit dug into the earth beneath the dais where the scales stood. Her eye sockets were empty in a seamed and hideously reptilian face that bore a passing resemblance to Sobek when he'd been in his crocodile guise. But there the similarities ended. The Soul Eater was nothing that could be found in the mortal realm. She was a primeval being. A chimera. Neither one thing nor another, but a meshing of forms. A lion's mane, thick and tangled and soaked in old, dried blood, swept back from her forehead and thickly furred the powerful leonine shoulders and torso that flowed down into front legs that more resembled arms, ending in paws that were almost hand-like, with scythe-like talons. The creature's hindquarters were the powerful, muscle-heavy haunches of a Nile hippopotamus, with a thick-folded bluish-purple hide, coated with greenish slime.

Fennrys felt his heartbeat lurch and then slow as he approached the scales. The hall, empty and thick with shadow, echoed with his footsteps, and the air burned in his lungs as he sucked in deep breaths, trying to still the urge to flee while the screaming voice in his head told him that if he did this thing—if he let himself be judged—he would die. Not just die, but be destroyed. Utterly.

As a Viking, all he'd ever wanted was to die honorably. To seek the reward of his ancestors, live his unlife in Asgard, feasting and fighting eternally in the afterworld. The reality of it had been something else—a dungeon cell, chains, suffering, torture for crimes he didn't even understand having committed. But then he'd been given a second chance, and returned from beyond the walls of death. What in hell did he think he was doing then, willfully walking back across that line? Why? For what?

For Mason.

The Soul Eater's black eye sockets fixed upon his breast.

Fennrys's heart was hammering in his ears. He could feel his pulse, thundering along the sides of his throat and in his wrists. A fire ignited in his chest, searing, terrible, glorious. The life in him fought back desperately against the will of the Soul Eater as she drew his very essence up toward the surface of his skin. His heart would burst from his chest any second and he would die spectacularly, messily, a pile of meat and bones left to decay and then crumble to dust. . . .

And he didn't want that to happen.

Because of Mason Starling.

The monster beneath the scales heaved itself toward him

with ungainly grace. He stared into those sightless eye sockets and couldn't tear his gaze away from the un-gaze of the black, empty pits. There was ageless hunger there. Never to be sated. The demon goddess, old as death itself, reared back on her grotesque haunches in front of Fennrys and reached for him with her taloned hands. For a moment, it could have been for a gentle embrace. Then pain—worse than anything that had gone before—flared like a sun. Burned his lungs to cinders and ash.

Mase . . .

The Soul Eater's claws slashed through the front of his jacket, tearing it to ribbon strips of leather, as she lunged forward, eager to rend the beating heart from his breast . . . and then her hand, furred and pawlike, stilled, hovering. Her sightless visage wavered with an expression of uncertainty. Questing. She reached out again and, with shocking delicacy, plucked from the breast pocket of Fenn's jacket the feather that he'd tucked away there at the doors of the library.

He'd forgotten he'd put it there.

Pale, tinged with silver and blush, infinitely fragile, yet strong enough for flight . . .

A thing of purity.

The Soul Eater's snout quivered, and holding the feather as if it was made of precious crystal, she backed away toward the scales. With her other hand, she plucked up the pristine, sun-white Feather of Truth—Ma'at—that had lain on a small obsidian table and placed it on the left scale dish. Then—and if Fennrys had thought that he'd still possessed functioning lungs, he would have held his breath—she placed Fennrys's mourning dove feather in the right scale. The finely balanced dishes seesawed, the delicate arms wavering up and down. . . .

And the balancing of the scales . . .

Perfectly even.

A soft gasp escaped Rafe's lips.

And the Fennrys Wolf's knees gave out and he fell in a heap on the cool, alabaster floor. For a long moment he hunched there, palms pressed to the smooth stone, the breath heaving in and out of his lungs, his heart—still nestled deep inside his rib cage where it should be—hammering, sending the blood surging through his body. He was alive.

Oh, Mase, he thought, savoring the sound of her name in his mind. *That was a close one, I think.* . . .

After a moment, Rafe dropped to one knee in front of Fennrys and put a hand on his shoulder. "I was right about you," the ancient god said. "You *do* deserve a second chance. Maybe even a third."

Fennrys mustered a smile. He'd been clenching his jaw so tightly, struggling to remain impassive, brave, in the face of what he'd been certain was his doom—finally—that it made the muscles of his cheeks ache.

"Thanks for the vote of confidence," he said, his voice a dry rasp. "I mean it."

Rafe helped him back up to his feet, and Fennrys saw that the demon Ammit, the Soul Eater, was nowhere to be seen. The mourning dove feather still lay on the scale dish, opposite the feather of Ma'at.

"It's not . . . it wasn't a cheat, was it?" Fennrys asked quietly.

Rafe shook his head. "You can't cheat Ammit."

He walked toward the dais and plucked the dove feather out of the dish. The scales wavered only slightly. He handed the feather back to Fennrys, who tucked it into the scabbard of the short sword Maddox had given him. His jacket was ruined, shredded by the demon's claws and he stripped it off, leaving it behind on the steps of the dais, like an offering.

"Not that I've ever seen something like *that* happen before. . . ." Rafe glanced back over his shoulder at the gaping hole in the floor beneath the scales. A deep, sonorous rumbling sounded forth—snoring. The demon slumbered once again. And Fennrys fervently hoped that it would be a long, *long* time before some other hapless soul awoke her to judgment.

Rafe led the way around to the back of the raised platform where a door Fenn hadn't noticed before, set into the hieroglyphic-adorned wall, now stood open. Above the door lintel, there was a painted depiction of a goddess, kneeling in a classic Egyptian pose, one knee on the ground. She had pale hair and her arms, outstretched on either side, bore feathered wings. A gentle golden light poured forth from beyond the door, and Fennrys felt hot, dry air on his face. But he could also hear the sound of rushing water. When they stepped through over the stone threshold, the temple room behind them vanished and Fennrys found himself standing in the water at the edge of a wide, shallow river, surrounded by tall, feathery sedge grasses—stands of papyrus. In the far distance, sand dunes shimmered in the heat.

Fennrys turned to see Rafe standing beside him, the pant

legs of his sleek suit wet to the knees.

"This isn't the River Lethe, is it?" Fennrys asked, instantly fearing for his memories again.

"No. Just a nameless bit of water. I think the ancient Egyptians figured that when you've lived one life on the banks of the mighty Nile, you don't need special rivers in the next. Now . . . follow me." Without hesitation, he waded forward, deeper into the river, where Fennrys saw a roiling disturbance ruffling the surface of the water. "If Hel can call in favors," Rafe murmured under his breath, "so can I."

Suddenly, a geyser of water shot skyward from the middle of the river, and the blazing desert sun turned it to a curtain of shimmering, rainbow-hued light. Just beyond that, Fennrys saw a woman, hovering above the surface of the waves on iridescent wings. She had long silver hair and held a staff in her hand. And she was smiling at him, the expression touched with wry amusement.

"I'm beginning to feel a bit like your personal chauffeur service, Fennrys Wolf."

"Lady." He bowed his head, recognizing the same bright figure who had transported him out of the Asgardian Hel at the behest of its mistress. It hurt to look at the shining silver figure, she was so bright and so beautiful. "I thought Iris was a Greek goddess," he whispered out of the side of his mouth to Rafe.

"Iris . . . Isis . . . it's only one letter of difference. Remember how I told you some of the Beyond Realms blur and overlap? Well . . . some of the gods and goddesses who dwell in them do, too."

"Lord Anubis," Iris/Isis said, turning her smile on her fellow immortal. "A rainbow in a desert land is a rare and precious thing. You know that."

"And beautiful, dear lady. Never more beautiful." He bowed gallantly, and her eyes sparkled. "But rainbows everywhere else seem to be in some danger these days. Rainbow bridges shattered, rainbow windows broken . . . and if darkness descends to blot out the light, they will cease to be entirely. Don't you agree?"

Fennrys glanced up to see her smile fade to seriousness.

"Whither goest?" she said, suddenly all business.

"Back into Asgard," Fennrys said, taking a step forward. "To bring Mason Starling home."

The rainbow goddess's expression became distant, and her gaze drifted over their heads as if she saw things that they couldn't. "You are too late," she said. "The Valkyrie is almost made."

"Almost?"

"The raven has shown her the spear," the goddess continued. "She will take it up. How can she not? And all will be lost."

"You said 'almost.'" Fennrys surged forward through the drag of the river current. "There's a lot of leeway in a word like that." He locked eyes with the goddess. "*Please*," he pleaded. "I need to go to her."

"Much evil has been done in the service of love, Fennrys Wolf." The shining goddess smiled down sadly at him. "Do not be one of those who sacrifice all else for its sake. Ammit has seen into the deepest corners of your soul and judged you worthy. Anubis deems you deserving of second chances. *I . . . see you as poised on the edge of a knife blade. I would have you cut your own heart out when the time comes to choose between the girl and the world."

"Would you? Make that same choice?"

"No. I did as you would." She shook her head, and her silver-bright hair shimmered. "I went to the ends of the earth and beyond to save *my* one true love. I bridged the gap between life and death and, in my arrogance, changed my world forever because of it. *Your* world might just cease to exist should you do the same."

"I'm willing to take that risk. Will you send me through?"

She gestured, and the rainbow spray plumed up out of the river again, shimmering like a curtain between them. "There is the way. Go in good fortune. May I not soon see you again."

"Likewise, Lady," Fenn murmured, and waded forward, through the middle of the diamond-bright veil, Rafe following close behind.

When the blinding brightness of the rainbow passage faded from Fennrys's eyes, his ears filled with the horrid, glorious sounds of men making war, coming from directly behind him. But in that moment it didn't matter, because right in front of him, less than thirty feet away, were the steps leading up to the soaring oak doors of the one place he'd always thought he belonged.

Valhalla.

He took a deep breath and—

"That's Odin's Hall. You can't go in there."

Fennrys raised both hands slowly, because he didn't want to

startle whoever had just slammed a hand down on his shoulder, and maybe provoke them into killing him. Not when he was so close to finding Mason.

"We can't go in until the fighting's done."

"I'm not here to fight," Fennrys said, turning around.

What in hell . . . ?

Fenn had expected to see an Einherjar. But the young man who'd accosted him was dressed—quite unlike all the other men on that field of death—in jeans and sneakers. And a letterman jacket from Columbia U with the designation of quarterback on the sleeve. Fennrys eyed him warily.

The guy had obviously had something of a rough go of it recently. And by "rough," Fennrys supposed he meant "lethal." The whites of his eyes were bloodred, and his skin was mottled. But his hair was still gelled and a hint of cheap after-sport body spray clung to him—mingled with the stench of a raging battlefield, it was more than a little disconcerting—making him seem just like any other college kid. From a horror movie.

"I don't think you're supposed to be here," the guy said, frowning at Fennrys.

"Yeah?" Fenn raised an eyebrow and gently plucked the hand from his shoulder. "And you are?"

A shadow of confusion flowed over the young man's face, but it passed quickly, replaced with an expression of stubborn mindlessness. "You can't go in there. Only the Einherjar feast in the halls of Odin. And not until the Valkyries call us to the feast." The way he made the proclamation made it obvious to Fennrys that the quarterback had pretty much no idea what he was talking about. The words were unfamiliar on his tongue and sounded as if he'd learned them by rote.

He didn't seem to know that there were no Valkyries left to call the men in from fighting. And there hadn't been for a very long time. Fennrys meant to keep it that way, but he had to get inside Valhalla to do that. He glanced at Rafe, who stood beside him, keeping a wary eye on the rest of the warriors and occasionally ducking out of the way when one got too close. The ancient god shrugged one shoulder.

"Like I said," Fennrys kept his hands up, palms out, "I don't want a fight. But I need to go in there, and you aren't going to stop me. You can try, but I'm going to go get Mason."

"Mason . . ." The young man's blocky features twitched with recognition. "Mason . . . Starling?"

"Yes!" Fennrys reached out a hand and grabbed a handful of the other boy's football jacket. "You know her? Have you seen her? Is she in the hall? Is she all right—"

"Let the man answer you," Rafe murmured, pulling on Fennrys's arm. "One question at a time. This dude is clearly a linebacker short of a huddle."

Fennrys backed off a step, and the kid nodded.

"Yeah. She was here. She was nice. . . ." He frowned again, swamped with uncertainty. "Rory shouldn't have done that to her. Putting her on the train like that. She's nice. Hot, too, y'know? I wonder if she'd go out with me. . . ."

So this guy had been with Rory when he'd taken Mason. He was probably the muscle that Rory had needed to accomplish the task. Fennrys wondered fleetingly just how the quarterback had then met his demise, and what had happened to Mason's shithead brother. But those were questions that could wait. Rafe was right. Death—or the shock of dying—had not been kind to whatever cognitive faculties Mr. Muscle had possessed in life. And Fennrys got the distinct impression that those had been somewhat limited to begin with. He clamped down on his impatience and took a deep breath.

"What's your name?" he asked quietly.

"Uh . . . Tag. Taggert Overlea. I shouldn't be here, either. I was on this train . . . and then . . . oh, man—"

"Tag." Fennrys shook him a little. It wouldn't do to let the kid spiral back into the memory of whatever death he'd experienced. It obviously hadn't been a pretty one, and the shock of those memories might just jar him out of his presently helpful state. "No. it's okay. You're here to help me. All right? You're here to help Mason. You said she was nice to you."

Tag nodded.

"Well, she needs us to help her out of a jam, okay? You have to let me pass. I have to go in *there*"—he pointed to the massive soaring doors of the feast hall—"so that I can help Mason. It's really important, okay?"

Tag nodded again. "Okay. But I told you—we're not allowed in until the battle's done. There's a . . . like an alarm system, y'know? You'll have to fight."

Fenn felt himself grinning. "I'm okay with that."

"You said you weren't here for a fight."

"I lied."

"Okay. Let's go."

A rune tattoo on the side of Tag's neck, just showing above

the collar of his jacket, began to pulse with a faint, reddish-gold glow. His meaty fist tightened on the hilt of the old, rusted blade he held, and he turned on his heel and lumbered forward in the direction of the feast hall.

Fennrys and Rafe followed close behind.

When Tag had said they'd have to fight, Fenn had thought he meant they'd have to fight the Einherjar. He'd actually sort of been looking forward to that—a good, clean, straight-up fight. No giant reptiles, no sea monsters, no storm zombies . . .

No such luck.

The second the football jock's foot hit the bare patch of ground in front of the mighty structure, the earth erupted as scores of gray, withered limbs suddenly punched up through the soil. Clumps of dirt flew, and Fennrys threw an arm up in front of his face to shield his eyes. When he lowered it, it was to see a small sea of draugr standing between him and the doors of Valhalla. The alarm system Tag had mentioned. It figured.

Draugr, he thought. *I hate these guys.*

He wondered for an instant how Mason had managed to run the gauntlet of zombie creatures to get into the hall herself. But then there wasn't much time to contemplate such things. The draugr, with their horrible white eyes and grasping talons and mindless, murderous rages, swarmed toward them.

Tag bellowed like a bull and surged forward, head down.

Rafe transformed with his usual elegance into the fearsome black wolf.

And Fennrys drew his sword, sank into a crouch, and

readied himself for the fight, the kill . . . for the wave of battle madness that would carry him forward to where a very special girl waited for him to bloody show up in time and help her out of a serious jam.

Because Fenn would be damned if he let Mason down again.

XI

*D*eath holds no fear for me. I shall conquer it as I conquer all things.

Fennrys had been joking when he'd said that to Mason. On the High Line, under a full moon, after she'd stabbed him and they'd kissed and she'd realized that maybe, just maybe, she might be kind of falling for him . . .

But in that moment, Mason realized that—even if he hadn't known it at the time—he'd also been speaking the truth. She knew now that he had, in fact, conquered death—after a fashion. He'd been to Asgard and made it out again. And even though she might have wished with all her heart that he was standing there, by her side, in that very moment . . . she was proud of him.

He'd made it out of there.

And she would too.

Gripping the iron medallion he'd given her as tightly as if

her life depended on it, and choking back the surge of panic clawing up from her chest, Mason squeezed her eyes shut and pictured Fennrys standing there in the hall with her. She pictured the torches flaring with clear golden flames . . . haloing his yellow hair as he smiled at her. Before she really even realized she was moving, Mason was suddenly about a third of the way down the vast hall, the sound of the closing doors still echoing in her mind. She was almost at a dead run by the time she reached the end, where a raised dais stood with steps leading up to a throne that looked as though it had been carved from the trunk of a thousand-year-old oak. Resting against one arm of the gnarled and knotted throne was a spear. And perched on the blade of the spear was an enormous midnight-winged raven.

Mason wondered fleetingly if it was one of Odin's fabled companions as the creature ruffled its oily, ragged-edged feathers and hopped up onto the back of the throne, where it hunched, glaring at Mason with one unblinking, ruby-red eye. It was probably far more likely that—judging from the state of the place—it was just some random bird that had made its home in the rafters of the deserted feast hall. When it opened its massive black beak to croak at her in a voice harsh as the north wind, Mason couldn't tell if the sound was a welcome or a warning. But she slowed her steps nonetheless and turned her attention to what she figured must be the Odin spear.

For a supposed object of magickal power, it was about as unimpressive as the rest of Valhalla. The long, slender blade of the weapon was etched with symbols—reminding her of the markings on Fenn's medallion—but the designs on the spear were almost entirely obscured, coated in a thick layer of dark, flaking rust.

It was only when Mason got closer that she realized that it wasn't rust.

It was old, dried blood.

Just . . . get it over with, she thought, shuddering. *Grab the damn thing and get out of here. Then it's back to Manhattan so you can find Fennrys and apologize for being such a bitch to him after the tournament. After that, you can hunt down your idiot brother, find out exactly what the hell he thought he was trying to pull with that insane train business . . . and* then *you are going to punch him in the face for shooting Fenn in the shoulder.*

Mason wasn't sure which of those things she was looking forward to the most. But both combined to fill her with a sense of urgency. As she ascended toward the massive throne, though, her steps faltered. This was the seat of a *god.* She wondered where Odin had gone—where all the gods had gone—and wondered if humanity was better off for their departure. She suspected as much. If what the other gods had done to Loki was any indication of how they dealt with unfortunate situations, then she didn't want to meet them. She just wanted to go home.

The raven on the throne cawed loudly, three times.

The blade of the Odin spear began to gleam with a sullen crimson light that modulated and seemed to match the hammering of her heartbeat as she took another tentative step forward, wondering what was wrong with her all of a sudden. The spear was her bus ticket out of there. It sang to her in her mind—a surging, insistent battle song that compelled her forward—so why then, beneath that urgent, crashing music, could Mason hear the clanging of warning bells loud in her ears?

She stared at the weapon resting against the great chair, propped up there as if its owner had simply forgotten it and would return any second to reclaim it. Mason hesitated, remembering something that Fennrys had said to her when he was mentoring her with her fencing technique. Something that hadn't been a joke. He said that you never just *pick up* a weapon. You *become* the weapon you pick up.

Mason did not want to become that weapon.

But what choice did she have?

The medallion tingled and grew warm in her palm, as if the magick within it was responding to the magick of the spear. Mason felt another desperate stab of longing. She wished Fennrys was there with her so bad it hurt. The red glow of the spear blade grew brighter. She reached out with her other hand and felt the waves of bloodred enchantment emanating from the Odin spear. It was the only source of light and heat in the entire gloom-filled hall.

Her hand hovered inches above the carved wooden shaft.

Just take the damn spear, she told herself. *You don't belong here. Only the dead belong here. You need to get out of this trap, out of this tomb, and go home. . . .*

Her hand spasmed, fingers cramping, but she couldn't make herself move any closer. The soaring roof of the hall seemed to be contracting, closing in on her. The darkness beyond the weapon's red glow was suffocating.

Suddenly, a booming crash echoed through the empty hall behind Mason. She spun around to see the massive doors at the far distant end of the hall swing wide. They crashed into the walls on either side of the archway, and the cold, pale light of the sunless Asgard sky poured into Valhalla. And standing there, silhouetted against the brightness, was the one person Mason desperately wanted to see. . . .

But not in this place.

"Fenn?" she whispered, horrified, but he was too far away to hear her.

No . . . , she thought, dread carving her suddenly hollow. *He can't be here!*

Framed by the massive doorway arch, Fenn's head was down and his shoulders hunched forward as if in great weariness. Backlit as he was, she couldn't see his face—or any defining features, for that matter—and yet she knew, instantly, just by the way he moved, who it was that had entered the hall of the gods.

The fingers of Mason's hand were clutching the iron medallion so hard that the edge of the disk had cut into her palm. She felt the blood, slick on the carved runes, and thought, *What have I done?*

She remembered Fennrys telling her—at the café in Manhattan, when they'd been attacked by monsters—that it was the power of her thoughts, the strength of her will, that made the magick of the talisman work. She'd done it then, used the magick to make a reality of what was in her mind. And her heart sank to think that, in her desperation to see him, to have him once more by her side, she'd done it again.

She'd wished Fennrys back to Asgard.

Which meant she'd wished that he was dead.

Mason heard the small, soft wail of anguish that escaped her lips. Rory had *shot* Fenn on top of the train. She flinched violently as the images assaulted her memory: the sight of Rory's face contorted in vicious rage . . . the flare of the gun muzzle . . . Fennrys's shoulder, bursting crimson as the bullet tore into him and he toppled off the top of the train car . . .

Mason squeezed her eyes shut, remembering how she'd just stood there, watching as Fenn's body tumbled along the rail tracks, legs and arms pinwheeling like a thrown rag doll's . . . and then the brightness of the Bifrost portal had swallowed her whole and she'd left him behind for dead.

Dead . . .

The Fennrys Wolf started toward her down the hall, his first few steps staggering and clumsy. From that distance, Mason couldn't see his wounds, but she knew they were there. They must have been terrible. A flood of guilt and bitter despair threatened to drown her where she stood.

"You can't be dead," she whispered, her voice gone parched and dust dry. "I'm going home. I'm going home to be with *you* again. . . ."

The touch of the spear would send her home.

She would leave this place . . . and never see the Fennrys Wolf again.

Behind her, the raven on the throne cried out in a harsh, urgent voice. Mason turned and saw that the spear was glowing so brightly it looked as if it would burst into flame. The image of it began to waver, like a mirage before her eyes, and

Mason sensed that she was facing a "now or never" scenario.

"Mase!" Fennrys called out, his voice shredded.

No. She couldn't bear to turn and seen him mangled by whatever death stroke had sent him there and so, instead, she turned away and reached for the spear in front of her. The music of it screamed at her. Still, she hesitated.

You could stay, whispered a voice in her head.

Stay there, in Valhalla, and be with him . . .

Watch Fennrys engage, day after day, in endless, mindless battle. See him turn into one of the Einherjar . . . A thing of senseless brutality, hacked to pieces again and again and put back together time after time but each time losing a little more of his humanity . . . Fennrys had told her that, growing up in the Otherworld, *this* was what he'd wanted all his life. This hall, this place. An honorable fate, a destiny. A glorious death that would guarantee him a place in Odin's Hall in Asgard, where he would battle and feast and it would go on and on until the End of Days. *This* was a Viking prince's reward for a life of violence lived. It was horrible.

It was Fennrys's.

"Mason!" he cried out again, closer now. "Stop!"

As she stood there, torn, a horrible image flashed through her mind—Fenn reaching her, taking her in his arms, winding her in a blood-soaked embrace as he clutched her to his ruined chest. . . .

She could almost feel the sticky-wet press of his wounds against her skin. . . .

"*Mason!*" He was running now, she could hear. Running toward her.

Mason didn't know what else to do. The pace of Fennrys's heavy, weary footsteps increased behind her, and a surge of panic crawled up her throat. She wasn't brave enough. She couldn't see him like that. It would kill her. . . .

Take the spear!

I can't . . .

"Mason! Don't touch the spear!"

I can't see him like that. . . .

Take the spear!

Mason squeezed her eyes shut and bit her lip so hard she tasted blood. She thrust her hand once more toward the spear, fingers hooked like the talons of the raven above her, reaching to grip it. She heard the raven's triumphant hiss—

A last ragged cry of "*Mase!*"

—and her fist slammed closed.

On warm, solid flesh.

Mason felt long, strong fingers closing around her own, and then she found herself pulled sharply back, away from the throne and the spear and the screeching black bird . . . and into Fenn's arms. He wrapped her in a fierce embrace and whispered her name over and over into her hair, and she clung to him.

She was sobbing into the torn material of his T-shirt. "Why are you here?" she cried. "Why are you *dead*? Oh god . . ." She could barely make out the sense of her own words through the thickness of the grief that clogged her throat. "I'm sorry, Fenn . . . I'm so *sorry*. . . ."

But he was shushing her. Rocking her back and forth, held tightly against the warmth of his chest. He was real and solid and *there*. And she felt no blood on his shirt, nothing sticky and congealing that bound them together.

"Mason," Fenn said, "I'm not dead. Not again. I *promise*."

A roaring silence filled her ears with those words.

Slowly, barely daring to hope, she opened her eyes and tilted her face up so that she could look into his eyes. They were red-rimmed with grief, or maybe it was fatigue, but they were Fenn's eyes, full of life. And—in that very moment— full of something that might just have been love.

"I'm *not* dead," he said again.

He dipped his head, and as if to prove to her just how very much alive he was, he kissed her. Mason's whole body melted, and she felt as though she might collapse, but he held her upright. Her lips opened beneath his, and she inhaled the breath from Fennrys's lungs, deep into her own. The warmth of his kiss felt like it was jump-starting her own heart back to life, and without even thinking, she reached up to wrap her arms tightly around his neck as he crushed her gently to him once again in a warm, real, *living* embrace. Mason could feel a flood of wetness on her cheeks, but she couldn't tell whose tears they were. She suspected that they were hers.

Fenn confirmed as much when he loosened his grip on her and reached up to brush them gently from under her eyes with his thumbs. He was smiling—that strange, rare, beautiful smile—and his frost-blue eyes gleamed brightly down at her.

"Hey, sweetheart," he whispered. "I missed you."

"How . . . ?"

He silenced her question with a kiss. And then another.

Then, reluctantly, he pulled away from her and took her face in his hands.

"We can talk later, okay?" he said. "Now? We need to go."

She put a hand over his beating heart—just to make sure—and nodded. He was alive all right. Even though the T-shirt he wore was so torn up it looked as though he'd just walked through a giant bread slicer. Aside from the shirt's decimation, though, Fennrys himself appeared to be unharmed. Breathing hard and disheveled, but unharmed.

"Yeah . . ." He covered her hand with his and pressed it to his chest. "There were a couple of draugr on the way in. And you know what a pain in the ass those guys are. But I had a little help. It's weird, but there's this guy out there in a letterman jacket—"

"You saw Tag?" Mason blinked up at him in surprise.

"Yeah. Friend of yours, right?"

"Friend of Rory's," Mason said, and watched as Fennrys's expression darkened. "Fenn . . . what the *hell* happened? And how did I wind up here?"

He hesitated for a moment. "I know some of it. But here—*especially* here—isn't the place to talk about it, Mase. Trust me. First we need to get somewhere safe."

She nodded, and exhausted and elated both, she let Fennrys wrap an arm around her shoulders and lead her down the dais steps. Questions could wait. As they walked down the long hall, a shadow swept over them. Mason flinched, ducking as the raven flew past, out the open archway, where it disappeared in the light streaming over the threshold of Odin's Valhalla.

As they approached the door themselves, Mason plucked at the material of Fennrys's shirt. It was hanging off the collar band in shredded pieces that flapped when he walked, and she noticed that it sported the remains of a Blue Moon beer logo on it. For some reason, she found that faintly hilarious.

"This is a truly unfortunate fashion statement, y'know," she said, grinning.

"My lifestyle is hell on a wardrobe."

"I think you should go Abercrombie. The boys in those ads never have to worry about ruining shirts," Mason said, not actually expecting that without missing a beat, Fennrys would reach up to the collar of what was left of his shirt and tear the thing effortlessly from around his neck.

He dropped the wrecked rag at the threshold of the hall and said, "Better?"

Mason felt herself smiling broadly for the first time in what seemed like forever. She stopped him before he could leave Odin's mighty feast hall and slowly ran her hands up his bare, scarred, beautiful chest. She felt him shiver at her touch, and she wrapped her arms around his neck and pulled his head down to hers.

"Definitely better," she murmured against his lips. And when he kissed her back, for a long, lovely moment, she let herself forget about everything else that was waiting for them beyond the doors of Valhalla.

XII

Outside the hall, the ground was littered with lank gray body parts and splashes of thick black blood. The field was ringed with Einherjar who stood like sentinels, weapons lowered, but still ready at hand. And Rafe was cleaning the edge of his bronze-bladed sword with a tattered rag that must have come from the tunic of one of the dead zombie warriors. Dead*er* zombie warriors.

"Wow," Fennrys said drily. "What did I miss?"

"You mean, aside from your shirt?" Rafe raised an eyebrow at Fennrys's lack of apparel. "I gave you that shirt."

"Fine. I owe you a shirt."

Rafe turned and winked at Mason. "Mason. Nice to see you again."

"You too. I think I owe you—"

"Unh!" Rafe held up a hand. "*Never* say that to someone

who might just collect one day. Do you hear me? Never say 'owe.'"

He smiled to soften the admonishment, but Mason remembered that she'd done something similar with a bunch of river goddesses. They had yet to make good on their claim, but hearing Rafe say that gave her a fleeting rush of worry, nevertheless.

Rafe glanced back at Fennrys. "The shirt-owing thing, I'll probably just let slide. It was just a promotional item anyway."

The coppery blade wiped free of gore, Rafe held it out in front of him and, with a flick of his wrist, made it disappear. Mason wondered fleetingly why he would need to clean a blade that was made of magick anyway, but she appreciated the gesture. She'd certainly never left a fencing practice without oiling and checking her weapon, filing it for stray burrs, making sure the hilt was properly tightened. . . .

At the thought of swords, Mason turned suddenly and ran for the stacks of weapons piled up outside the doors of Valhalla. She sighed in relief to see that her sword was still there where she'd left it, resting on top of a heap of old rusted weapons. She plucked it from the pile and slung the black leather strap over her head so that it hung properly across her torso. The weight of the sword hanging at her side made Mason feel instantly, infinitely better.

Until she turned back and saw the tall, black-cloaked figure of Hel gliding through the ranks of the Einherjar, who shifted uneasily to make way.

"Daughter." Hel's eyes flicked over Mason, her glance

taking in the sword at her hip and the obvious lack of Odin spear in her hands.

Mason lifted her chin and steeled herself for whatever wrath was about to fall upon her, but before Hel could say anything, Fennrys stepped forward, almost—but not quite—interposing himself between mother and daughter.

"Hello there," he said. "Again." There was a wary edge to his voice.

Mason looked up at him and then back at her mother. From the corner of her eye, she saw that Rafe had quietly circled around so that he was standing on Mason's other side. She suddenly felt like she was flanked by bodyguards.

"You two know each other?" she asked Fennrys.

Fennrys nodded, his eyes never leaving Mason's mother. "This . . . lady looks an awful lot like the one who busted me out of Asgard the first time."

"She's my *mother*," Mason said to Rafe. "Can you *believe* that?"

"Huh," Rafe murmured. His gaze, too, was fastened firmly on the slender, dark-haired woman. "I really can't. . . ."

Hel turned a bleak, frosty glare on Rafe. It was fairly clear to Mason that she knew she was in the presence of a fellow deity. And wasn't very happy about it.

"I dunno. I can see the family resemblance," Fennrys said. "The eyes . . . the hair. Can't believe I didn't put two and two together, but it's all starting to make a bit more sense now. Listen . . . I never got the chance to say thanks for the jailbreak last time." His posture belied the casual tone of his voice. "So, y'know . . . Thanks. And now, if you'll excuse us, we have to go."

Mason was a little startled by his reaction. For one thing, it was her mother he was talking to, and even if Mason herself didn't exactly harbor warm, sentimental feelings toward the woman, she would have thought that Fennrys would have exhibited his usual gruff charm. Especially if, as he'd said, she was the one who'd helped him escape from the torturous dungeon he'd been confined to. Just knowing that, in fact, went a long way toward softening Mason's feelings toward Hel.

"Of course you must leave." Hel inclined her head. "For the good of all. But my daughter still needs the spear of Odin to return to the mortal realm."

"Yeah . . . I'm a little bit fuzzy on something here," Fennrys said.

He didn't *sound* the least bit fuzzy on anything, Mason thought. Instead, he just sounded a little bit dangerous.

His voice lowered to a warning growl. "*I* didn't need a spear."

Hel's expression suddenly turned from hard and cold to blazing with ill-repressed fury. Mason could see it smoldering in her eyes.

"All *I* needed," Fennrys continued, "was your rainbow pal."

"*My* rainbow pal," Rafe interjected.

Fennrys ignored him. "I'm not sure why you wouldn't just call her up again to get your daughter home, if that's what you wanted."

"Iris is a goddess in her own right." Hel shrugged. "She does not always come at my bidding. Nor should she."

"But she did. For me. Because *you* asked her to," Fennrys said. "Didn't you? I find it hard to believe that getting me out of Hel was more important to you than getting Mason home."

"Fenn . . ." Mason put a hand on his arm. *Where is he going with this?* she wondered.

"You were needed to protect her," Hel said. "Time was of the essence."

"Right," Fennrys said. "But I recently got to thinking . . . I mean . . . here's Bifrost, the rainbow bridge between the mortal realm and Asgard, and it comes out right smack in the middle of Manhattan. So then I got to thinking that maybe you—maybe *Hel*, that is—had some kind of beef with the bridgekeeper of the Aesir. What's his name again? Heimdall?"

On the other side of her, Mason heard Rafe draw in a sharp breath.

Fennrys ignored that, too, and continued on. "I remember him from the stories. Grumpy sort, I seem to recall. Didn't really get on with some of the other gods, like . . . Loki. But this Heimdall guy is a bit of a slippery character too. Isn't he?"

Mason was listening very carefully to what Fennrys was saying, even though she still wasn't entirely certain what his point was. But then he glanced sideways at her, and his meaning became crystal clear with the next words out of his mouth.

"A couple of the Aesir are kind of like Rafe, here. They're *shape-shifters*. Heimdall is one of them. Could turn himself into a seal, among other things, which never sounded particularly useful to me, but there you go." Fennrys's voice was hard and blunt, his gaze flinty as he turned it back on the Asgardian standing before him. "The thing is, Heimdall always had this horn that he carted around with him everywhere, so no matter what shape he wore, you could always tell it was him. Dead giveaway . . ."

Mason's gaze went to her mother's belt, where a polished, gold-chased horn hung at her side . . . right beside the silvery-furred sealskin pouch. She felt the blood draining from her face.

That's not my mother.

A crushing weight of disappointment descended on her. All this time, Mason had thought she'd found her mother, when really, she'd just been played for a fool. The idea of her mother slipping away from her again was almost too much, and she felt a tightness in her throat that threatened to become a flood of tears.

Hang on, the voice in her head interrupted what was about to become a full-fledged bout of self-pity. *All this time you thought* this *was your mother. And all that time you thought your mother was kind of a jerk.* She took a step toward the imposter god. Anger instead of regret boiling in her chest.

"Take it off," she snapped. "Now."

"Speakest thou so to—"

"Don't," Mason snapped, "give me any of that wrathful god-speak thee-and-thou bull crap. Take off my mother's face before I take it off for you."

She loosened the silver rapier in its sheath.

Not-Hel's eyes glittered wildly, glancing back and forth

from Mason's face to her fist, wrapped around the hilt of the silver sword, and Mason drew the sword an inch or two from the scabbard. As she did so, a wild wave of energy pounded like a riptide, surging up her muscles from her fingertips all the way to her shoulder.

"Whoa there," Rafe murmured in Mason's ear as he stepped forward and gently drew her hand away from the sword. "Best not brandish a weapon on the steps of Odin's house unless you absolutely have no choice in the matter. Even if Odin's not here."

There was a moment of tense standoff, and then suddenly Yelena Starling's features blurred and shifted. The light of the day seemed to bend and reshape itself around her, and when it settled and coalesced, Hel was gone, and a tall, regally handsome man with burnished-copper hair and a sharply trimmed beard stood in the place where the image of Mason's mother had been only a moment before. His eyes—now a deep shade of amber—still glittered fiercely, but he had schooled his features to blankness.

"I knew it." Fennrys shook his head in disgust.

"Well, well," Rafe drawled. "Heimdall Bridgekeeper. You must be pretty pissed about the whole Hell Gate kaboom thing, yeah?"

"Mind your own matters, Dead Dog," Heimdall snarled at the Egyptian god of the dead through clenched teeth. Then he turned on Fennrys. "Had it been my decision, you would rot still in your dungeon cell. Hel deemed otherwise, and for that, there will be a reckoning, doubtless."

Fennrys's knuckles went white as he clenched his fist, but

other than that, he gave no indication that he'd even heard the insult.

"And as for you, Mason Starling, I sought to grant you a boon. To return you to the world of men. The Bifrost bridge is broken." There was a note of barely suppressed rage in Heimdall's voice as he said those words. "How will you get home now without my help? Without the magick of the spear?"

Mason frowned, but Rafe just laughed.

"Don't worry about that, friend. The Aesir and their toys aren't the only game in town. Folk seem to be getting in and out of Asgard just fine without crossing over your precious bridge. C'mon, you two," he said to Fennrys and Mason. "We don't need the spear, and you sure as hell don't need to stand here talking to this jackass anymore."

As they turned and started toward the ring of Einherjar who'd stood by during the whole exchange, Mason heard Heimdall say, "This is not the end. 'Tis but the beginning of the end."

Mason snorted in disgust and spun back around.

"Thank you, Mr. Cryptic," she said. "Man. I'm *so* glad you're really not my mother. But if you ever try to pull something like that again? I'll definitely make you wish you were someone else." She took a step forward. "Fennrys said your name is Heimdall?"

The god nodded once.

"Fine. Heimdall. You just made the list."

With that, Mason turned on her heel and, grabbing Fennrys by the hand, stalked toward the wall of warriors,

Rafe trailing in their wake.

"There's a list?" Fennrys said, increasing the length of his stride to keep up.

"There is now."

One last glance over her shoulder showed Mason that Rafe was stifling an amused grin and Heimdall had vanished completely. Which was probably a good thing, because it was getting hard for her to maintain a furiously dignified demeanor as they went. Mostly because she found that she kept stumbling over draugr bits.

"Seriously." She gestured at the carnage underfoot, which was extensive and more than even a guy like Fennrys could have accomplished on an average day, fighting his way into Valhalla to rescue her from a fate, she now suspected, might very well have been worse than death. "What happened?"

Rafe kicked a rubbery, ashen-hued arm out of his way and explained. "After Fennrys fought his way through into the hall to get you, a whole bunch more of those gray-skinned freaks showed up." He pointed to where a familiar figure stood among the Norse warriors. "But then your buddy Tag there, sort of . . . rallied the troops. The Einherjar banded together and kept the draugr from storming the doors of Valhalla."

Mason stared at the erstwhile football hero in open astonishment. Tag Overlea was apparently much cooler in death than he'd ever been in life.

"These boys haven't had anything to fight except each other for so long that this was kind of like a holiday for them," Rafe said. "Once he convinced them that they should take on the draugr, they . . . well. I mean, look around you. They had a little fun and made short work of your zombie pals. The kid's kind of a homecoming hero to these boys."

"Hey, Starling." Tag waved at Mason a bit shyly.

"Hi, Tag," she said. "Nice, um, work."

"Thanks." He hooked a thumb at the warriors standing behind him. "They did most of it. I just kinda pointed 'em in the right direction. Kinda like quarterbacking."

Mason glanced around at the ring of Einherjar and noticed that—even though they were all still a bunch of great, grim hulking lumps of muscle and menace—a couple of the glory warriors were actually smiling. And on the whole, there was a kind of . . . *spark* about them, a liveliness that hadn't been there when she'd crossed the field with her mother—no, *not* her mother, some liar god *disguised* as her mother—and it made Mason glad to see it. At least, it seemed, something good had come to the Einherjar because of their interloping presence there.

"Okay. So." Fennrys slapped his hands together briskly and turned to Rafe. "I told Mason that you could get us out of here. How do we do that?"

Rafe raised an eyebrow and pointed over Fennrys's shoulder. Mason looked and saw a strange, miragelike distortion that was just shimmering into view. Snaking tendrils of arcane energy, writhing up out of the battlefield carnage, began to coalesce . . . twisting together to form something that looked like a glowing, jagged-edged rip in the air. Beyond it, there was darkness, and flickering weird flashes of light.

"What *is* that?" Mason asked.

"The rift that's been growing between the worlds ever

since Fennrys crossed over into Asgard the first time," Rafe explained. "The thing has a fixed point in the mortal world, but now, for some time, it's been randomly manifesting in the Beyond Realms, providing doorways for entities that have long been absent from the world of men to sneak back in, and compromising the integrity of the entire fabric of reality. It's like a crack in a car windshield: it starts with one tiny flaw . . . and then it spiderwebs out in all these different directions."

"Wait. *That's* how you were planning on getting us home?" Fennrys shook his head in disbelief. "A *random* manifestation? And you're just telling me that now?"

Rafe lifted a shoulder. "I didn't want to burden you with uncertainty. I grant you it was a bit of a long shot—the rift's incredibly unstable—but it seems to draw energy from death and chaos"—Rafe glanced around—"and I figured there might be some of that once we got here. At any rate, it worked. I was right. Let's go."

"I don't understand *any* of this." Mason shook her head. "Why did Hel—or Heimdall or whoever—tell me the spear was the only thing that could get me back home? What would it *really* have done? Why am I even here in the first place?"

Rafe and Fennrys exchanged a laden glance.

"What?" Mason said flatly.

Fennrys shot a glare at Rafe, who pinched the bridge of his nose and scowled fiercely, muttering to himself.

"I was going to tell you all of this when we got home," Fenn said as he turned toward her.

"Why don't you tell me now," Mason replied, clearly in no mood to be coddled.

He turned and cast a pleading glance at the Egyptian god. "Rafe?"

Rafe huffed a sigh. "Okay. I'll try to explain this so it makes sense, but then we *have* to go." He gestured at Fennrys. "You already know his story."

"Yup." Mason clasped her hands together and nodded. "Viking prince. Raised by Faeries. Saved me from monsters."

Rafe nodded. "And you accept that."

"I don't have much choice. It happened," Mason said. "It was real."

"Yeah? Well, so's this." Rafe said, waving a hand at the fantastical landscape of Asgard. "I know it seems like a dream—or maybe a nightmare—but it's not. It's not an out-of-body experience, or a hallucination. It's not a trick. You just managed to walk into Asgard, the home of the ancient Norse gods, Mason Starling . . . and we're here to make sure you walk right back out again."

Mason felt a cold knot of apprehension twisting in her guts. "And why exactly did I do that? I mean . . . how?"

"Well, the *how* is that you crossed Bifrost," Rafe explained.

"You mean the Hell Gate." Mason nodded. "On the train."

"That's right. The magick of the Asgardian's rainbow bridge was woven into the Hell Gate way back in the early 1900s by the men who built it. Men who were the descendants of families who served the Norse gods. Men with ulterior motives and long-range goals, who hoped that one day, such a thing might come in handy."

"The *why*," Fennrys continued, "is that . . . someone else who currently shares those long-range goals thought you could come in handy, too."

Mason blinked at the two of them, utterly mystified. "Handy for *what*?"

"Do you know what a Valkyrie is, Mason?" Rafe asked quietly.

Mason snorted in grim amusement and gestured to the surrounding mythic environs. "Of *course* I know what a Valkyrie is. Although I haven't seen any around here, and I'm actually a bit disappointed by that. Winged warrior girls with swords?" She tapped the hilt of her rapier with a fingertip. "I think I might have imprinted on that when I was little. They were the only fun part of the stories my father read to me and my brothers before bedtime. The rest of it bored me—it's all so grim and apocalyptic—but Rory would freak if he didn't get his nightly dose of Nordic doom. If he knew this stuff was actually *real*? I can only imagine what he . . . uh . . ."

Her amusement faded as a creeping realization insinuated itself into her thoughts. A cold understanding and an even colder dread flooded her from top to bottom. The horror of the truth.

"Rory . . ." Mason felt like a hand was squeezing her throat. "He . . ."

"He wasn't just pulling some asinine stunt gone horribly wrong on you when you were on that train, Mase," Fennrys said quietly. "Your brother has an agenda. He's not the only one."

Mason was starting to feel a bit light-headed. Whether with apprehension or a slow-building rage, she wasn't sure. "Who?" she asked, her voice a dry whisper. "Who else . . ."

Rafe's dark, timeless gaze filled with compassion. "To some people, Mason, the old tales aren't just bedtime stories."

Her gaze swung back and forth between Rafe's and Fennrys's faces, reading the things there that neither of them could bring themselves to say.

"You mean to say . . . Rory and my *father* . . . ?"

Rafe nodded. "Remember those long-range goals I was talking about?"

Rory she could believe. But Gunnar Starling?

Her father . . . *No.*

"I'm sorry, Mason. Your dad's kind of a . . ." Rafe's dark brows knit in a deep frown. "Let's just say he's well-respected among the more arcane social circles of the power elite. And by 'well-respected,' I mean, 'greatly feared.' Rory, on the other hand, hasn't actually pinged anyone's radar where this kind of thing is concerned. He's just an opportunistic little rat, I guess."

"You're saying that my *father* is like some kind of supernatural mob boss."

"That's actually a pretty accurate description."

"And Roth?" Mason asked. "Did he have anything to do with this . . . this . . . ?"

Fennrys shook his head. "No. Roth was trying to find you. To warn you. In fact, he told me that he'd been sent by your father to find *me*, but he was worried about Rory getting to you first before he could warn us both. I do know that it was never in your father's plans for *you* to be the one to cross over, Mason. It was a mistake."

He leaned forward, forearms on his knees and hands clasped loosely in front of him. Mason couldn't help but notice the scars on his wrists. The ones he'd gotten when he'd been chained in a cell somewhere in this awful place that her father—and his father before him—thought was so great.

"They thought that *I* was the only one who could travel *into* Asgard," Fennrys continued, "and then be able to travel back *out* again. On account of the whole 'I'm kind of dead' thing and seem to be prone to doing that as a result. The plan, as I understand it from Roth, is that they were going to coerce me into crossing the Hell Gate. *You* were only on that train because you were supposed to be the . . . uh . . ."

"What?" Mason voice was tight. "I was only supposed to be the *what*?"

Fennrys turned his head, and his blue gaze was bleak. "The bait."

Rage—yes, it was definitely rage now, hot, liquid, incandescent—coursed through Mason's veins. *Bait*. Now that . . . *that* sounded like Rory. But the thing that cut Mason like the blade of the sharpest knife was that her father—her *father*—had known. More than known. He'd actually—what—sanctioned it? Approved of Rory stuffing her in a bag . . . locking her in the trunk of his car . . . He'd almost killed her. He'd shot Fennrys.

That, in itself, was enough to blind Mason with hideous anger.

But the fact that her father, who she'd loved all her life

more than anyone else, who she'd always known would protect her from hurt, was somehow involved in all of this . . . More than involved, it seemed . . . The rage evaporated and something worse—cold grief—washed over her in its place.

"The spear wouldn't have sent me home." Mason hugged her elbows to keep from shivering with the sudden chill that suffused her body. "Would it?"

"No." Rafe's pencil-thin dreadlocks swung as he shook his head. "That's not its purpose. Not exclusively, anyway— although I'm pretty sure it would have given you the power to go between realms all on your own. It would have given you the power to do an awful *lot* of things. That's why they were trying to get Fennrys to retrieve it. So that *then* they could have given it to you."

She'd known. Somehow, Mason had known. She'd felt it. Heard it in the crashing music in her head when she'd been so close—so *very* close—to wrapping her fingers around that ancient, terrible weapon.

"You're telling me that if I had picked up that spear, it would have turned me into a Valkyrie?" she asked, needing to be sure.

"According to a very old prophecy." Fennrys nodded. "Yeah."

"An old prophecy that my father knows about."

"Not really his fault, that." Rafe's gaze turned darkly inward, as if he was examining a memory. An unpleasant one. "A trio of delightful ladies called the Norns made damned *sure* he knew about it."

The way Rafe said "delightful" made them sound anything but.

Mason had read about the Norns—agents of fate, or destiny, or whatever you wanted to call it—and she'd read about Valkyries. Odin's shield maidens. His choosers of the slain, who would fly over battlefields and decide which of the most valiant warriors would die a glorious death in order to be admitted to the halls of Valhalla as Einherjar.

"Are there others? Other Valkyries, I mean?"

"As far as I know, the Valkyries are no more. Over the millennia they began, one by one, to abandon the All-Father of the Aesir. Some were sickened by the unending bloodlust, some probably just got bored. Some met their ends, and some rebelled against the gods and their pointless petty bickering and selfishness and rush toward a fated doom that the Valkyries began to see as less and less glorious and more and more a stupid, blind waste. Those that rebelled were banished to the mortal realm. I only ever met one who managed to tough it out and make something of a life for herself there."

"Who was that?" Mason asked.

"Her name was Olrun," Rafe said, and there was an uncommon hint of respect in his voice as he said the name. "She became a carriage driver in Central Park and vowed never to return to the halls of Asgard. But sometimes, one's calling is simply overwhelming. And when a real hero was on the verge of death, his spirit called to Olrun. She appeared to take him into the Beyond Realms. Something got in her way."

Fennrys lowered his gaze, and his shoulders sagged. "Me," he said.

"Yeah. You," Rafe said. "And in an act of selfless brav-ery—I usually like to call those kinds of things by their *proper* names: 'act of monumental stupidity'—you offered to go in his place. That, and the fact that you returned again, made you a harbinger of a prophecy and opened up a whole new can of magickal worms for the mortal realm."

Over Rafe's shoulder, Mason saw that the dark, glitter-ing rift—the tear in the fabric of reality—had grown large enough so that it dwarfed the doors of Valhalla, stretching from the ground to the vault of the sky. A strange and surreal portal. But it was crackling and flickering wildly now.

"We should probably go." She nodded at the rift. "Looks like it's getting temperamental. That thing I said about telling me everything now? I retract that. You can tell me all about why my father thinks it's such a good idea to turn his only daughter into a chooser of the slain once we're home."

Her voice caught, hitching a bit on the word "father," and she drove her nails into the palms of her hands to keep it from turning into a sob. Fennrys nodded and he, Rafe, and Mason stood and walked toward the dark, sparkling rift where it undulated and writhed, ominous and beckoning at the same time. Mason thought she could see things moving in what-ever it was that lay on the other side of the tear.

"That's what we call the Between. We're going to have to travel through that to get back to the mortal realm." Rafe rolled an eye at Fennrys. "And, yes, this time you *are* going to have to hold my hand. I'm not happy about it, either. But I strongly suggest you *not* let go. The things that exist in the Between aren't things you want to tangle with."

Before they stepped through, Mason stopped for a moment, turning back to Tag Overlea, who still stood there with a sword in his hand.

"Hey," she called. "You coming with?"

"Naw," Tag said. "Mr. Rafe kind of explained it to me. Far as I understand it, I'm here for good. I leave this place and I'm a ghost. But it's cool." He shrugged and blinked at her. Mason noticed that the redness was fading from the whites of his eyes and, with it, the dullness of his wits. He actually looked more like a normal person than he ever had. He grinned lopsidedly at her. "At least I can get these chowderheads doing something interesting for a change. And then maybe if we fight good enough, we can get some of that awesome grub and booze they're all on about." Tag started to turn away, back to where the other warriors seemed to be waiting for him. But then a shadow of a frown crossed his brow. He turned to Mason. "Hey . . . uh, seriously, Starling. I'm real sorry about, y'know, all that stuff. Tell Palmerston for me when you see her again, 'kay?"

"Sure." Mason smiled at him.

"And honestly? I know I said he was okay . . . but your brother really is kinda a douche. Don't turn your back on him, all right?"

"Trust me. I won't."

With that, Tag Overlea turned back to the Einherjar, who were waiting for him. Mason shook her head as she turned to follow Rafe, who'd shifted into his transitional man-jackal form, probably just in case anything in the Between decided to question his godly identity. A few yards from the rift, he stopped. Mason reached out to take the ancient deity's offered hand. Paw. Whatever.

"This whole thing," she muttered, "is incredibly weird."

On Rafe's other side, Fenn grimaced sourly and took the god's other hand. "It really is," he said. "Sadly, I don't think it's going to get any *less* weird."

XIII

Rory lay in a dull fog of painkiller-induced numbness, listening to the voices outside his door. When he'd first regained consciousness, he'd been disoriented and confused. Now he knew at least he was in the guest bedroom of the posh penthouse condo his father kept in midtown Manhattan—and he knew that whatever they'd pumped him full of, it wasn't anything even remotely over-the-counter. Only something magick-infused could make him feel that good. Especially considering the beating he'd taken . . .

Rory Starling had never had a very high pain threshold.

And so when Fennrys had attacked him and shattered his arm in an attempt to make Rory drop the gun he was pointing at Mason, the pain of that injury might have clouded his judgment. After all . . . shooting the one guy they needed, the only known, readily available soul who'd crossed the barrier into the Beyond Realms and walked back out again whole and *re*-alive . . . well, that might have been a little hasty. Because if the Fennrys Wolf was dead, then their one shot at retrieving the Odin spear from Valhalla was gone.

Or maybe not . . .

Rory couldn't remember exactly how he'd gotten to the penthouse. The last clear memory he had was watching his father destroy the rune gold that Rory had been using to augment Taggert Overlea's strength and speed. Of course, Rory had pumped so much rune magick into Tag—hoping to use him as a point man for building his own personal warrior band—that destroying the acorn had also destroyed Tag.

But Rory, more to the point, had destroyed the Fennrys Wolf first.

I put a bullet in that son of a bitch, Rory thought. *If that didn't kill him, the bridge exploding must have. I mean . . . there's gotta be a limit as to how many times a guy can die before it sticks, right?*

And even though a dead Fennrys would probably nullify any chance of setting Ragnarok in motion, Rory felt a small, grim sense of satisfaction at the thought of the Wolf's demise. But as he struggled to concentrate on the voices in the hall, it became increasingly apparent that the situation was a lot more complicated than Rory had stopped to consider.

"I would dearly love to know who, exactly, is responsible for the destruction of the Hell Gate," Gunnar said in a tight, angry voice. "And I want to know where your sister is!"

"Don't you think *I* do, too?" Roth snapped. "Why don't you ask Rory what *really* happened on top of that train? He was there—he should know, damn it!"

Whoa, Rory thought blearily. *Roth's pissed.*

That didn't happen. Ever.

"I already asked him," Gunnar snapped back. "He said he couldn't see for the brightness as the train passed over the Hell Gate. And then, once it reached the other side, she was simply . . . gone. He has no other explanation—"

"He's useless," Roth snarled.

"—and *I* can come up with no viable scenarios either. At least not ones that don't involve the death of your sister, Roth." Gunnar said those words carefully. Quietly. "It's a possibility that we're going to have to consider—"

"NO!"

Rory flinched at Roth's roar of outraged denial and a sound like a fist punching through plaster. The wall of the room he was in shuddered, and he felt a sympathetic pain in his own hand. He tried to turn his head to look at the limb he vaguely remembered having injured. . . . But it was just too hard to move, and his head rolled back on the pillow, his eyelids sinking shut. He thought he heard noises in his room—chittering and scrabbling sounds, like insects, and the clink and hiss of metal—but he couldn't make himself seek them out.

Stupid Roth, he thought, drifting on a soporific tide, *throwing a stupid tantrum . . . serve him right if something terrible had happened to his precious Mason . . .*

Rory felt a distant twinge of envy, followed by an even more distant twinge of guilt. He seemed to be the only one who knew just how much of a screwup his sister was. She'd proved it in spades at the fencing competition when she'd gone down in flames. He also happened to know that Cal Aristarchos blamed her for the damage he took the night of the storm. She was a phobic mental case. And she'd spent the last couple of weeks sneaking around with that muscle-bound creeper with the ridiculous biker-gang name.

What the hell's wrong with her?

When he'd first found out about it, Rory could barely believe that it was his sister's destiny to become a Valkyrie. That was way too cool for Mason. As far as he could see, she didn't have it in her, and it galled him intensely that she was the linchpin to his own damn destiny. Especially now that she'd gone and royally screwed up his and Top Gunn's grand plans for Ragnarok by simply vanishing into thin air as they'd crossed the Bifrost. Maybe she'd fallen off the train into the river below. Maybe she really was dead.

"Roth . . . Rothgar!" Out in the hall, Gunnar was trying to shout down Roth's stream of furious invective. "I know how you feel about your sister. Mason is more precious to me than gold. You know I never *ever* want to see her hurt— and we have no evidence to say that she is. All we have to do now . . . is find her."

"What about the Odin spear?" Roth asked, seeming to have calmed down somewhat, but there was still a hard edge to his voice. "We can't even begin to fulfill the prophecy without it. To get that, we still need *him*. And a way to get him into Valhalla—which would seem to me to be something of an impossibility now that the bridge has been destroyed."

Surprisingly, Gunnar actually chuckled.

"Roth," he said, "you disappoint me. Think for a moment. The Hell Gate hasn't always been here . . . but there was always travel between the Beyond Realms and the world of men. It just hasn't always been easy. And harder still for us 'mere mortals.' That's why this so-called Fennrys character was such a godsend, as it were. Wherever *he* came from, whatever his story, whoever named that lad after the Great Devourer was courting Fate."

"Like we're doing now," Roth said.

There was a pause. When Roth spoke again, he sounded calmer.

"What if we can't find him?" he asked Gunnar. "Do we leave it at that?"

What? Rory thought. *No! Shut up, Roth. . . .*

"If the prophecy is meant to be, it's meant to be," Gunnar answered.

Rory could almost hear his father shrug, and the sheer passivity of that statement made him want to scream.

"I believe it *will* happen," Gunnar continued. "If it does not . . . then we simply weren't fit to accomplish so monumental a task."

If Rory could have raised his voice in hollering protest, he would have. But whatever they'd given him was utterly paralyzing. The room noises were getting louder. . . .

"You're giving up?" Roth asked.

"How likely do you think that is, son?"

Roth was silent in response.

"Now," Gunnar continued, "our first priority is finding Mason and this Fennrys Wolf. And we'd best do it before the situation in the East River becomes untenable."

What? What situation? Rory struggled desperately to concentrate.

"What have you heard?" Roth asked.

Gunnar sighed gustily. "The destruction of the bridge seems to have made an unstable situation even more dangerous. The rift between the realms is widening, and if we cannot harness the power that is flowing through that mystical spillway before our rivals do, then all could very well be lost for us."

"Rivals. You mean Daria Aristarchos."

"Yes." Rory heard the bitterness in his father's voice. "There are others, of course, but they are weak and scattered. I respect Daria's strength and her determination. She's the most dedicated high priestess the Eleusinians have ever had. And she is a worthy adversary. But if she gets in my way, I *will* crush her."

There was a long silence, and Rory wondered why Roth wasn't cheering on that sentiment. It sounded like a good idea to him. Then again, he knew perfectly well that Cal Aristarchos's beautiful, bitchy mother was the head of a family dedicated to the Greek pantheon of gods in the same way his family was sworn in service to the gods of the ancient Norse. *Kick her ass, Dad,* Rory thought.

"Now . . ." Gunnar's voice sounded as if he was moving farther away, down the hall.

That's okay, Pops . . . don't mind me. I'll be fine here all by myself. . . .

"Find your sister, Rothgar," Gunnar said. "Use whatever resources of mine you need."

As the footsteps drifted away, Rory sank deeper into his pillow with a weak groan. The act of struggling against the medication to overhear that conversation had proved exhausting. But now he could sleep. Now that he knew Gunnar was still moving forward. And as soon as he'd rested up a bit, he'd prove to his father that he was still a vital part of the team. He went to close his eyes, but a surge of pain coursed through him.

"Holy *sh*—" He flailed spasmodically in the bed and swore, but a hand came down to cover his mouth, silencing him. Rory's eyes flew wide. The soporific effect of the drugs had suddenly, shockingly vanished. When he managed to focus his gaze, he saw Roth standing over him, holding an IV tube in his hand—the hand not covering his brother's mouth. He'd bent the tube in the middle, stopping the flow of a gently glowing, bluish liquid from entering Rory's arm.

"That wasn't anybody's gun but yours, brother," Roth said quietly.

Rory's protests were muffled squeaks beneath Roth's palm.

"Shut up. I've known you had a gun stashed in the glove box of your car for months now. I'm assuming it was part of the payment you got from your lunkhead buddies for the magickal performance enhancers you've been providing them with. Which, by the way, is right up there on the list of stupidest possible things to do *ever*." Roth's voice grew harsh with barely suppressed rage. "The family doesn't *deal*, Rory. That's a *rule*." His gaze bored into his brother like a drill. "But don't worry, I'm not gonna tell Dad that you fudged that little detail of your story."

He glared coldly down at his brother and, after a moment,

took away his hand from Rory's mouth. But Rory knew better than to make any noise. If he cried out and brought Gunnar running—as if *that* would ever happen—Roth would just renege on his promise and tell their father Rory had lied to him.

"What do you want, Roth?" he asked, his voice barely above a whisper.

Roth looked at him like he was beneath contempt. "What I want . . . is to know what *else* about your little story is a steaming pile of crap. I want to know what you did to Mason."

"I didn't do anything to her!"

"I don't believe you."

"All I did was get her on the train."

Rory was sweating now with pain. And fear. Truthfully? Roth had always scared the living daylights out of him. He was always so damned quiet that if he *did* ever say anything, you knew you were in trouble. But for some stupid reason, Rory decided to try and tough it out.

"*You* were the one who screwed up, Roth—you were supposed to bring that Fennrys dude over the bridge. I did *my* part. I'm the one who—"

"How?" Roth ignored Rory's counteraccusations. "How did you get her on the train?"

Rory swallowed nervously. If his brother found out that he'd essentially tortured Mason—that he'd ruthlessly wielded her claustrophobia against her like a devastating weapon— Roth would probably kill him. Or close enough, which might actually be worse. The pain had begun to flare like wildfire through Rory's whole body. His face felt like it had met a brick wall up close and personal, and the nerve endings of his right hand and arm felt as though someone had dipped them in a vat of acid. He knew Fennrys had broken his arm—badly—but he couldn't even lift his head to see the extent of the damage.

Roth held the crimped plastic IV tube up in front of Rory's face.

"I hear this stuff's pretty sweet. I have no problem whatsoever denying you access to it if you don't tell me what I need to know," he said, smiling dangerously. "You know . . . the Wolf busted you up pretty bad. The regular docs didn't think there was much they could do for your arm besides putting half a dozen pins and a couple of plates in. The rehab alone would have taken months. So Dad called in favors to get you taken care of, Ror, if only so you wouldn't end up as a totally useless waste. Even still . . . there's only so much the witchmechs can do, y'know?"

Witchmechs? Rory thought, his brain screaming with pain. And then he remembered. "Witchmechs" was a kind of derogatory term Gunnar had used in his diary in a couple of entries to describe the dwarves of Norse myth. They were repugnant things—evil little creatures that lived belowground and created wonders out of precious metals in return for dark bargains—but sometimes useful. Half witch doctors, half sorcerer-mechanics. Still, Rory wasn't at all sure what they had to do with *him*. . . .

"Maybe you were just too hurt," Roth was saying. "Maybe you never even regained consciousness. . . ."

"Jeezus, Roth," Rory gasped. "We're brothers!"

"And Mason is our sister." Roth shrugged. "Honestly? I've *always* liked her better than you. Now. *What* did you do to her?"

"Nothing! I swear!" Rory's brain went into spin mode. "She was with that Palmerston chick. And—uh—me and Overlea . . . we—we just told them we were going to a party. We told them to come along. That's all."

"And Mason just went with you. Just like that. Even after losing the competition?"

"Yeah. Yeah . . . I guess she was pretty upset. Maybe she just wanted to forget. I think that's what Heather said to her . . . I mean . . . I'm sure she did. Y'know. That a party would help take her mind off it." A flare of pain sizzled up from his arm to explode in fireworks behind his eyes. "C'mon, man! Let go of the tube—"

"Why the hell did Mason wind up on top of the train car?"

"'Cause she's so damn stupid!" Rory gasped. "You know she does crazy shit, Roth! I was—y'know—partying with Heather in the front of the salon car, and I guess things got out of hand between Overlea and Mason."

"You left that overgrown ape alone with her?"

"I didn't know. I guess . . . I mean, yeah. That was totally my fault. I should have been looking out for her, I know. I guess he got a little too aggressive. Dumb jock probably thinks he's a real Romeo. . . ."

What the hell, Rory thought. Dead men tell no tales, and if he was lucky—and Mason really was out of the picture for good—then he could pin his whole sorry screwup on a football player who his dad had just offed probably less than a couple of hours earlier. At least he could buy himself some time.

"I think maybe Mason told him off and went into the other train car to be alone," he continued, spinning a pretty plausible tale as he went. "I think Tag followed her. He's used to college girls. He probably cornered her and Mason . . . y'know. She probably got all phobic. You know how she gets. I think the most likely scenario is that she just freaked."

And, in fact, that *was* a pretty likely scenario. Even Roth, knowing Mason's history with claustrophobia, couldn't deny that. Roth's eyes narrowed, and he stared down into Rory's face for what seemed like half an hour. Rory held his gaze and silently willed his brother to believe him. The strange, restless, meaty-metallic noises he'd heard earlier had paused, and the clock ticking on the bookshelf across the room was now the loudest sound in the quietest room Rory had ever heard. He felt his heartbeat slowing to match it, each beat thrumming against the insides of his ears.

Roth let go of the IV tube.

"I have to go see what I can do about cleaning up this mess you've made," he said, and shook his head in disgust. "Maybe I can stop things from spiraling too far out of control . . . but I doubt it."

Rory almost wept with relief as the glowing blue magick flowed once more into his veins and wrapped him in a cloud of euphoria. He was going to be fine. He was going to be better than fine. He didn't realize just how much improved, though, until Roth turned to go. Before he did, he glanced back at his brother, and his gaze drifted to Rory's right arm—the one opposite to where the IV needle pumped such sweet elixir. The one that Fennrys had shattered, trying to wrest the gun from Rory's grasp.

"I told Gunnar he was making a mistake, having them fix you up like *that*. I'm still not sure you deserve it," Roth said. "All I can say is . . . don't waste it."

Rory blinked at his brother in confusion, his brain already cottony again with the painkiller. But as Roth left the room, Rory forced his head up off the pillow to see, finally, what had become of his wounded limb. He was just in time to see a strange, stunted creature tearing away the last, fibrous bits of flesh that held his forearm attached to the rest of him. There were two more misshapen, dwarfish things who carried Rory's arm away as he tried to scream, but the glowing blue narcotic that fogged his mind had also stolen his voice. He could only watch in silent horror as another witchmech crawled up through a strange, shimmering hole in the penthouse floor, carrying a bundle wrapped in oilcloth. As he was unwrapping it, Rory caught sight of the ragged stump where his forearm used to be . . . and passed out cold.

When he awoke some time later, Rory flailed around in terrified remembrance, struggling frantically to prop himself up. In the dim light filtering through the curtains, he saw his right arm, where it lay on top of the covers.

It was only a dream, he thought. *A nightmare.*

He still had his hand.

Whole and sound, his fingers and wrist moved with supple strength as he bent and flexed the joints. But something was strange. Different. As he contracted his fingers into a fist, they felt cool and too smooth against one another. He reached over and turned on the bedside lamp. In the glow from the single bulb, Rory saw that the skin of his arm gleamed with a watery, metallic sheen. Rory lifted his hand up in front of his face and gasped. His arm—his real, flesh-and-blood arm from the elbow down—was gone.

In its place was one made—impossibly—out of living silver.

Rory watched, mesmerized, as with a thought his shining fingers slowly clenched again into a fist. It felt like a sledgehammer. He smiled to himself at the thought of bringing that hammer down on the head of the Fennrys Wolf the next time they met. Because there would be a next time. And *that*, Rory vowed silently, was exactly what he was going to do.

XIV

For the life of him, Fennrys couldn't figure out how Rafe knew which way was which in the Between. Everything was a sameness of bleak, oppressive, darkly luminous fog. Yet somehow, the ancient god seemed to unerringly negotiate the murk and the press of wraiths, the shades of the unquiet dead.

Fenn was really only worried about what would happen once they actually reached their destination: North Brother Island—the anchor point of the rift where it manifested in the mortal realm.

"Once we get to where we're going," Rafe said, as if in answer to Fennrys's thought, "we'll need to leave. *Quickly.* I have a boat standing by."

"A boat?" Mason asked, ducking to avoid something smoky and toothy that drifted past her head.

"The rift opens up on an island," Fennrys explained, and then turned to Rafe. "This wouldn't happen to be the same boat that took so long to get to us last time that I almost got eaten by a sea monster, would it?"

Rafe grinned sourly. "I told Aken that if he's not waiting when we get there this time, I'm actually gonna make him *pay* his bar bill. All of it."

"Sea monster?" Mason raised an eyebrow.

"*Dead* sea monster," Fennrys reassured her.

"Right. Okay. So . . . an island." Mason waved off another wraith that was doing its best to tangle itself in her hair. "Sounds . . . nice?"

Fennrys snorted.

"Oh, come on," Mason said. "How bad can this place be? I mean, I like islands. Y'know: Coney . . . Hawaii . . ."

"Rikers . . . Devil's . . ." Fennrys rolled an eye at her.

"Here we are!" Rafe sang out. "Last stop, all exits, no waiting, people!"

The god surged forward, and the swirling dimness that pressed in upon the trio suddenly split, spilling brilliant crimson light into the Between. Rafe hauled Mason and Fennrys in his wake through a kinetic surge of storm-cloud energy that wrapped around them and snapped at their limbs and hair and hands. Together, they tumbled through from the Between, to land sprawling in a place that resembled a moss-thick, leaf-strewn clearing on the edge of a forest in a fairy tale. The kind of forest that small children and comely maidens of virtue true were always being told to avoid entering at all costs.

Fennrys shrugged out of Rafe's grip and pushed himself to his knees, gazing all around. Opposite the trees, a ragged little

cove and a refuse-strewn, rocky beach gave way to a view of
the East River. The sun was close to setting, and streamers of
bloody-red clouds unfurled against the burnished gold back-
drop of the sky. Behind them, beneath the trees, the shadows
were deep purple, and the twilight contrast clarified every
little detail of leaf and twig, picking them out in sharp, stark
focus.

"Did it work?" Mason asked, rolling over and pushing the
hair from her face. "Are we there?"

"Yeah. It did. We are." Fennrys hauled himself to his feet
and held out a hand to help Mason to hers. "Welcome to
North Brother Island, Mase. The place I died."

Mason's eyes went wide, and her mouth drifted open. Her
hand tightened convulsively on his, and he could see her gaze
fill with concern for him. Fennrys wasn't quite sure how he
felt in that moment, revisiting the place where he'd sacrificed himself and gone to Valhalla so that another man could
live. He'd thought it might have been hard to take—that it
might've hurt coming back. But in fact, all he felt was a kind
of hollowness. Echoes. It felt like that life had belonged to
someone else. The only thing that mattered to him was who
he was *now*. And who he was with.

He reached out a hand and smoothed Mason's hair, the
strands slipping through his fingers like spun silk, midnight-
hued and shining. Her eyes never left his face as he did so,
and the warmth and compassion in that sapphire gaze made
everything Fennrys had gone through to be there, in that
moment, completely, totally worth it.

He felt himself smiling as he reluctantly turned his gaze

from her face to their surroundings. In the distance, he could make out the contours of several buildings, their outlines softened by the massive overgrowth of vegetation that had taken over the island since it had been abandoned. The island had once been home to a quarantine hospital and had seen more than its fair share of tragedies, but now the whole place looked as though it was being consumed by nature. It was eerie. As were the strange, will-o'-the-wisp-ish lights that sparkled and danced in the deep shadows under the trees.

"As islands go," Mason murmured, "this place is less resort-y than I generally prefer." She shivered and hugged her elbows. "It feels kind of . . . haunted."

"It *is* haunted," Fennrys said.

In the west, the glass-and-stone towers of Manhattan lay glittering far beyond the restless gray stretch of the Hell Gate strait like some fairy-tale kingdom. The sun was sinking swiftly behind the artificial horizon of the city line, and a deep indigo blue tinted the vault of the sky in its wake.

"I wonder what time it is," Mason said.

"Yeah? I wonder what *day* it is," Rafe muttered, then shrugged when Mason glanced questioningly at him. "Time passes a little differently in the Beyond Realms. Until I see a calendar, even I can't be sure how much of it passed *here*, while we were *there*." He turned to the water and scanned up and down the shore, a frown creasing his forehead.

Mason sighed. "This isn't going to be one of those 'hapless mortal returns home after a night of revels to discover a hundred years have passed and everyone she knows is long dead' folktale things, is it?" she asked drily. "Because that would suck more than all the other weird things that have gone on in the last few hours of my life."

"Hey, there are worse fates," Fennrys said, striving for lightness.

But Mason had obviously heard the edge in his voice, and he mentally kicked himself. It wasn't her fault that what she'd just described was, fundamentally, almost exactly what had happened to him.

"Oh god." She winced. "I'm so sorry, Fenn . . . I didn't mean—I wasn't thinking—"

"Forget it, Mase." He shook his head and forced the smile back onto his face. "It's okay. Really. *I'm* okay. Hell . . . if I'd lived and died when I was supposed to, I never would have met you, right?"

"I'm starting to think that's maybe not such a bad thing."

"Stop." He gripped her by the shoulders—hard enough to make her blink up at him. "Don't *ever* say that. Nothing about this is your fault, and you are *not* the guilty party here. We will figure out how to make all of this right and then, when all this is done, we will go back to the Boat Basin Café and we will sit at that pain-in-the-ass waiter's table again and we will finish those beers and order those burgers like we were supposed to. Okay?"

"Okay."

"Damned ferryman," Rafe muttered, still scanning the boatless river. "I'm going to go see if I can spot our transport farther down. You two find somewhere safe to hunker down and wait until I get back. With darkness falling, I don't want Mason wandering around out in the open in this place."

Fennrys agreed, even though he could feel Mason bristle a bit at his side. But then, in the near distance, something horrible-sounding yowled, yelped, and went crashing through the shadow-bound underbrush. Mason's hand flew convulsively to the hilt of her sword, but Fennrys just smiled at her and shook his head, covering her hand with his own.

"Don't give them a reason," he said. "This is the kind of place where the best offense is strictly defensive. Flight first," he said. "Fight only when you have to, remember?"

"Right." Of *course* she remembered. It was the same thing he'd said to her in both real life and real scary dreams. "Run."

"If you have to."

She nodded and relaxed her grip, flashing him a brief smile and taking a breath to calm herself. Fennrys looked around and spotted the shell of one of the island's old service buildings looming up through the trees like a medieval castle.

"We'll hole up in there until you give us the word," he said to Rafe.

Rafe nodded. Then, in the blink of an eye, his form blurred and a sleek black wolf took off at a run down the ragged beach, disappearing around a weedy promontory.

When he was gone from view, Fennrys took Mason by the hand and led her along a barely discernible path and through a gaping hole in the brick wall of the outbuilding—the actual door was impassable, blocked by a stand of saplings—and into a blue-shadowed, vaulting room. Half the roof had collapsed, and the floor was carpeted with fallen leaves that gathered in knee-deep drifts in the corners. In the gloom, Mason and Fenn could barely make out each other's faces, so Fennrys gathered up a small pile of fallen twigs and branches and cleared a space in a crumbling alcove that could serve nicely as a makeshift fireplace.

"Here . . ." He fished in his pocket for the lighter he carried. "Why don't you start a fire for us?"

Mason blinked up at him. "Really?"

Fennrys reached out and tapped the iron medallion hanging on the leather cord around Mason's throat. "Do you remember that night back in my loft?"

Mason nodded, the hint of a wicked grin tugging at the corner of her mouth. "Only every second of it, yeah . . ." She reached up to trace her finger lightly along the line of the scar she'd given him.

Fennrys smiled, his eyes gleaming in the dimness. "Okay. Good. No stabbing this time, all right? I just want to see if you can conjure a little fire. Like I taught you in the boat basin—use your mind to shape the magick."

"I'm not like you, Fenn. I'm not trained for this stuff. Should I really be doing this?"

"I don't see why not. I believe in carrying as many tricks in your bag as you can. Never know when they might come in handy." He flicked his thumb on the wheel of the lighter, and a little blue-and-yellow flame sprang to life on the wick.

Hesitantly, Mason reached out with thumb and forefinger. . . .

"Ouch!" she yelped, and drew back.

Fennrys grinned. "You're playing with fire, Mase. You have to will yourself to *not* get burned. Try again."

He watched as her other hand drifted up, fingertips resting lightly on the face of the iron medallion. A tiny crease formed between the dark arches of her brows as her face settled into an expression of fierce concentration. She took a deep breath, reached out again, and gently plucked the flame from the wick of the Zippo. The delighted grin that spread across her face, lit by the tiny fire's glow, made Fennrys's heart constrict in his chest.

Mason turned her hand over and nudged the flame from her fingertips to her palm, where it flickered and danced, cycling through shades of orange and blue and green . . . then, suddenly, the blazing little teardrop turned violet and shot into the air like a bullet. Fennrys ducked as it rocketed past his head and began to ricochet wildly off the crumbling brick walls. Mason threw her arms up over her head and crouched, and Fennrys bent his body around her, shielding her from the incendiary little missile. Suddenly, they were both in very real danger of getting badly burned, and there wasn't anything Fennrys could do. It wasn't his spell.

Beneath him, he could feel Mason struggling to wriggle free of his protective embrace. He made a grab for her as she slipped free and thrust her hand high above her head—fingers spread wide as if she wore a baseball glove—and snatched the fiery little projectile out of the air. In one fluid motion, she snapped her fingers shut on it like a cage, spun around, and hurled the flame at the pile of kindling . . . where it burst in a miniature explosion of orange and crimson, splashing sparks onto dry branches that blazed up into a crackling, cheery little fire.

Gasping, Mason collapsed forward, propping her hands on her knees, and Fennrys started to laugh. From behind the curtain of her hair, she cast an incredulous look at him as his mirth almost doubled him over.

"See?" he said. "You're a natural!" Still chuckling, Fennrys walked over and stomped on a pile of leaves smoldering in one corner of the room. He pointed to the campfire. "Look. All we need is marshmallows."

"Great. *You* can conjure those. I'd probably wind up calling forth a tiny horde of tasty, demonically possessed puff balls." She slipped the medallion from around her neck and handed it back to Fennrys, shaking her head. "I'm gonna leave the spell casting to the pros, thank you."

Fennrys grinned and fastened the charm back around his neck. Instead of the metal shocking him with a chill against the skin of his bare chest, it was warm. He didn't know whether the heat was from the magick or from Mason, but both were welcome. There was a substantial pile of leaves in a drift near the fire and they sat down in it, Fenn wrapping his arms around Mason and pulling her close.

"You know, this place really isn't so bad," Mason said, leaning her head on Fennrys's chest and gazing up at the broken windowpanes glinting in the last gleam of twilight.

The firelight reflected off her smooth, fair skin, turning her face to pale gold. She gestured at the leaf-and-rubbish-strewn space where the shadows crawled, writhing up the walls and gathering in the broken corners of the roof rafters. As the very last of the day's light leached from the sky, it felt to Fennrys as if nightmarish things might come seeping through the holes in the walls at any moment.

"All it needs is a good sweeping up," Mason continued. "A

few pieces of art on the walls. Maybe some nice curtains . . ."

The temperature was dropping precipitously with the onset of night, and Fennrys felt the shivering that ran through Mason's limbs despite her game face. He hugged her close, gazing down at her. She gazed back; brave, trusting, beautiful.

"Curtains," he said.

"Yeah. Curtains."

"You're a weirdo." Fenn shook his head. "Must be why I love you."

And time suddenly stopped.

Right there. With those words. That word.

He hadn't meant to say it, but he knew—in that moment—that he meant it.

Love . . .

Love . . .

Mason's breath caught in her throat, and her heartbeat slowed to nothing.

She was stranded in a derelict ruin, surrounded by a haunted forest on a phantom island in the middle of the East River with a dead guy, having just escaped from a place that wasn't *really* supposed to exist, and her family seemed to be plotting sinister things for her future, and . . .

And none of it mattered. *None* of it.

Because Fennrys had just told Mason that she was a weirdo.

And that *he loved her.*

Stunned to silence, Mason looked up into his eyes and saw that he meant what he'd said. And that he felt the exact same way as she did about every other damned thing in that moment. *None of it mattered.* Smiling his strange and ridiculously beautiful smile, he bent his head to hers, and Mason reached up to wrap her arms around his neck. Her mouth opened under his, and she felt as though she could devour him whole and still be hungry for more.

The way he kissed her back, she could feel that he was just as ravenous. As they pressed against each other, everything else fell away. All Mason could feel was Fennrys's lips as they moved over hers, his hands—fingers strong and splayed wide, roaming over her back and shoulders as if he needed to touch as much of her as he could all at once—and the beating of his heart as they fell back into the bed of leaves beneath them. The broken walls that sheltered them loomed like the battlements of a medieval fortress, and overhead, Mason thought she saw stars peeking through. The lonely cry of a hunting owl echoed in the distance, the firelight cast Fenn's profile in crimson and shadows, and Mason felt as though she had fallen into the pages of a fairy tale. Even prefaced by all the madness that had led to that moment, she could hardly find cause for complaint. She just gave herself over to passionately kissing her handsome prince.

So far, this is one of the fairy tales with a happy ending. . . .

She could feel the corners of her mouth turning up at the edges beneath Fennrys's lips, and he broke the kiss, pulling his head back a few inches so that he could gaze into her eyes.

"Did that tickle?" he asked, his winter-blue eyes glinting with amusement.

"No . . ."

"Then why are you giggling?"

"I was smiling." She ran her fingertips over the dark-gold stubble that shadowed his jaw and chin. "You *could* use a shave."

"I've been a little busy."

"But you're still not a werewolf, and *that*, at least, is a great comfort to me." She felt her grin widening. "Only that's not why I was smiling."

"I really think you were on the verge of giggling."

"I'm *happy*."

"You are?" he said, and Mason could hear the apprehension in his voice.

"In spite of everything—"

"And in the middle of all this chaos."

"—and in the middle of all this chaos . . . *yes*. I'm happy."

Fennrys traced the curve of her cheek with the fingertips of one hand. His expression was starkly unguarded in that moment, and Mason was worried suddenly that it might all be too much for him. But then he saw the way she was looking at him, and his mouth bent back into that insanely kiss-worthy smile again.

"Hey," she whispered against his fingertips as he ran them beneath her cheekbone and across the curve of her lips. Just the slightest touch from him left her skin tingling. "Don't knock it." He raised an eyebrow, and she explained. "I think that in a situation like this—not that I've ever really *been* in a situation like this before—you might as well try to find whatever joy you can and make the most of it. I mean, you never know what's thundering on down the road toward you."

"Speaking metaphorically, of course," Fennrys said wryly.
"Of course."

Mason grinned and reached up and pulled his head down
so she could kiss him again. She had the distinct feeling she
was going to enjoy being able to do that whenever she wanted
to. Now that she knew how Fennrys felt about her . . . she
wanted to tell him in that moment that she loved him, too.
But at the same time, she was almost afraid to. She didn't
know why, but it almost felt like if she did, she'd break some
kind of spell or something. It was stupid. But she also wasn't
willing to tempt fate. Everybody else seemed to be doing that
for her, and—what was worse—she'd let them. She'd let herself be blind to her father's dark obsession. She'd let Rory use
her claustrophobia against her. She'd let Heimdall manipulate
her, using her dead mother's face.

She'd stopped asking questions. . . .

Suddenly, a chill traced down her spine, in spite of the
warmth of Fennrys's body pressed against her, as Mason realized that she hadn't even asked the biggest question of all.

"Hey." Fennrys finally broke her long silence, putting a
finger under her chin and tilting her face up so she had no
choice but to look up into his eyes. "What is it? What's both-
ering you?"

There were things moving through his gaze. Shadows.
Secrets . . .

Mason shifted up onto her elbow so that she was looking
down at him. She put her hand on his chest and felt the steady
beating of his heart, thrumming against her palm.

"How did I cross over into Asgard?" she asked.

When his mouth opened and no words came out, Mason was pretty sure she knew. She just needed to hear him say it.

"Fenn?"

The muscles of Fennrys's neck moved convulsively as he cleared his throat and found his voice. "Yeah?"

"It's okay," she said. "I can handle it."

Are you sure? whispered a small voice in her head.

"I know you can. I know. Mason . . ." Fennrys closed his eyes.

She waited.

When he opened them again, she saw the answer to her question in the depths of his blue gaze before the words were past his lips.

"You died."

A sap pocket in one of the branches of their campfire suddenly popped loudly and hissed, spitting sparks and brightening the air with a brief orange flare that dwindled almost instantly to nothing. The shadows in the room crowded closer. Mason could almost feel them. It was as if the shades that haunted North Brother Island had suddenly realized that she was kindred to them.

You are.

Dead.

She'd asked and he'd told her. And there it was. No sugarcoating.

It felt as if the world was falling away from her. The crumbling bricks, the leaves, the firelight . . . everything but Fennrys's face, clouded with concern, was becoming insubstantial. As if the world was the ghost. Not Mason.

But you are.

Fennrys sat up and pulled her with him. Her head lolled on her shoulders, her ability to make her muscles work properly fleeing from her in that instant.

"Mason," he said, giving her shoulders a shake. "Mase!"

She tried to focus on his face. She tried to breathe.

Am I supposed to breathe? Do I do that?

"Sweetheart . . . *listen* to me."

He breathes . . . his hands are warm . . .

"It was a long time ago. And it doesn't change a *thing*. It doesn't change who you are, or how I feel about you."

Dead girls don't cry. . . .

But there was wetness on her lashes. It turned the firelight into golden spangles and made it seem like she was looking at Fennrys through a curtain of rain. He gazed at her, eyes locked on her face, unblinking, unfailingly steady. He was there. He was real. And he was dead too.

Mason drew a sudden, deep breath.

And the world snapped back into focus.

"How?" she asked. "When?"

"I can't be sure, but I think it was probably right around the time that your claustrophobia first manifested."

"Oh my god," Mason murmured. "The hide-and-seek game . . ."

"Yeah," Fennrys said. "I think so. I mean, it makes sense. I think your phobia is a result of the fact that you died. I mean, it didn't take—obviously—but you crossed the threshold."

"Something sent me back."

Fennrys nodded.

Mason knew what the something—some*one*—was. "My mother."

Fennrys nodded again. "That's what I was thinking, too. I mean, I'd say that's a pretty fair guess."

"It's *not* a guess. I know it was her," Mason said. There was a sense of utter certainty as she said the words. Her mother was a queen of the underworld, and her mother had sent her back. Just like she'd sent Fennrys back.

And the thing was . . . Mason knew. She'd known it all along. Even though she had no memory of the event, no sense of what had actually happened to her, trapped in that shed, she had always, since that time, felt different. There was a distance . . . a detachment. A feeling that she was always on a slightly different vibrational plane from all the other students at Gosforth. Then there were the nightmares . . . the claustrophobia . . .

No. Not anymore. I will not be afraid of anything anymore.

Mason closed her eyes and felt herself grow light as air.

The air flowed into her lungs, her blood sang through her veins. Her hands were still on Fenn's chest, and she could feel the beating of his heart. And then her own . . . as her heart began to beat along with his.

She was dead. *Was* dead. And now . . .

And now she felt more alive than she ever had.

Mason left one hand over Fennrys's heart and put the other over her own. Her heartbeat was light and quick, strong and vibrant. Fennrys's was deep and steady and powerful. With those two beats coursing through her, rhythm and counter-rhythm, Mason strangely, surprisingly, didn't care that she was dead. Or had been. Or however that had worked out. She didn't care because the very same thing had happened to Fennrys, and that meant that the two of them were special in the same way.

If he could handle it, so could she.

Fenn was still gazing steadily at her, a shadow of worry twisting in the depths of his blue eyes. He needed to know that she was all right. She leaned forward and wrapped her arms around his neck and let him know she was. He pulled her close, and Mason let herself drift on the sensation of kissing Fennrys, but suddenly, he froze. She thought for an instant she'd done something wrong, but she saw that his head was cocked to one side . . . listening . . .

Then she heard it too.

Howling.

Sorrowful, soul-deep, and fiercely, frighteningly angry.

Fennrys was up on his feet and loosening the blade he carried strapped to his leg in its sheath. The howling built to an echoing cacophony, and Mason shivered when she realized what it was. Wolf song.

Rafe.

Something was terribly wrong.

Mason leaped to her feet and kicked at the little bonfire until it was extinguished. Then she and Fennrys were running before Mason even had a chance to wonder what the hell was going on. As they rounded the southernmost tip of North Brother Island, Mason and Fennrys saw that their ride was waiting for them.

Just not quite in the way they had expected.

XV

Aken the ferryman floated in the water about ten feet from shore.

More precisely, pieces of him floated in the water. The boat that Aken had been meaning to transport them from the island in was smashed right through the middle, upended and jammed against a shoal of rocks. Its two distinct halves bobbed awkwardly just off shore.

Rafe hunched in the shallows of the water; a huge, sleek black wolf howling at the dark night sky. It was the most heart-wrenching, mournful sound that Mason had ever heard. As she and Fennrys slowed to a stop, the howling died and Rafe's outline blurred until he knelt on the shore in his transitional man-wolf state.

Mason heard him swear in what she could only assume must be his ancient Egyptian tongue, and she was glad she couldn't actually understand what he was saying. It sounded like curses—in the original sense. After his outburst, Rafe seemed to deflate a little, his shoulders sagging. He mumbled something about needing to perform a ritual of passage for the dead demigod Aken's spirit, and began uttering a low, singsong incantation full of raw, welling emotion.

Fennrys and Mason moved off down the shore to give him privacy, both of them pretending not to notice the tracks of bloodred tears that marred the fur of his cheeks as he did. As they walked down the beach, Mason couldn't help but notice that Fenn's hands were clenched into white-knuckled fists. He glanced over and saw that she was staring at him.

"Random boating accident?" she asked, hearing the tightly controlled anger in her own voice.

"Yeah." Fennrys snorted in disgust. "What are the odds?"

"I think it's fairly clear that someone doesn't want us getting off this island," Mason said quietly.

She sat down on a moss-covered rock at the edge of the trees, and her gaze drifted across the East River, toward the dark, glittering shapes of the towers in the city. Her father had offices in one. And a palatial penthouse apartment in another.

And what else?

There was a whole, hidden side to Gunnar Starling that Mason had never known about. Or maybe she'd always suspected it was there and she'd never been able to bring herself to wonder further. . . .

"Looks like there's a fog rolling in," she said, nodding toward where the lights of the skyscrapers were starting to shimmer with distortion, haloed in the evening light. She wasn't even sure she wanted to broach the subject. But of course she would have to eventually. It seemed there were a lot of unpleasant truths she was having to face up to all of a sudden. She wasn't sure just how much more she could handle. But she had to know.

Fennrys sat down beside her and waited.

"So tell me. As a . . . a Valkyrie, I would . . ." She hesitated, trying to frame the question in a way she could understand as she asked it. "I mean . . . what, exactly, was it my father wanted from me? What was I supposed to do?"

For a moment, she thought he wasn't going to answer her. But then he did. And she almost wished he hadn't.

"There's Valkyries and then there's *Valkyries*, Mase," he said. "Just like everything else, it's a matter of degrees. The Valkyrie that your dad was trying to make out of *you* was to be the one who would choose a third Odin son to lead the Einherjar out of Valhalla."

"A third."

"Rory, Roth . . ." Fennrys ticked them off on his fingers. "You were, it seems, supposed to be the third. A son. And when you turned out otherwise, it seems Gunnar just assumed that the prophecy was flawed. Unattainable. According to Rafe, he was on the verge of letting it go for good. But then, thanks in large part to *my* dumb ass, the rift between the worlds opened. And I could walk between them. That's when Gunnar's plans got dusted off and adjusted. If I could fetch the Odin spear for him, Gunnar could make a Valkyrie. A Valkyrie can make an Odin son." Fennrys glanced sideways at Mason from under his brows. "That's what your dad wants."

"Because, according to this prophecy, these Odin sons are needed to lead the Einherjar," Mason said, struggling to understand, even though she strongly suspected that she already did. "Lead them to what?"

"Ragnarok."

Mason closed her eyes, and all she saw was red.

Ragnarok. She had always feared that word. Harsh and guttural, it was made of sounds that stuck in the throat like a death rattle. Which, she supposed, it was. Death. Ending. Mason had never understood the myths of her forefathers. She hadn't embraced them the way Rory had—with his gruesome enthusiasm and sneering disdain for humanity—nor had she ever emulated them the way Roth had, with his silent, stoic, fatalistic approach to life. And she certainly hadn't aspired to manifest them, as it appeared now her father always secretly had.

"Ragnarok. The end of the world." Her voice echoed hollowly in her ears.

"Yeah," Fennrys said quietly. "That certainly seems to be the direction your father's pointing toward."

My father . . .

He'd promised Mason, after that time with the game—the hide-and-seek game when she'd been lost, locked in the abandoned shed for three days—that he'd keep her safe. For what? So he could sacrifice her humanity later in life to fulfill some kind of twisted global death wish? She could barely believe it. And at the same time, something about it made absolutely perfect sense.

Bastard.

For the second time in less than an hour, Mason felt as if she might actually faint. Her vision was starting to tunnel, even in the darkness, but there was no way she was going to give in to the despair that washed over her at the news of this . . . this . . .

Betrayal.

That was the only word that seemed to fit at the moment. Suddenly, Mason saw everything with a startling clarity. And she knew somehow that her mother—her *real* mother, wherever she was—had known. About the prophecy, about the fact that Mason was supposed to be born a boy. She *must* have. And she'd . . . she'd *done* something. Made some kind of bargain or willed Mason to be a girl or sacrificed herself somehow to alter that doomed outcome.

No wonder Loki had granted Yelena Starling the power of a goddess. Her mother must have had extraordinary strength of character. Or maybe Mason was just deluding herself in order to feel better. Certainly, it was only a guess, but she felt sure that in life, Yelena had done everything she could to save Mason from her prophesied fate. Because, in *death*, her mother had sent her Fennrys. For that alone, Mason would be forever grateful.

"There's irony for you," she murmured softly.

"What's that?"

"You told me that Hel—the *real* Hel—sent you to me. My *mom* sent you to me so that you could help keep me from becoming an instrument shaped for ending the world. *You.*" She smiled wanly at him. "A guy who was so eager for his own ending. And now? You're back, fighting to keep me from fulfilling the most sought-after destiny of Vikings every-where. I find that ironic."

"I probably would, too." Fennrys shrugged. "If I hadn't gotten the chance to get to know you, Mase. Some things are worth dying for. Some are worth living for. And some are both. I suspect your mom had a suspicion I might think that way about you. She struck me as pretty insightful."

Mason blinked against the sudden sting of tears that threatened. "I wish I'd met her—the *real* her—while I was in Asgard. She sounds cool."

"I can vouch for that. And I kind of got the impression that you mean everything to her, Mase," Fennrys said gently. "Stopping the end of the world notwithstanding."

"I wonder if she even knew I was there. I wonder . . ."

"Look." Fennrys reached over and took her hand in his. "If we can—I mean, when all of this weirdness has settled itself out—I promise we'll go back and look for your mom. Okay?"

Mason smiled at him, but she shook her head sadly. "I know that's never going to happen," she said. "It's okay. Thank you for saying so anyway."

Fennrys squeezed her hand tightly and said, "*Never* going to happen? I don't know if you noticed, but Asgard is in real danger of becoming my local hangout. I spend more time there than I do at my apartment. If we live through this— whatever this turns out to be—we'll go. And if we don't . . . well . . . hell." He shrugged. "We'll probably just wind up back there anyway."

Mason actually found herself laughing at that.

With the toe of her boot, she kicked idly at a small rock. The thin line of foam that marked the water's edge was only a few feet away, gleaming bone white in the darkness, and

Mason got to wondering exactly what had happened to Rafe's ferryman. She frowned and reached down with her free hand to pluck up the stone and then heaved it out into the river.

There was a moment of stillness as rings of ripples flowed outward and faded. And then, suddenly, the whole surface of the river erupted.

Only nine or ten feet from the shoreline, the lithe, shimmering figure of a gorgeous girl suddenly breached the surface of the water like a dolphin, followed by another and another. The first one's head whipped around toward them, spinning her iridescent green hair out like streamers, and Mason saw that, beautiful as she was, the sea maid's eyes blazed with a cold fire and her open mouth was full of serrated teeth. She bared them at Mason in a terrifying grimace before she dropped back into the water and disappeared beneath the surface.

"Whoa . . . ," Mason murmured, shocked to stillness by the sight of a whole school of what were clearly some kind of mermaids or sea nymphs or something. "I guess that explains what happened to Aken."

"*What*, yeah," Fennrys agreed, trying to look casual as he drew his feet back from the edge of the water. "But *why* is another matter."

"I wonder if those are Calum's psycho playmates," Mason mused tartly. "Funny . . . Cal talked about them being gorgeous, but he never mentioned the teeth."

At her side, Fennrys suddenly went rigid with silent tension.

Mason turned to look at him, but he sat there, silent, his lips pressed together in a white line. It looked as if he was about to say something, but he didn't. Mason decided not to push him. Whatever it was, he'd tell her if it was important. She turned back to where the frenzied, boiling surface of the water had turned still and calm once again.

"Cal's gonna freak when I tell him one of his new girl-friends ate poor Aken," she said.

"I . . . no," Fenn said. "He's not."

"Maybe you're right." Mason shrugged. "I can't honestly predict how he'll react to things these days. It's like I don't even know him anymore. And anyway, I don't even know if I'll get the opportunity to tell him. I don't actually think we're speaking at the moment."

"Mason . . ."

She kicked a smaller rock, which rolled to a stop just before the water's edge. "We had this huge argument right before the competition," she said, "and I really let him rattle me. It's a big part of why I lost. And . . . Fenn . . . I'm *so* sorry for taking it out on you afterward."

"Mase . . ."

"I know, I know . . ." She pushed a strand of hair back behind her ear. "It's just that it all seems so stupid now with everything else that's happening. But at the same time, I *knew* Calum was upset, and I didn't do anything to make it any better for him. I mean, maybe I really am partly to blame for what happened. I just—"

"*Mase*—" Fenn's grip on her hand tightened spasmodically.

She winced as the bones of her fingers ground together. "What is it?"

He loosened his grip, grimacing as he looked down at their

clasped hands. "Cal's . . . gone," he said finally.

Mason looked at him, blinking in confusion for a moment. She saw something in his expression that might have been guilt and thought she knew what he was talking about. He must have run into Cal at the gym after the competition. She could only imagine how *that* little conversation had gone. . . .

"It's okay," she said.

"It is?" Fennrys frowned at her.

"Fenn . . . Whatever Cal might have said to you—or you to him—I don't care. He hates me? He never wants to see me again? It doesn't matter." She smiled at him and shook her head. "I'll always consider him a friend, but it's probably for the best anyway if he wants to distance himself from me. I just seemed to keep pushing all the wrong buttons with him. And anyway, I . . . I don't feel like *that*," she said. "Like I feel about you."

A whispered groan of anguish escaped from Fennrys's lips as Mason looked up at him, her eyes shining, full to the brim with *exactly* how she felt about him in that moment. A moment that should have been perfect. She was so beautiful, her hair a gleaming dark curtain lifting on the breeze, her pale skin washed with moonlight, lips curved in the hint of a smile. . . .

She was perfect. She was *his*.

And Fennrys knew she was on the verge of saying she loved him.

All he had to do was nothing. Let her say those words that no one else had ever said to him. Take her in his arms and kiss her and forget all about telling her how brave, handsome, stupid Calum Aristarchos had died helping Fennrys as he tried to rescue Mason on the Hell Gate.

You don't have to do this. You don't have to tell her.

No, he didn't. He could just keep his mouth shut.

"Mason. I have to tell you something *else*." There had already been so many awful revelations for her to absorb, he thought. And yet, this one might be the worst. One of the beautiful things he'd discovered about Mason was that she cared more about other people than she did about herself. And she'd cared deeply for Cal.

The smile in her eyes wavered the longer he stayed silent, trying to figure out what he could say that would soften the blow. To the south, a cascade of lightning flashes illuminated the distant twisted wreckage of the Hell Gate where it clawed at the sky with broken iron fingers. Fennrys couldn't even look at it. And he couldn't bring himself to look at Mason, either.

"What is it, Fenn?" Mason asked quietly.

Fennrys took a deep breath.

"On the bridge," he said, nodding downriver. "When I got to you on the bridge, it's because Cal was the one who got me there. When Roth came to tell us what was happening, Cal insisted on coming along. . . ."

You don't have to tell her that he was a hero and got you to the train on time—and then you didn't do much of anything particularly useful. You don't have to tell her the details.

Except, yeah. He did. Cal deserved that much.

"He was driving the bike that we were both on. It was rough on the bridge, but he managed to keep it steady long enough for me to jump the train and then . . ."

"Then *what?*" The muscles in Mason's throat jumped as she swallowed convulsively.

"Then something happened. I didn't see it—Rafe told me about it afterward—but there was an accident. Cal lost control of his bike and drove off the bridge into the river. Rafe said he hit one of the girders and—"

"Where is he?" Mason interrupted. "Is he okay?"

He shook his head. "No."

"What do you mean *no?*" She grabbed him hard by the arm. Hard enough to bruise. "Who found him? Where *is* he?"

"Mason—the bridge blew up. We didn't have time to even look."

He didn't bother reminding her that he'd also been shot and fallen off a train and that Rafe almost had to carry him out of there, because in light of what had happened to Cal, that just seemed like, so what? Fennrys should have stayed. He should have been able to do something for the kid.

"But even if we had . . . Mase . . . I'm so sorry. I saw the cracks on his helmet—it must have come off in the crash—but even if he'd still been wearing it when he went over the side of the bridge . . . it wasn't a survivable fall."

"But . . . *we* died," Mason said, a desperate hope in her eyes. "And *we're* here. What if—"

"I don't think it's the same thing." Fennrys's heart felt like something was squeezing it. He would have rather punched himself in the mouth than have to say these words that made Mason look like she did in that moment. "Cal was in an accident, Mase. That's all it was."

Mason bit her lower lip and squeezed her eyes closed. Twin teardrops spilled over her lids, leaving tracks that gleamed in the moonlight. Fennrys reached out and pulled her into his lap, enfolding her in an embrace. She sagged against his chest, her knotted fists pressed against him, and he held her, smoothing her dark hair while tears ran silently down her cheeks.

After what seemed like hours, but was probably only minutes, Rafe appeared, walking toward them out of what was now full dark. He was back in his human form, his suit immaculate, not a dreadlock out of place. He seemed composed and calm, but his dark eyes held a weight of regret that hadn't been there before. And a dangerously simmering fury.

Mason lifted her head off Fennrys's chest and brushed the side of her hand across her cheeks. Rafe frowned when he saw that she'd been crying. He glanced at Fennrys.

"You told her?"

"Everything. Ragnarok, her death . . . Cal. I think that's everything."

Rafe shook his head. "It's enough. How're you holding up, Mason?"

She lifted her chin and said, "I'll live. I mean . . ."

The ancient death god held up a hand. "I know what you mean. Good."

"I'm sorry about your friend," she offered.

Rafe nodded tightly. "*I'm* sorry about your ride." Looking back over his shoulder toward the black expanse of the river, he sighed. "I wanted to get you off this rock, but for the time being, I think we'd best head back to shelter."

"Couldn't we wait here for a passing boat?" Fennrys asked.

"Maybe flag a coast guard vessel—"

"No . . . ," Rafe said, his eyes narrowing as he noticed the wispy, blurred blanket of silvery mist stretching out over the water. "It's not safe to be out in the open. Especially with that fog rolling in. I don't trust fog."

Mason suddenly paused and took a step toward the water. "Guys, I think that fog just called my name."

XVI

Heather lay sprawled on the bed in her dorm room, weighing the two crossbow bolts that Valen had given her on the subway, one in each hand. The golden one was featherlight, slender, and the metal grew instantly warm to the touch. It almost seemed to writhe against her skin, tingling with energy. The little leaden bolt, in contrast, was shockingly cold and heavy, and made her fingers ache. Heather slotted that one into the tiny crossbow and cocked the trigger. In the back of her mind, she suspected that she might have already figured out what the weird little weapon was for—especially if the guy who'd given it to her was who she *thought* he was—but she still had no idea under what circumstances she would ever actually use it.

But Heather was bored. Bored with being cooped up, bored with studying. Not that she'd been studying for *school*—she hadn't been to class since she'd gotten back to the academy— more like she'd been trying to find out as much as she could about the differences between the Greek and Roman gods . . . while trying to decide whether she believed she'd actually *met* one of them three days earlier on a subway ride from Queens to Manhattan.

So she'd retrieved the crossbow from where she'd hidden it in her underwear drawer and started messing around with it.

"Yeah," she muttered. "Because in the last couple of days, I've either crossed over a very scary line . . . or I've just completely lost my mind." She stood up and struck a gunslinger pose, pointing the strange little weapon at a picture of Cal that hung on her wall beside her door. The one she still said good night to every night when she turned out her light. Even after he'd broken up with her. Even after he'd . . .

I wish I could get you out of my head, she thought.

"What do *you* think, Cal?" she murmured, closing one eye and sighting down the crossbow at his smiling face. "Am I crazy? If I am, it's probably your fau—"

Suddenly Heather's door slammed open, crashing against the wall, and a slender, wild-eyed, purple-haired girl burst through. Heather's finger squeezed the trigger, and the leaden bolt shot from the crossbow and buried itself in Cal's picture—right in the middle of his chest.

"Holy—" Gwen Littlefield flinched violently away from the projectile that had hit its mark less than six inches from her aubergine-dyed locks. She froze, pressed up against the open door frame, her eyes white-rimmed with shock.

"Oh, hell *no!*" Heather exclaimed, just as shocked as Gwen was. "I don't believe this!"

After a moment, she recovered herself enough to throw

the crossbow onto the stack of mythology texts that lay open on her bed and cross the room to yank the other girl out of the way of the door. She glanced up and down the hallway to make sure there weren't any other students around and slammed the door closed, breathing heavily. Then she stalked back into the middle of her room and rounded angrily on the other girl.

"What the hell are *you* doing here?" she snapped.

"Looking for you," Gwen gasped, the breath heaving in her lungs. It looked as though she'd been running, and her hands and the front of her shirt were stained with dirt. And . . . blood. "I need help."

Heather could feel her own eyes growing wide at the sight, and she edged back toward the door. "With what? Dumping a body?"

"Relax . . . it's only dinner," Gwen panted, following Heather's gaze to the deep red stains marring her pale skin, almost to the elbows. "They're serving liver in the dining hall tonight. I needed to do a reading, so I stole some before they could cook it."

"Well, thanks for the heads-up," Heather said. "Guess it's Pizza Eatsa for me tonight. Again." She edged farther toward the door. "I'd invite you along, but you're probably not that hungry—"

She made a break for it, but Gwen was faster and got to the door first, jamming her shoulder up against it and holding the solid oak closed with surprising strength.

"Out of my *way*, Littlefield!" Heather yanked hard on the brass doorknob to no avail, mentally kicking herself for having forgotten to lock it after her last stealth trip to the girls' bathroom down the hall. She'd just been so preoccupied with trying not to be seen by any of her fellow dorm mates while she holed up in her room.

The thing was, she didn't actually need to go *out* for a slice. The only other living person Heather had seen in the last three days had been the Pizza Eatsa delivery guy, two nights in a row, and there were undoubtedly leftovers in at least one of the boxes sitting on her desk. Since the incident on the train, Heather had locked herself in her room, only gone out after hours, ignored the calls and texts to her cell phone, and kept the curtains drawn.

Toby Fortier had said to get back to the school. He'd said it was safe. Protected. Heather knew that it was a huge risk. That coming back to Gosforth—where Gunnar Starling was actually the head of the board of directors—was essentially hiding in plain sight. But she just didn't know what else to do.

And Toby had promised.

It was easier than she'd thought it would be to stay in the dorm undetected. Quite a few students had been called home by their parents because of the strange fact that over the last day or two, New York—a place that wasn't exactly known for its earthquakes—had been experiencing a series of mild to worrisome tremors. Add to that the Hell Gate Bridge exploding, and most people seemed to think that the city was under some kind of siege, either natural or man-made. Heather suspected that they were right about the siege, but wrong about the origins.

Most of the faculty still seemed to be hanging tight on the

campus, though—at least as far as Heather's furtive glances out bedroom and bathroom windows told her—but even at the risk of announcing her presence back at Gosforth, Heather desperately needed an excuse to flee her room just then. She just needed to get away from Gwen Littlefield.

"Damn it, let go!" She put a foot against the wall and heaved at the door.

"Heather, you have got to listen to me—"

"No! I do *not!*" Heather let go of the handle in frustration and turned on Gwen, suddenly furious. "The *last* time I listened to you"—she stuck a pointing finger right in Gwen's face—"I got kidnapped, threatened, lost one of the only real friends I've ever made in my whole sorry tenure at this prison camp they call a school, and watched my ex-boyfriend *die!* I *don't* listen to you anymore. There is nothing you can say that I have any interest in hearing whatso—"

"She's gonna kill Roth."

"I—what?"

Gwen bit her lower lip, and her hands clenched into fists under her chin. "I know how you felt about Cal. How you . . . *still* feel. I feel the same way about Roth Starling."

Heather blinked at the other girl dumbly.

"And Cal's mom is gonna kill him."

"Cal's . . ."

Heather backed off, her brow knotting in confusion. Just like the last time she and Gwen had spoken, the weirdo pixieish eggplant-hued Gosforth outcast was virtually incomprehensible at first. When Gwen had first tracked her down, days earlier, to tell her that Mason was in some kind of trouble—or at least, *about* to be—it had taken Heather the better part of an hour to figure out what the haruspex was trying to say. That was before Heather had even known what the hell a haruspex was, or that Gwen Littlefield was particularly gifted—or rather, burdened—with that unique skill set.

But once Heather had figured it all out and, more to the point, decided to *believe* it . . . enough time had been wasted and events had slotted into place anyway. The very same events that Gwen had come to get Heather's help to stop from happening. The whole exercise had turned into a colossal fail of majestic proportions. And Heather couldn't bring herself to go through something like that again. Even if it had something to do with Cal or his mom or . . .

No. She wouldn't listen to another word Littlefield had to say. That was that. As she glared at the other girl, Heather watched two of the biggest teardrops she'd ever seen gather on the bottom lids of Gwen's storm-gray eyes. They grew, finally spilling down her flushed cheeks to drop onto her shirt, where they left two perfect round spots beneath her collarbones.

Heather rolled her eyes and let out a heavy sigh. "Shit. . . ."

"Please, Heather. I didn't know who else to go to."

"Right. Because I was *so* damned helpful last time," she muttered.

Heather wilted down onto her bed and dropped her head into her hands. Her hair, she could feel as she ran her hands through it, was an unruly mess. She knew from the single time she'd bothered to glance at herself in the mirror that there were dark circles under her eyes.

"Fine. Tell me. What did you see *this* time?"

As Gwen began to speak, Heather reached over to snag a long-sleeved T-shirt from the back of her chair and yanked it on over her head. Then she raked her fingers through her hair, pulling it back into a messy bun. By the time she'd slipped into her runners and collected her jacket, and shoved her keys and cell phone into her shoulder bag, Gwen had spilled most of the, admittedly somewhat vague, details of what she'd "seen" in the liver.

"You stare at animal guts and can see the future." Heather shuddered in revulsion. "That's *seriously* messed up."

"Why do you think I'm a vegan?"

Heather did a double take and then burst out laughing at the rueful expression on the other girl's face. After a moment, Gwen started to laugh too.

"So, does any old viscera do for your little party trick?" Heather asked. "Or does it have to be, like, grade A guts?"

Gwen rolled an eye at her. "Ritually sacrificed on a marble altar is ideal."

"Are there a lot of those kicking around Manhattan?"

Gwen snorted. "I used to get deliveries from a butcher in the East Village—and yeah. He had an entire sacrificial altar setup in a locked room in the back of the shop devoted to the goddess Demeter. Marble altar, pure silver knives, statues . . . the works."

Demeter, Heather remembered from a class on the subject, was the goddess of agriculture and civilization. She frowned and glanced at the textbooks on the bed, remembering the things she'd read about the ancient secretive worshippers of

Demeter at a place called Eleusis. They were fanatics, cultish, strange.

"He supplied me with the good stuff," Gwen said with equal parts revulsion and longing. "See . . . if the offering isn't pure . . . prepared under strict conditions and, uh, really fresh . . . I get—um—interference. Static. Sometimes it's hard to tune into just exactly what's happening."

"So you could, theoretically, be wrong about all of this," Heather said.

"Yup." Gwen shrugged. "But I'm kind of a 'better safe than—'"

She broke off as the air in the room became suddenly, electrically charged.

Heather felt a moment of queasy disorientation before she realized that the walls were trembling and the floor felt as if she was standing on the deck of a ship. Another earthquake. That made eight—or was it nine?—tremors in the last twenty-four hours. Heather reached out a hand to steady herself against the wall as the overhead light began to sway and a framed picture—this one of her and Cal together, sitting waterside at his place on Long Island Sound—toppled off its perch on her bookshelf, the glass in the frame shattering as it hit the floor.

Heather glanced at Gwen, who was frowning fiercely, two deep parallel lines forming between her brows, beneath the fringe of amethyst hair.

"Yeah," she said. She didn't bother to reach out to steady herself, but just flexed her knees and rode the trembling floor like a surfboard. "It's worse in the catacombs. You can really feel it down there. And one of the older tunnels caved in yesterday, but I think it was just a dead end."

"*What* catacombs?" Heather asked.

"The ones under the school."

Gwen shot out a hand to grab one of Heather's trophies, which had tipped off the shelf, before it, too, smashed on the floor. Heather snatched it out of her hands before Gwen had a chance to read the plaque and see that it was for winning second place in some grade eight nerd-o-rama science fair.

"Some of the tunnels go pretty deep," Gwen continued, her eye line following the swift progress of a crack that suddenly zigzagged up the plaster wall, shedding flakes and dust that floated down between the two girls.

Heather walked unsteadily to the window and twitched the curtain aside an inch or two. The afternoon sky outside looked angry and unsettled. It had been like that all day, churning with storm clouds and flashes of lightning, but had yet to shed any rain on the city, and the heat and humidity was becoming oppressive.

"I've only checked out a few of the easier ones to access," Gwen said, still talking, for some reason, about catacombs. "And some of the chambers that don't have warning sigils or curse runes carved above them."

"What the hell is a 'sigil'?"

"An arcane symbol," Gwen huffed impatiently. "Magick. This is Gosforth. Don't you pay attention in class?"

Heather's glare, when she turned back from the window, was so flat it was probably comical. She was beginning to weary of this bizarre little person using words like "catacombs" and "sigils" and "runes" and "chambers" and talking about the academy like it was frickin' Hogwarts.

"What exactly were you doing crawling around a bunch of creepy old—"

"I'm living there."

Again Heather was reduced to just standing and blinking.

Gwen shrugged and brushed self-consciously at a dirt stain on her shirt. "Only for the last little while. It was Roth's idea when he knew I had to go into hiding. Things got hot, so I went underground. Literally."

"Hot . . . *how*, exactly?"

"Remember how I mentioned Cal's mom?"

"Yeah," Heather said. "What does Daria Aristarchos have to do with any of this?"

"I used to work for her," Gwen said. "The butcher I told you about is one of Daria Aristarchos's people. Devotees, really. Your ex-boyfriend's mom is, like, the high priestess of the Eleusinian mysteries cult."

And—*wow*—did that ever totally make sense all of a sudden.

Heather had always suspected that Cal's mom was one of those ravenously power-hungry types. She was a control freak to end all control freaks. And what better way to control the people around you than by claiming that you were the conduit to their gods?

Secret, mysterious, ancient gods . . .

"When I prophesied what was going to happen to Mason, Roth freaked," Gwen said. "And not just about his dad, but about all of it. All of *them*. All the heads of the Gosforth families. He thought it was too dangerous for me to work for her anymore."

"I think Roth might have been onto something there," Heather said drily, and gave Gwen a rundown of what she'd gleaned from her encounter on Gunnar's train.

"Look. All I know is that I *saw* Roth confronting Daria about something. I don't know what—the visions don't always come with audio tracks—and the next thing I see is her freaking out. Then there's static . . . and when the vision comes back online, Roth's unconscious." Gwen squeezed her eyes shut, as if she was seeing the vision replay in her mind's eye. "I get, like, a time lag . . . and then the vision changes and she's taken him somewhere. Someplace where I just *know* she's going to kill him."

"Do you have any idea where?" Heather asked.

"Somewhere . . . high up." Gwen opened her eyes and shook her head. "In the vision, I could *feel* it when another tremor hits—it's bigger than any of the ones we've had so far—and I felt as if I was surrounded by glass walls and marble columns, almost like a palace or a temple, and everything was swaying. And I was afraid that I'd fall right through the glass and out into the sky. But . . . I don't know exactly where I was. I think I could see the park—I mean, there were a lot of trees in the far distance, beyond tall buildings. . . ."

"Right." Heather thought for a moment.

Fall into the sky . . .

The park . . .

She knew where Roth was.

Reaching up, Heather suddenly yanked the leaden bolt out

of Cal's picture. She felt a corresponding twisting in her own heart at the sight of the hole it left behind. She turned and saw that Gwen was staring at the stubby little arrow in her hand.

"Is that—"

"I don't *know* what it is. Not exactly." She still wasn't sure she wanted to.

"Who—"

"I don't exactly know who gave it to me, either." She moved back over to the bed and picked up the weapon, stuffing both bolts and the crossbow into her shoulder bag. It was the only thing she had that resembled a weapon of any kind, and so she took it. Just in case. "I have some ideas."

"You should be careful with that," Gwen said in a hollow, quiet voice. "Really, *really* careful."

"Yeah." Heather offered up a brittle smile. "That's one of my ideas. Now let's go. I know where Daria has taken Roth Starling."

XVII

The sound of a boat engine drifted over the surface of the water. The moon had disappeared behind a cloud, casting the island into darkness. A rumble of thunder drowned out the engine sounds for a moment, but when it faded, they could clearly hear the growl of an outboard. And it seemed to be coming closer.

"Are you expecting someone?" Fennrys asked Rafe quietly. "Besides Aken?"

The god shook his head. "No. But clearly someone was expecting us."

Someones, Mason thought. *First Cal's mer-girl, and now this.*

She took another step forward, her head cocked to one side as she listened intently. She heard it again. A voice . . . calling softly, as if its owner didn't want to be overheard by the wrong party.

The voice was calling Mason's name.

"Mase," Fennrys hissed, grabbing her hand and drawing

her back behind a scraggly stand of trees as the narrow beam of a small searchlight clicked on from somewhere out on the surface of the water and began to sweep the margins of the beach. Rafe ducked behind a rock and motioned for them to stay hidden.

"Mason?" the voice called out again, and the sweep of the beam swung up and down the shore. The call was quiet, the voice deep, the tone hovering somewhere between wary and hopeful. "Are you there?"

Mason opened her mouth to answer, then paused. She recognized the voice now beyond a shadow of a doubt. But while she trusted her ears to identify the source, she didn't necessarily trust the source itself. Heimdall masquerading as her mother had seen to that. But she definitely recognized those gruff tones. She'd spent far too many hours getting barked at by them on the fencing piste not to.

"*It's Toby,*" she mouthed to Fennrys silently.

"*Maybe,*" he mouthed back, equally wary.

"Mason . . . ," the voice called out again. "It's Toby Fortier. If you can hear me, I'm here to help."

Mason drew a deep breath and glanced back over her shoulder at Fennrys. It was clear he had no more idea than she did what her fencing instructor was doing out in a boat in the middle of the East River at night, off the shores of North Brother Island, looking for her. Fennrys narrowed his eyes and stared hard into the darkness. Mason followed his gaze, and then she saw it: an inflatable type of boat gliding across the water's surface. She vaguely recalled from a documentary she'd once seen that the boat was called a Zodiac, and it was a preferred mode of transport for marine researchers and Navy SEALs. Then she remembered something that she wasn't really supposed to know. Toby Fortier used to be a SEAL.

The matte-black rubber craft was almost invisible in the darkness, and so was its pilot—Mason could only just make out a figure behind the handheld search lamp, clothed in black and wearing a black watch cap. She opened her mouth to call out to him, but Fennrys put a hand on her arm and a finger to his lips, gesturing for her to remain silent. Then he stepped around her and walked out toward the water, his boots crunching loudly on the gravel as he strolled casually, not attempting to hide his presence.

"Mason?" Toby called, and the beam of light swept up from Fennrys's feet to his face.

Fennrys put a hand up in front of his face to shadow his eyes and squinted into the spotlight. "Evening, Coach," he said.

"Well," Toby said, idling the motor. "You are not the first person I expected to find here, I gotta say."

Fennrys shrugged. "The feeling is strangely mutual."

Toby cocked his head to one side, and Mason could see the glint of his dark eyes as the moon made a sudden, brief appearance through a hole in the racing clouds. "I thought you were out of commission. What are you doing out here, son?" Toby asked.

"Picnic. You?"

"Boat cruise."

"I see." Fennrys paused for a moment and then asked, "What's your boot size, Coach?"

"Excuse me?"

"You heard me. Boot size. Yours. What is it?" Fennrys glanced over his shoulder to where Mason was peeking out from around the bushes. She had one hand clamped over her mouth to keep from laughing at the way Fennrys had chosen to confirm Toby's identity. Seeing as how Fenn—who'd appeared out of nowhere on the night of the raging zombie storm without the benefit of clothing or footwear and thus had been obliged to steal Toby's boots as the fencing master slept—knew *exactly* what size those clodhoppers were.

There was a pause out on the water.

And then the man in the boat chuckled and said, "I wear a twelve wide in combat boots, which you damned well know. Thanks for returning them—next time, run 'em through a shoeshine stand, will you?"

Mason exhaled a sigh of relief.

"You're probably wondering what I'm doing out here in this boat," Toby said, and Mason could almost hear the wry smile on his face.

"It had crossed my mind," Fennrys said.

"You saved my kids the night of that storm." Toby's voice was serious and quiet. "You saved me. Me, I don't care about so much. But I hate wasted potential, and my fighters are exactly that. They're also my sacred charges." Mason could see him shaking his head. "I don't take particularly well to having my ass kicked by monsters when I'm trying to do my job. And I don't like having to rely on someone else to kick monster ass back on my behalf. But that doesn't mean I'm not grateful, and it doesn't mean that I don't repay debts. I do."

"That's good to know." Fennrys crossed his arms over his chest. "But you weren't expecting to find *me* here, Coach. You just said so yourself."

"That's true. But I thought you should know that before I tell you what I am doing here. Because that reasoning is something that impacts upon my decisions here."

"Fair enough."

"I assume Mason's with you?"

"I'm right here, Toby," she said, stepping out from behind the trees and walking up to stand beside Fennrys.

They both heard Toby sigh with relief and murmur, "Thank the gods. . . ."

Mason and Fennrys exchanged a glance at Toby's particular word choice. Fennrys raised an eyebrow, and Mason shrugged.

"I'm going to beach the Zodiac. You two can climb onboard, and we'll get out of here."

"We *three*," Mason corrected him. "There's three of us here."

"Who else is—oh . . ." Toby fell silent as Rafe stalked out of the darkness to stand beside Mason, and the beam from the searchlight illuminated his decidedly inhuman form. Which Toby clearly recognized immediately. "Humble greetings, mighty Lord of Aaru, Protector of the Dead," he said, with a respectful bow of his head. "I offer myself in service to you."

"Gee," Rafe said drily. "Thanks. 'Cause it just so happens I'm fresh out of boatmen."

Mason and Fennrys exchanged another glance as the fencing master maneuvered the flat-bottomed boat up onto the ragged little beach, and Fennrys helped steady Mason as she climbed into the boat.

"The good news is," Toby said to Mason as Fennrys handed her off to him, "the fact that you're still alive is one less thing your father will want to kill me over."

Mason went stiff and instantly cold at the mention of Gunnar Starling.

"The bad news is," Toby continued ruefully, "he'll still want to kill me anyway over what I'm about to do."

"And that is?" Fennrys asked warily.

"*Not* take you and Mason directly to him. Now get in."

Fennrys climbed over the side of the boat, followed by Rafe, who shoved them off, and Toby reversed the engine, then pointed the boat downstream and steered westward. No one spoke for a few minutes as they glided across the black expanse of water. Downriver, banks of portable floodlights had been trucked onto the two severed ends of the Hell Gate Bridge, illuminating the wreckage in a wash of white light that rendered the twisted metal girders in stark black silhouette. The whole thing looked like some kind of abstract sculpture and was strangely beautiful.

And they were passing directly beneath it.

There were police and coast guard boats patrolling the waters of the Hell Gate Strait on either side of them and workers clearing debris above, but Toby kept the Zodiac's engine purring at just barely over an idle, and the little black craft slipped past utterly unnoticed. Of course, that might have had something to do with the fact that Fennrys had, for the duration of the ride, been clutching the iron medallion at his throat and murmuring. Mason figured he was drawing on some of the power of the charm's Faerie magick to keep them hidden as they swept past the patrolling boats.

A look of understanding had passed between him and Rafe as he'd begun to cast the veiling spell. The ancient god seemed grateful and more than willing to let Fennrys do some of the arcane "heavy lifting." The trip through the Between, Aken's death, and the ritual Rafe had performed for him . . . it all seemed to have taken a bit of a toll on the Jackal God. He sat in the bow of the boat, shoulders slumped and head hanging. His dreadlocks swept forward, curtaining his face.

When they were well past the Hell Gate, Fennrys sat back and looked over at Toby, who sat in the stern, steering the Zodiac. "Hey, Coach," he called out softly. "Earlier, you said you thought I was out of commission. What exactly would have led you to that conclusion?"

"Oh, I don't know." Toby took a sip from the travel mug that was his constant companion and wiped the corner of his mouth on the back of his hand. He kept his voice low, and his eyes never left the river in front of them. "Maybe it was the bullet through the shoulder. Or the cartwheel off the train. Or, y'know"—he pointed with the mug—"the bridge exploding while you were still on it."

"You know all about our little train trip then," Fennrys said.

"Of course I do." Toby grunted. "I was *driving* the train."

Mason stared at Toby, her mouth drifting open. She cast her mind back to the fencing tournament she'd so spectacularly crashed and burned in . . . and tried to remember what

Toby had said to her. How he'd dealt with it. And then she remembered . . . Toby hadn't been there.

"You missed the competition," she murmured, shaking her head in disbelief that she hadn't, at the time, even noticed. How screwed up was *that*? "It was for the Nationals and you missed it."

Toby blinked at her, as if startled by the accusation leveled at him. "I know, Mase . . . I'm sorry. You didn't get my note?"

She shook her head, mute. That whole evening—*how* long ago had it been now? a few hours? days?—seemed like a kind of fever dream. She'd been so thrown by her confrontation with Calum, by everything, even though she'd thought she'd had a handle on it all. But now, in hindsight, it seemed almost as if the entire thing had been staged to catch Mason at her most vulnerable. Like Fate had stepped in to mess her up. She wondered . . . if Toby *had* been there, would she have so totally blown the competition? Stormed out afterward and right into Rory's trap? Maybe she never would have wound up on that train in the first place. The train that Toby had been operating . . .

What. The. Hell . . .

Mason felt a stab of cold in her gut. "Wait. If you were driving the train that night—but—that would mean—"

"That I work for your father, Mason." Toby's gaze was steady and calm as he looked at her. "Yeah. I do. Sort of. And Gunnar damn well ordered me to be on duty that night. In an 'offer I couldn't refuse' kind of way." He shook his head. "You know how proud I am of you, Mase, and you know how badly I wanted to be there. For the team, but mostly for you. I wanted to see you win."

"I didn't. I lost." The dull hurt of her failure had faded into the background with everything that had happened since, but sharpened suddenly to a new stab of pain at the memory. "I imploded."

"I'm sorry." Toby's eyes never left her face. "And I'm still proud of you."

Mason felt a corner of her lip curl. "Are you *sure* you're really Toby Fortier?"

"Let's see . . . you ever even *think* of performing that badly again, Starling, and I will *bench* your lame ass for life." He grinned and then reached over and patted her reassuringly on the knee.

"Okay, Coach." Mason blinked back a sudden sting of tears.

Fennrys sat back, letting the two of them share the moment. Then he leaned forward slightly and cleared his throat. "So, you *work* for Gunnar Starling? And we just got in a boat with you?"

As he asked the questions, Mason saw Fenn's fingers twitch in the direction of the long dagger he carried. Toby saw it, too, but he didn't flinch.

"That's right," he said, nodding. "What Gunnar doesn't know—at least, I sincerely *hope* he doesn't know—is that he's not the only one I work for."

"Don't tell me," Rafe said with sour mirth from where he still sat hunched on the bow bench seat. "Daria Aristarchos?"

"No." Toby grimaced in distaste. "Not directly. I can't stand the woman, to be honest. But her ends and mine are sometimes . . . in agreement. Much as yours are, I would imagine, lord. I just don't necessarily approve of her methods. Look, my primary goal is the safety of my charges. The students at the academy. That's what I signed on to do. Keep them—keep *you*—safe. For a while, working for Gunnar Starling on the side seemed like a good way to help make that happen."

"Know thine enemy?" Mason said drily. She felt a twinge in her heart at those words.

"Until recently, I wasn't entirely convinced that he was," Toby said quietly. "Gunnar seemed like he'd pretty much abandoned the whole idea of a Norse apocalypse after your mother died, and I saw that as being a step forward for him. In some ways, Mason, I actually believe in the same things as your father. At least Gunnar believes in free will. More so than Daria and her ilk. He believes that humanity has done what it's done to itself, without much in the way of interference from the gods—for better or worse—and that we get what we deserve. The other Gosforth families—some of them— actually want to not only keep the memory of their gods alive, but bring them back into the world. So that humanity could one day worship them again."

"You know that Cal's dead, right?" Mason said quietly.

Toby, pale in the scattered moonlight, went even paler. He swore softly under his breath and squeezed his eyes shut for a moment. "No. I didn't know."

Fennrys put an arm around Mason's shoulders and did her the kindness of telling Toby for her what had happened. Mason could feel her muscles shivering beneath his arm as she struggled not to cry for Cal again.

The shadow of the Triborough Bridge cast them into a deeper darkness as they passed beneath it. Mason could hear the honking of car horns and the distant murmur of raised voices. There seemed to be a traffic backup of some kind, but she couldn't bring herself to care about something so mundane as that just in that moment.

Toby angled the craft around the southernmost point of Wards Island and aimed it toward the shores of Manhattan, revving the engine so the rubber boat surged forward.

"There's a ferry terminal and an industrial shipping jetty around East Ninetieth Street," he said. "I can tie up the boat and we can flag a cab to take you somewhere safe from there."

"You know," Mason said, trying hard to reconcile her suddenly *radically* expanded view of her coach, "I never would have thought you were the kind of guy to give all that much credence to gods and goddesses, Toby."

"My views on gods and goddesses are . . . complicated, Mase." The fencing master's placid expression shifted, his gaze clouding. "That's kind of what happens when you actually fall in love with one—*and* they fall in love back."

Mason blinked at him, speechless.

Toby shook his head and twisted the throttle on the outboard. "It's a really long story, kiddo, and it'll have to wait." He grunted and torqued the steering handle, gunning the engine. "It seems we're going to have a bit of a fight on our hands making landfall. . . ."

Toby had the nose of the inflatable boat pointed toward the city, but even though he was running the outboard motor now at top speed, it seemed as though they were making little to no headway—almost as if some invisible force was pushing them back. The current began to carry them rapidly downstream. Mason noticed that it was getting harder and harder to discern individual buildings on the Upper East Side.

The fog they'd seen earlier, gathering near North Brother Island, seemed to have moved off westward, as if drawn there by some kind of magnet. On the eastern bank of the river, the lights of Queens still shone brightly, unobscured, but all around Manhattan, a shimmering, silver-gray fog barrier was rising up from the surface of the water to hang like the fifty-foot-high battlements of a medieval fortress.

An impassable barrier between the boat and the city.

"I'm starting to understand what you meant when you said you didn't trust fog, Rafe . . . ," Mason said.

She eyed the fog bank piling up around Manhattan with suspicion. But then she noticed something even more worrying. A pale shape—no, *shapes*—moving just below the surface of the dark water, alongside the Zodiac.

Mason opened her mouth to warn her companions, but suddenly, in spite of all Toby's best efforts to steer, the boat began rotating in a slow circle, as if caught in an unseen whirlpool.

The little craft heaved up out of the water as something huge and heavy hit one of the float chambers from below. Toby was thrown backward, and the engine sputtered and threatened to stall as he clutched the rope handholds on the side of the boat, managing somehow not to tumble into the water.

A good thing, too, Mason thought, frantically grabbing for her own rope. Because not far off the port side of the boat, one of Cal's mer-girls rose up out of the water in a plume of spray. Her mouth was open wide in savage song, showing her teeth, which were like long white knives. In a flash, the vicious sea maid had closed the distance to the Zodiac and was trying to scrabble her way up over the side with her grasping, talon-tipped webbed hands. Without a second thought, Mason hauled off and kicked the creature in the head as hard as she could. The heel of her boot connected with a loud *crack*, and the nymph squealed in pain and rage and disappeared back down below the surface.

Suddenly, she surged back out of the water, snarling and thrashing, blood running from the side of her mouth, and this time Mason scrambled out of the way as Fennrys shouted for her to move. Wielding an oar like a club, he bashed the creature repeatedly over her green-haired head, punctuating his blows with angry words that echoed Mason's sentiment: "*Why* . . . does *everything* . . . that *lives* . . . in these *rivers* . . . have *fangs*?"

On the other side of the boat, Rafe picked up a gas can and smashed it down on another of the things trying to scrabble over the pontoon and into the boat. "People keep flushing expired meds down the toilet," he said, grunting with exertion. "All that stuff was bound to have adverse effects on the marine life, eventually."

"You're a god!" Mason called to Rafe as the surface of the river boiled with thrashing movement. "Can't you *do* something?"

"I'm a *desert* god!" he called back. "Water-based magick is a little beyond me!"

Still, he had a pretty good swing, and between Mason's boot heel, Fenn's devastating oar wielding, and Rafe's gas-can smashing, their assailants seemed wary about approaching again. For a long moment, everything went still. The little rubber boat still spun in a lazy circle, but the river seemed suddenly calm and empty. As silently as she could, Mason loosened her rapier in its sheath and prepared to draw.

Fennrys noticed and shook his head. "It's too close quarters for a long blade," he said in a whisper. "If you puncture the boat, we'll wind up in the river."

"That would suck," she whispered back.

"It really would." Fennrys grinned. "Take this."

He handed over the oar and drew his short sword. But when several long minutes ticked by and all was silent, she started to think that maybe she wouldn't need to use the oar, either. Toby eased himself back onto the bench seat in the stern and gripped the motor handle. He twisted the throttle, the engine revved, the boat plowed forward a few precious feet . . .

And then a geyser erupted at the bow.

Fennrys was flung forward and cracked his head against the rigid bench seat, splitting the skin above his eyebrow. Blood poured from the wound, and his face went slack as he lost consciousness. Mason caught a fleeting glimpse of a seaweed-draped nymph riding on the back of an enormous, fish-tailed, snow-white bull in the instant before she lost her footing on the slick, wet floor of the boat. The oar flew from her hand

and disappeared over the side into the black water. And then Mason followed it, toppling over the side of the boat to vanish beneath the waves with barely a cry for help.

For some strange reason, her last thought as she sank into darkness was of Cal—of his smile . . . and his laughter. And his sea-green eyes.

XVIII

The sound of waves washing the shore, lulling him with a constant, steady rhythm—like the beating of a giant heart—gave way to the insistent beeping of a heart monitor. He listened to it for a very long time before he realized that it was beeping in time with *his* heartbeat. There was cool, dry air on his face where before there had been the chill caress of water. Through closed eyes he could sense light where only moments before—or so it had seemed—there had been deep, profound darkness. He heard the sounds of gasping and realized it was his own parched throat that had made the noise. His lungs were uncomfortably dry. Arid. He was drowning in the way a fish drowns, and he felt his hands reaching, grasping at the nothingness in front of his face as if he could swim back into the watery embrace where he had felt so at home. So at peace . . .

"Easy . . ."

Calum Aristarchos felt a hand on his arm.

"Easy, son."

Strong, gentle fingers circled his wrist. Cal tried to open his eyes, but it was as if all the moisture had been sucked out of them. His eyelids felt stuck together and it was hard, painful to try to pry them open. When he finally managed the feat, everything was blurry and wavering. It seemed to take a long time for his vision to clear enough for him to be able to tell that he was lying in a bed in a room with greenish-white walls. Pale curtains billowed slightly in the breeze that came through a window, and stiff, starched sheets rubbed his skin like sandpaper as he moved weakly. Looking up, Cal saw a bag with a clear liquid hanging from a hook beside his bed. It flowed through a tube and into a needle stuck in the back of his hand.

Cal swallowed painfully. He was so thirsty.

Remembering the voice that had spoken to him, Cal turned his head away from the IV and saw that on the other side of his bed, there was a man. A stranger. At first Cal thought he must have been sitting on a very low stool, but then he caught the gleam of chrome-rimmed wheels and saw that the man was, in fact, in a wheelchair. There was a plaid blanket tucked tightly around his legs and feet.

Cal shifted his gaze to the man's face and felt a strange sense that he'd seen him somewhere before. The stranger's face, above a neatly trimmed beard, was deeply tanned and his hair, pulled back into a short ponytail at the nape of his neck, was thick and wavy, a shade of rich chestnut brown shot through with highlights. His eyes were green. Sea green.

The same color as Cal's eyes.

"How are you feeling?" the man asked, his voice a pleasing baritone.

"Where am I?"

"Hospital." The man shrugged one heavily muscled shoulder. "It's actually a specialty care facility on Roosevelt Island. They don't usually take in emergency patients, but seeing as how you washed up half-dead and mostly drowned pretty much right on their doorstep, they didn't really have much choice but to give you a bed. When I got here, I convinced them not to transfer you to a facility in Manhattan."

"And how did *you* do that?" Cal asked warily.

"Money talks." The man grinned. His teeth were almost blindingly white in his tanned face. "You know that."

Of course he knew that. Cal's family was one of the wealthiest in New York. "So you know who I am, then," he said.

The man nodded.

Cal gritted his teeth. "And who are you?"

There was a glint of wry amusement in the man's eyes. "You mean to tell me your mother didn't keep my picture on the mantel? I'm wounded."

"You're . . ." Cal had, of course, known in an instant. He knew it now, with bone-deep certainty.

"Your father. That's right, Calum." His gaze flicked away for a moment, and one hand clenched tightly for a brief instant on the rim of the chair's wheel. But when he looked back at Cal, his gaze was calm. "Don't worry. I don't expect you to call me 'Dad.' My name is Douglas—"

"I *know* your name. You're Douglas Muir."

He shrugged, unfazed by Cal's less-than-welcoming tone.

"I wasn't sure you would. It wouldn't have surprised me if Daria had banned the speaking of it in her house."

Cal's glance strayed, once again, to the blanket that was tucked tight across his father's lap. "She never said you were . . . uh."

"She doesn't know." Douglas waved a hand dismissively. "It happened after I left. Boating accident. One of the hazards of my . . . lifestyle."

"You sail?"

He laughed, a low, mellow sound. "That's how I got *here*. My sloop is moored at a jetty just south of the hospital grounds. I came as soon as I could. As soon as I got word."

Cal frowned. There was something very weird about this situation. It was all a bit surreal, and he wasn't entirely certain that he wasn't just experiencing some kind of side effect of pain medication. "No offense," he said, "but why did the hospital call *you*?"

"Hospital administration *didn't* call me. They don't yet know who you are." He wheeled to the end of the bed, plucked Cal's chart from the hook where it hung on a clipboard, and tossed it onto the bed beside him, where it landed with a thump.

Cal fumbled to pick it up with prickly-numb fingers and looked at it, his frown deepening. In the space for his name, it actually said "John Doe." In the notes section, it made reference to the scars on his face—almost fully healed—and to the injuries to his head—inconclusive as to extent, but indicative of recent trauma. Also, the chart noted the fact that Cal's lungs had been full of water when he was found, and the nurse who'd accidentally stumbled across him had had to revive him using mouth-to-mouth resuscitation and CPR.

His father wheeled back to the head of the bed. "They were pretty sure you were a goner when they first found you and—"

"What the hell do you *mean* they don't know who I am?" Cal interrupted. He was more than a little afraid now and starting to get angry. "If that's the case, then how did *you* find out I was here?"

"The girls told me."

"What girls?"

His father's green eyes glittered. "The Nereids. Daughters of the sea god Nereus. Lovely things. I believe you've made their acquaintance recently?"

Cal felt as if a sudden frost was spreading icy fingers throughout his chest.

Nereids . . .

His thoughts turned to the recent nights when he'd been home on his mother's estate on Long Island Sound. Nights spent down by the water, watching silently as dozens of beautiful girls cavorted in the waves, swimming and diving, riding on the backs of beasts that were half bull or horse or lion at the front end, half fish with scaly, silvery tails at the back. Cal remembered the feelings of longing to join them . . . the dangerous, scintillating temptation that he'd only narrowly avoided, and sometimes wished he hadn't.

The strange, dreamlike visitations had started just after he'd been injured in the attack on the school—a nightmarish encounter with monsters in a storm that had left Cal injured, his face disfigured by scars. He'd spent most of his daylight hours since trying to convince himself that the water nymphs were a product of his imagination. Some kind of coping mechanism to deal with the stress of his injuries.

And with Mason Starling's subsequent rejection of him. Because of those injuries.

You still trying to convince yourself that's what's really going on with her?

No. Not really. But it was easier to think that she was repulsed by his disfigurement, rather than to consider that maybe she just didn't feel the same way about him as he felt about her. That maybe she felt that way about someone else . . . The sudden gut-punch sensation Cal experienced every time he'd even thought such a thing was almost overwhelming. It was the main reason that when the Nereids had called to Cal a second time, he'd gone to them.

Not *joined* them—his instincts had told him that he would be forever lost if he went so far as to swim with the beguiling creatures—but rather, he'd hovered about on the fringes of the nightly gatherings. As an observer, he could forget for a time the desperate stirrings of deep longing he harbored for Mason. He could distract himself with other desires. In the beginning, it had worked. But the more he went down to the water, the more the water girls implored him with their seductive songs to stay, to join them. . . . He soon found himself torn between two equally fruitless yearnings. One of them devastating to his heart, the other . . . a danger to his very life.

"Wait . . ." Now he remembered. It all flooded back to him in a painful wave of memory and sensation. "I heard them," he murmured. "When I was on the bridge. On the bike. They were singing—and then *screeching*—in my head. It was like somebody suddenly filled my helmet with acid. . . ."

Cal remembered the sensation of scorching jealousy filling his thoughts. He'd been on the bridge, near to the waters where they swam. The Nereids had called to him and he had ignored them. Because of Mason. Because he and Fennrys were trying to save her.

The daughters of Nereus the sea god hadn't taken that very well.

Cal remembered the corrosive anger in their voices—it had set his brain on fire—and he remembered shaking his head like a dog, tearing wildly with one hand at the chin strap to get the thing off his head, as if the helmet was holding the sound in. He would have done anything to make that terrible pain go away. And then, distracted by that—and by the blinding white light that had suddenly blazed up in front of him—he remembered losing control of the bike.

Then blackness . . .

Silence . . .

Cal looked over at his father, who'd gone very still.

"They didn't mean for you to get hurt," Douglas said quietly. "They don't understand how fragile our humanity makes us sometimes. How vulnerable. They just wanted you to go to them—"

"They almost got me *killed*." Cal glared at the older man. He took a breath. "Why didn't I drown?"

"It's called Amphitrite's Kiss." Douglas's mouth bent in a one-sided grin. "If you were anyone else, it would have saved your life. As it is, the kiss just . . . awakened something already inside you. And next semester? You should really think about trying out for the swim team. You'd win every gold medal there is."

Father and son lapsed into silence, and Douglas reached over and poured Cal a drink of water from a pitcher on the table beside the bed. Cal took a grateful sip and lay back on the pillow and closed his eyes . . . And there it was again.

The distant sound of roaring tidal waves.

It hadn't been his imagination on waking. He could *feel* the distant pulse of the East River as it flowed around the contours of Roosevelt Island. He could sense the ebb and flow of the waters of Long Island Sound. And, farther still, he could reach out and, in his mind, touch the salt swell of the Atlantic. He knew that the nurse who'd found him hadn't saved him. Calum may have been suffering from the effects of the head injury he'd sustained, but he hadn't succumbed to drowning.

He *couldn't* drown. Not anymore.

His eyes flew open, and he bolted up in bed. When he turned to his father, Douglas nodded, reading in Cal's gaze that he understood. Cal could feel it in his bones. Bones in a body that wasn't entirely human anymore.

Maybe, a voice whispered in his head, *it never has been.* . . .

"This," his father said, "*this* is your mother's worst nightmare—this newfound fate of yours. You'll be even more like me now. More like your grandfather. And his grandfather." He laughed mirthlessly and shook his head.

Cal just stared at him. "I really, *really* don't know what you're talking about," he said.

Douglas sighed. "Feels a little funny to be having 'the talk' with you now, but I guess that can't be helped. Your mother, while she is devoted to the gods of her ancestors in her own . . . exceptionally dedicated ways, does not approve of those same gods, uh, *consorting* with mortals. She considers human/immortal pairings to have been the essential source of all the troubles, back in the day. She didn't know that I had Olympian blood in my veins. That my great-grandfather happened to have been a god who'd taken a shine to a mortal woman and . . . well, taken a *shine* to her. In the old stories, they talked about that kind of stuff happening all the time, but by the 1800s, it wasn't exactly common anymore."

Cal knew that he'd probably gone a bit pale. "You mean you're—we're—"

"Demigods? More like . . . *semi*-gods. Not exactly half-divine, but still. Even in minuscule amounts, god blood has a pretty potent kick to it. If your mother had suspected before we'd gotten married that I had it running through my veins, you wouldn't be here right now. But she didn't know. Hell, *I* didn't even know until I was in my twenties, and by then it was too late." Douglas shrugged. "I was already in love with Daria, and I wasn't about to let a little thing like the occasional manifestation of gills come between us. Of course, your mother figured it out eventually. When your sister, Meredith, was born, Daria suspected something was different about her, even though no one else did. She was just a perfect little baby. But when *you* arrived, it was fairly obvious. You were a child of Poseidon right down to the bright green eyes and webbed fingers and toes."

Cal glanced at his hands . . . which were perfectly normal. He raised an eyebrow at his father.

Douglas nodded. "Plastic surgery when you were two. I'm surprised she waited that long, but there wasn't a doctor she could find that would do the procedure when you were any younger. The membranes were very fine. Didn't take much to remove them. And our breed heal better than the average human, so of course, there wasn't any scarring."

Cal snorted. "I call BS on that. Look at my *face*." He couldn't quite manage to keep the acid from his voice.

"Something . . . *other* do that?" his father asked quietly, leaning forward in his chair. "Something supernatural?"

Cal nodded reluctantly.

"Thought so. But I'm betting the gash you came in with on the other side of your head—the one from the bridge accident—is probably pretty much gone already."

Cal raised a hand to the opposite side of his forehead from where the draugr's claw marks still seamed his flesh. There was a bandage there, taped to the skin just under his hairline. He peeled the whole bandage off and looked at it. The underside had a fairly large bloodstain on it, but when Douglas held a small mirror out for him to take a look, all Cal saw was a faint pinkness to the skin. Like a fading strip of sunburn. His gaze slid once again to his father's blanket-wrapped legs.

"So." He nodded. "Fishing accident, huh?"

"Big-game fish. Really big. Titanic, you might say."

"A . . . Titan?"

"One of 'em, yeah." Douglas shifted in the chair. "A lesser one, but still . . ."

"I'm sorry."

"Don't be. I had to do something useful with my life after your mother cut me out of hers. And yours. Meri, at least, still sends the occasional letter. . . ." He shrugged and waved a hand at his blanketed legs. "That's how this happened, actually. I was doing her a favor."

"And the rest of the time you just, what? Sail up and down the East River, waiting for your errant offspring to drop from bridges?" Cal tried to lighten his tone, but even to his own ears the words were laced with bitterness and bewilderment.

Douglas, to his credit, seemed prepared to shrug off his son's not-so-veiled hostility. "No," he said with a smile. "As a matter of fact, I was diving off the coast of Antigua when the Nereids caught up with me."

"Antig . . ." Cal felt his jaw drop open. "How long have I *been* here?"

"About seventy-two hours."

Cal shook his head, his patience wearing thin. "You just said your boat was docked here. There's no way you could get here from Antigua in under three days."

"You mean there's no way I could get from there to here in under three *hours*," his father corrected him. "Because that's how fast I had to move to get here in time to square things with the hospital administration."

"Hours . . . ?"

"You'd be surprised how fast a boat can move with fair winds, calm seas, and the help of a dozen sea goddesses motivated by guilty consciences." Douglas's green stare was sharp, unblinking. "Let me ask *you* something, son. What were you

255

doing on that bridge in the middle of the night? Right before it blew up?"

"I was helping a friend—wait . . ." Cal went silent as his father's words registered, and an ice-cold hand of fear lay its palm across his chest. He tried to keep the tremor from his voice as he asked, "Right before the bridge did *what*?"

"I guess *that* part of the night's festivities occurred after you fell." Douglas's mouth hardened into a straight line. "Somebody saw fit to blow the hell out of the Hell Gate."

Mason . . .

Fear spread across his chest and punched straight through Cal's rib cage to encircle his heart. What if something had happened to her? Cal wasn't sure he could live with himself if Mason had been hurt. He still felt the sharp sting of knowing that a large part of the reason she'd even been on that train, crossing that bridge in the first place, was because of him.

Because you were such an ass to her.

"Mase . . ." Cal struggled against the tight-tucked sheets. "I have to get up . . . I have to find her. She has to be okay—"

Douglas reached up and clamped iron fingers around Cal's arm, keeping him from pulling out his IV needle. "Calm down. Cal! Calm *down*. Who are you talking about? What's this all about?"

Cal swung his feet to the floor and stood, shakily, steadying himself against the side of the bed. He glared down at his father and after a long moment, when it seemed like he wasn't going to pitch forward onto his face, Douglas let go of his arm. Cal yanked off the strip of medical tape holding his IV in and pulled the needle from his hand. He felt the cessation of the hydrating drip like a swiftly ebbing tide, but he also felt strong enough to do without it.

"I was trying to help save a friend. Mason Starling—"

"Gunnar's little girl?"

"Yeah." Cal nodded. "She was on a train going over the bridge. There's this guy who was trying to stop it. . . . Look. I really don't understand everything that was happening. It's . . ." He lifted his hand in front of his face and spread his fingers wide. His father had said there would be no scars there, and he was right. But Cal could also vividly picture what his hands would've looked like with the webbing between his fingers intact. He could almost feel it. He dropped his hand to his side and looked at his father. "It's just as weird as all of this. Stuff about gods and other realms and the end of the world as we know it . . ."

"Ragnarok," his father murmured, his green eyes drifting slowly closed. "Damn you, Gunn."

"So it's true then?"

"It's the reason Gosforth exists," Douglas said. "The reason you go to school there. A long time ago, the founding—or should I say *feuding*—families, all of them dedicated in service to one ancient pantheon of gods or another, decided that their children would all grow up together. Sort of a joint hostage exchange program. Because, yes. The gods, the Beyond Realms, the monsters and the magick . . . it's all real, Calum. *All* of it. And you're a part of it now."

Cal turned and saw that his clothes had been laundered and folded and placed in a pile on a chair in the corner of his room. He walked over to it and started to get dressed.

"Where are you going?"

"I have to find Mason," he said, stuffing one foot into a leg of his jeans. In the very back of his head, beneath the sounds of waves and water that whispered through his mind, Cal suddenly heard a shriek, almost like the discordant cries of a flock of angry seagulls.

The Nereids.

Cal's gaze flew to the window. The curtains billowed and he could see, beyond trees and a rolling lawn, the slender stone finger of the old Blackwell Lighthouse that stood at the very northern tip of Roosevelt Island, its lamp lit like a candle to drive back the dark.

He heard the shrieking again—louder—and then . . .

Mason's faint, startled cry for help.

XIX

The bored-looking security guard shook himself out of his lazy slouch and cut across the lobby of the Top of the Rock. It was full of milling, vaguely disgruntled tourists, who were being turned away from the elevators that accessed the observation deck at the top of 30 Rockefeller Plaza.

"Miss Palmerston, isn't it?" he said. "Welcome back to the Rock. It's been awhile. We thought you'd abandoned us."

He just barely managed to keep his eye line from drifting south of Heather's face. She'd tugged her shirt as low as it would go and did a quick hair and makeup job in the cab on the way over. Hopefully it would prove to be enough of a distraction.

"Oh . . . Paulo," Heather said, shooting him a sly smile, having already scoped out his name badge from behind her oversize mirrored sunglasses—which she then pushed up on her head so she could turn the full wattage of her gaze on him. "Would I do such a thing? I just didn't want anyone to suspect we were madly in love, that's all. People get jealous, you know?"

She shot him a wink, and Paulo actually blushed outright. But then, as Heather breezed past the tourists, heading toward the security checkpoint that led to the elevators, with Gwen following in her wake, the guard hurried to get in front of them. "You know the observation deck is closed for the rest of the day, right?"

Heather tilted her head and gave him a questioning look.

"It's the tremors," he explained. "The earthquakes . . . you know. We've been getting a lot of sway up there. I mean— it's nothing to worry about, the building's not going to come down or anything—but, it's a little disconcerting. There was a bit of panic last time. And, uh, motion sickness."

"Ooh," Heather said. "Barfing tourists. How charming." She reached out and rested her hand lightly on Paulo's wrist. "So the deck's closed to 'gen pop.' That's fine. We're not here for the view, sweetie."

She bestowed a *knowing glance* on him and nodded at Gwen—who was playing the role of bored, sulky hot girl, crossing her arms tightly under her chest to hide the blood-stains on her hands from the cafeteria liver that she hadn't had time to wash off.

"Right," Paulo said with a wink. "Ms. Aristarchos is doing one of her exclusives up in the Weather Room. A cocktail party or something like that, right?"

"Something like that," Heather agreed.

"Anybody else and management would've canceled it along with shutting down the decks, but you know, that lady's got a lotta pull. I'll just get the guest list so I can check you off." He started to move back toward the desk. "The others have all been up there for a while. You ladies are fashionably late." He frowned faintly, glancing back at Heather's jeans and sneakers. "And just . . . a little casual?"

"We're the entertainment, sweetie." She cocked her head, her smile tight. "They already have our costumes up there." Heather felt her patience thinning and her nerves dangerously close to showing through. Their names weren't *on* any list— guest or otherwise. But then Gwen suddenly stepped forward and pressed a fingernail into Paulo's chest, keeping him from the desk.

She smiled a lazy, catlike smile and virtually purred, "And if they don't, then we'll just have to come back down and entertain *you*." She traced a little heart on his chest above his name tag, and a flush suffused his face.

Paulo went a little glassy-eyed and murmured, "Yeah, sure. Of course . . ."

Heather held her breath, hoping he wouldn't look down and see the stains on Gwen's hand. But he didn't. He just turned and escorted them to the elevators, where he activated the call button and, when the doors slid open, stepped aside to let the girls into the elevator cab. Heather blew him a kiss as the doors slid closed, and when the elevator began its ascent, she leaned against the back wall and exhaled the breath she'd been holding.

"I thought we were busted," she said, and rolled an eye at Gwen. "Way to be, there, sex kitten. Didn't know you had it in you."

Gwen, who'd gone so pale she looked like she was either going to hurl or pass out, grinned wanly. "I didn't either. Please tell me that was the hardest thing we'll have to face in all of this."

Heather bit her lip and said nothing. She watched the floor numbers climb swiftly upward and felt the palms of her hands grow slick with cold sweat. She suspected that Gwen had tapped into some kind of magick, even if Gwen herself wasn't actually aware she'd done so. Heather began to wonder if this wasn't all some kind of huge mistake. What were they going to do when the elevator doors opened and they suddenly came face-to-face with Daria and who knew who else?

"So . . . yeah. About that. It would be really helpful to know what, exactly, we *will* be facing once these doors open," Heather prompted.

"I keep telling you—I don't know. It's never that clear." Gwen frowned in frustration. "There are still things about what's *already* happened that I don't understand, because what I *know* has happened doesn't mesh with what I *saw* happening. But that's because I never see it all."

"I don't get it," Heather said, not for the first time. "What don't you see?"

"Well, for one thing, I never see what happens to *me*."

Heather snorted. "I think that's probably for the best. Who wants to know their own future?"

"I just want to know that I *have* one," Gwen said almost in a whisper.

Heather winced at the pain in Gwen's voice. She had an incredible ability. A gift. But more than that, it was a burden. "Have you ever been able to stop something that you saw?" Heather asked gently.

"No."

"Then why—"

"Does that mean that I should stop trying?" she asked fiercely, and Heather could see tears glimmering on her lashes.

Heather shook her head and looked up through the glass roof of the elevator as they climbed upward toward the sixty-seventh floor. They were almost there—at the Weather Room, an indoor observation gallery with soaring windows and its own separate terraces where New York's elite held super-swank private events, high above the city. Like the party Daria Aristarchos had thrown there just last year for Calum's eighteenth birthday.

Gwen was staring at her, waiting for an answer. Instead, Heather asked her a question of her own. "Is that why you didn't tell me about Cal?" she said quietly. "So that I'd try and help Mason and not him? Because she's Roth's sister?"

"No," Gwen said, reaching out to grip Heather's hand hard in hers. "I swear. I didn't tell you about Cal because I didn't see him die, Heather. I've *never* seen him die—"

"Stop!" Heather pulled her fingers from the other girl's grasp. "Just . . . don't do that. Don't give me false hope." She switched to a slightly less painful subject. "Can you see

Starling?" she asked. "Mason, I mean? Do you know what's happened to her?"

Gwen shook her head, a frown creasing her brow under the fringe of purple hair. "She's gone. Not . . . dead. Just *gone.*"

Heather thought about the blinding flash of light that had swallowed the train as it had thundered across the bridge. *Gone where?*

"I don't know where," Gwen said, as if answering her silent question.

The elevator made a soft *ping* sound and the doors slid open, admitting a rush of incense-sweet air. Gwen and Heather exchanged glances and stepped hesitantly out into the dim elevator lobby. There was nobody there, and the place was as silent as the grave. Through twenty-five-foot-tall windows, they could see the sweeping vistas of the city lights spilling out into the distance, but all the lights in the Weather Room were turned down low. Most of the illumination came from colored spotlights, artfully hidden behind panels of fabric that hung from the high ceiling. White couches were scattered everywhere, draped with crimson throws, grouped around low tables holding large, shallow silver bowls filled with rotted fruit. The sickly stench of decaying pomegranates and moldy, fermenting bunches of grapes was overwhelming, and Heather wanted to gag. There were razor-sharp silver sickle-shaped blades hanging suspended from the black branches of leafless olive trees scattered around the room in white marble planters. Bunches of barley stalks hung upside down, tied to marble pillars with wide white ribbons like festive garlands. Heather reached out to touch one of the feathery stalks, but

Gwen grabbed her hand, pointing to a grayish, sickly-looking growth on the barley that Heather hadn't noticed.

"Ergot," Gwen said. "It's a fungus. And it's super toxic. In ancient Europe they called it Tooth of the Wolf."

"What's it doing *here*?" Heather asked, drawing back in revulsion.

"It's also a powerful hallucinogenic. Sometimes the priests or priestesses would give it to sacrificial victims before ritually killing them— –to put them into some kind of mystic trance or something, I think."

"That's delightful."

Maybe Gwen wasn't overestimating the amount of danger Roth was really in, Heather thought. If he was even there. The hall felt deserted. . . .

"It's also widely thought to have been a key ingredient in *kykeon*, a concoction specially prepared for rites performed by participants in the Eleusinian mysteries."

Daria's little cult, Heather thought, her blood running cold.

"I guess we're in the right place, then."

"Sure. *We* are. But where's everybody else?" Gwen said, looking around. "The guard downstairs said that a bunch of other guests were already here."

Heather shrugged and walked cautiously out into the main room. The small hairs on the back of her neck rose, and she felt as though someone was watching them, even though the place was empty and echoing. The only movement came from the billowing of more white draperies at the far end of the room, where a door leading out onto the north-facing private terrace stood wide open. Heather nodded at the door, and the girls moved silently over to the exit and out onto the terrace.

The space was empty and unadorned except for a massive slab of what looked like carved black granite, table-high, supported by two stone plinths and flanked by a pair of freestanding fountains that burbled away in the corners of the terrace, the water falling musically, hypnotically, from the eyes of weeping stone maidens into marble pools.

"Oh *no* . . ." Gwen went pale. Pal*er*. If that was even possible. "Look at the altar."

"What about it?" Heather walked forward and peered at the top of the granite slab. It was decorated with a carving of a horse's head—only with snakes in place of a mane—and it was surrounded by a circle of wheat sheaves and poppies.

"This isn't just a standard meeting of Daria's Eleusinians." Gwen pointed at the stone. "It's a dedication to Demeter *Aganippe*. Also called the Night-Mare. Also known as She Who Destroys Mercifully."

"Destruction and mercy?"

Gwen grabbed her by the wrist and pulled her back inside, her voice cracking with panic as she said, "We have to get out of here! Now!"

"But what about Roth?" Heather asked, running to keep up with the other girl as she headed back toward the elevators.

Gwen didn't answer her, and Heather almost knocked her over when Gwen screeched to an abrupt halt in the elevator lobby and stood, staring up at the glass observation window of a room two floors up that overlooked the Weather Room. It was called the Breezeway, and under normal circumstances, it housed a cool interactive-display art installation—a computerized lightshow—one of the tourist attractions at the Top of the Rock. But in that moment, it looked more like a nightmarish crystal prison. All the lights in the room cycled to red, silhouetting the figure of Roth Starling—who was pressed up against the window glass above them, his limbs spread-eagled and his eyes wide . . . vacant.

His mouth was open in a silent scream.

"Roth . . . ," Gwen whispered, frozen where she stood. "What have they *done* to you?"

Heather grabbed Gwen by the arm and yanked her away, dragging her toward the nearest elevator. She stabbed wildly at the call button, but it didn't light up. She couldn't hear any indication of the elevator motor working to lift the cabs. The only sound was that of Roth's hands clawing at the glass wall above them. . . .

Heather spun around in panic, just as fifteen or twenty figures—men and women dressed in long, white, hooded robes—came gliding around a marble corner on silent feet to surround Heather and Gwen in a circle. The women each held a silver sickle blade in one hand, and they looked like they would use them without hesitation, if the girls decided to make a run for it. Heather made a grab for her purse, where she'd concealed the little crossbow, but one of the women snatched the bag from her shoulder and threw it the length of the elevator corridor, out of reach. Not that Heather even knew what she would have done with it. Two bolts against a room full of crazies . . .

Daria Aristarchos's dark eyes flashed coldly at Heather as she stepped forward and pushed her hood back from her face.

"This is unexpected," she said. "I didn't think Gwendolyn would bring along a guest, but I suppose it's only fitting. Since you loved him, you can stand witness to the consequences of my son's death." She turned back to Gwen. "While you . . . will help me protect this city from that madman, Gunnar Starling, whose son is proving himself to be so very useful to me. And such a perfect, tempting lure to draw you here."

"I won't do it!" Gwen struggled against the hands of the devotees who held her. "If you hurt Roth or Heather, I won't read the future for you anymore—I swear!"

She winced as Daria grabbed her by the face and forced Gwen to look her in the eyes. "I don't want you to just *see* the future anymore, Gwendolyn," she snapped. "I want you to *create* it. Together we will call the Miasma down upon Manhattan."

"That's a terrible idea," Gwen said through clenched teeth.

Daria smiled coldly. "You are so much more than a haruspex, I've always known that. You are a conduit. A sorceress, more powerful than even ancient Circe or Medea. Use your gifts to call down the Miasma—the kin-killer curse—and ring this island with a Sleeper's Fog. Then I will sow the dragon's teeth and keep our people safe."

Heather cried out a warning, but there was nothing she could do as one of the robed women stepped up beside Gwen and put a hypodermic needle to the side of her neck. Gwen shrieked in terror as the woman jabbed the thing into her flesh, pushing the plunger on a syringe filled with a faintly gleaming, silver-gray liquid.

The screams stuck in her throat and Gwen's expression

went slack, her pupils dilating until her eyes looked black. Heather felt hot tears of frustration and despair welling up in her eyes as Daria smiled with grim triumph, and overhead, in his glass cell, Roth Starling cried out like a lost, damned soul.

XX

The first thing Fennrys noticed once he regained consciousness was the sharp pain in his head. The second, that there was too much room in the boat. Someone was missing—

"Mason!" Fennrys shot to his feet, and the Zodiac rocked wildly as he lurched toward the empty space. "What happened? Where is she?"

"She went over!" Toby was leaning over the side, one hand thrust into the murky water almost up to his shoulder. "Mase! Mason! . . . *Shit!* I can't feel anything!" He hissed sharply in pain and jerked back from the water. His arm, dripping wet, was scored with three long, shallow gashes and the sleeve of his jacket was shredded.

"Move!" Fennrys shoved past the fencing coach, intending to launch himself into a dive—only to be tackled to the floor of the boat by Rafe. "Get the hell off—"

"Stop!" The god put a knee on Fenn's chest to pin him

down. "You can't help her dead. The Nereids are like pira-
nhas. They'll strip the meat off your bones before you even
have a chance to drown."

"But Mase is—"

"*Stop*," Rafe said again.

There was an echo of power in his voice that hit Fennrys
like a shock wave. The Jackal God's dark eyes flashed, and he
released Fennrys so he could sit up in the boat. Rafe's gaze
went out over the water that still frothed white from where
the sea bull had almost capsized them.

Rafe lifted his hand, as if he felt something in the air.
"There's something . . ."

Stillness descended like a shroud. Even Fennrys, near
panic-blind desperate to find Mason and save her, sensed it.
And—whatever it was—it stopped him cold.

"Something . . ."

Fennrys and Toby moved to flank Rafe as he stared out
over the river.

"Here."

Beneath the black-glass mirror of the water, Fennrys saw
lights. Flickering, shifting, cycling through blues and greens
and purples. Shapes moved. Shadows . . . and then something
shot to the surface from deep in the water, and a head broke
the surface.

Calum Aristarchos.

And he was carrying Mason, cradled in his arms.

The two of them rose out of the water, lifted on the back
of one of the Nereids' fantastical creatures—a cloud-silver
water-horse—and Fennrys couldn't help but notice that Cal

sat astride the animal as easily as he had a Harley-Davidson. He looked born to it. Majestic. *Different* . . .

Fennrys heard the breath whistle from between Toby's clenched teeth.

"I really wasn't expecting *that*," the fencing master said of his erstwhile student.

Cal's face was serene, the golden-brown hair swept back from his brow and dripping water onto his bare chest and shoulders. All he wore was a pair of jeans, and Fennrys saw that there was a bandage wrapped around his ribs and another one circling his left forearm. A fading rawness marked the skin on one side of his forehead—the same side as where the terrible damage to the motorcycle helmet had been. The other side of his face was still seamed with the scars left behind by that first encounter with the draugr. The claw marks showed bone white on his tanned flesh. But he still managed somehow to look . . . princely.

The heads of a handful of the mer-girls that had attacked the Zodiac popped up above the waterline, and they swam in a loose circle around Cal as he kneed his mount in the direction of the inflatable boat and gently shifted Mason in his arms so he could hand her over to Fennrys and Rafe and then climb into the boat himself. As the water-horse disappeared back under the waves, Fennrys saw that Mason wasn't moving.

Panic gripped Fenn's heart, but Cal shouldered him aside and knelt down beside Mason, lifting her head and gently lowering his mouth down over hers. He stayed like that for a good long time, and it started to look less like resuscitation and more like a lingering kiss. Fennrys was about to grab Cal and heave him back into the river when Cal sat back and pushed the dripping hair back from his forehead.

Out in the water, the Nereid that Mason had kicked in the face scowled and swam closer, a mewling, hissing sound escaping her pouting lips.

"Back off, Thalia," Cal said to her in a voice that sounded deeper than Fennrys remembered.

"Nice friends you've got there, Calum." Rafe eyed the sea maids warily. "You know they sicced a sea monster on us."

"I'm not surprised," Cal murmured, focusing his attention on Mason. "They're the ones who almost got me killed on the bridge. Nereids, I've been told, don't really get the whole 'human frailty' thing. And they don't really overthink things, if you know what I mean. They just kind of react." He lifted one of Mason's hands in his, rubbing warmth back into her blue fingers. "C'mon, Mase . . ."

"Be *careful* with her. . . ."

Fennrys reached for Mason himself and almost collapsed with relief when suddenly her whole body spasmed and she coughed raggedly, her arms flailing as she struggled to sit upright. River water trickled from the side of her mouth, and her dark lashes fluttered on her cheeks as she opened her eyes.

"Cal . . . ?" she murmured, looking up into his face. There was bewilderment in her voice.

Cal grinned down at her, and she gasped.

"Cal!" Mason shouted with joy and threw her arms around his neck. Laughing and crying at the same time, she hugged him tight, and Cal returned the embrace. He buried his hands in the long wet waves of Mason's dark hair, eyes closed as he held her close against his chest. The smile on his lips was one of pure, perfect happiness. But then he opened his eyes and Fennrys caught a glimpse of something in their depths: raw, dangerous hunger.

Fenn's flesh went even colder than from the chill of the water, and he clenched his jaw to keep from ordering Cal to back the hell off. Mason was, Fenn understood, ecstatic. She'd only found out, less than an hour earlier, that Cal was supposedly dead—killed while trying to help save her—and of course she was overjoyed to see him there, unexpectedly, impossibly alive. . . .

Fennrys noticed Rafe's gaze was locked on Cal, too. And there was a deep crease between his dark brows. He turned and shared a worried look with Fennrys. By the time they looked back to Cal and Mason, though, Cal was laughing along with her . . . the greedy, needful longing Fennrys had seen in his eyes masked behind a lopsided grin.

"I'm *okay*, Mase," he was saying. "Seriously. I got a little banged up. That's all. I've been in a hospital on Roosevelt Island for the last couple of days. Ever since the accident. But I'm okay."

"What are you doing here?" she asked. "How did you know how to find us?"

Cal tapped the side of his head, where the bruise from his fall was fading. "Just . . . couldn't get you out of my head, that's all."

Fennrys suspected he meant his heart, not his head.

It was then that Mason seemed to notice that there was

something distinctly different about her erstwhile fencing teammate. Out in the water, the Nereid who Cal had called Thalia bared her teeth at Mason again in a threatening grimace. Cal frowned and, seemingly without thinking, flicked his hand in her direction. As he did so, a rogue wavelet rose off the surface of the water and thrust the mer-girl several feet away from the boat.

"I said back *off*," Cal murmured, then turned his attention back to Mason.

"What the *hell* . . . ?" she whispered.

"C'mon," Cal said, nodding at Toby. "Let's get you back onto dry land."

Fennrys sheathed his weapon and reached out to help Mason climb up to sit on the bench seat as Cal steadied her.

"Hey, Aristarchos." Fennrys kept his tone casual. "Thought we'd lost you there a while back."

Still holding Mason by the hand, Cal said, equally casual, "You almost did. Good thing I swim like a fish."

Which, of course, explained absolutely *nothing* about how he had survived the devastating crash and plunge off the Hell Gate or why he'd suddenly shown up in the middle of the East River in such a unique fashion, but Fennrys decided to let that slide for the moment.

Mason reached out for Fennrys with her free hand, her eyes shining with happiness. Fennrys laced his fingers with hers, willing himself not to reach over and pry her other hand out of Cal's grasp. He kept a firm grip on her as she settled onto the middle bench seat beside him, and if she wondered about the suddenly possessive nature of the gesture, she didn't let on.

"You're hurt," she said, as she lifted her hand to where the gash on his head still seeped blood down the side of his face.

"I'm fine," he said, and smiled at her.

Then he looked over the top of her head at Cal, who wore a carefully composed, neutral expression. Cal turned from him to grin at his fencing coach.

"Hey, Tobe," he said. "I'd ask you what you're doing here, man, but I'm kinda getting used to people just sort of popping up unexpectedly lately."

"Calum." Toby nodded. "I'm damn glad to see you in one piece."

Cal turned then to Rafe—a little warily, Fennrys thought—and said, "Uh, hey. Nice to see you again too, there . . . Rafe? Did I get that right?"

"You did." Rafe inclined his head.

"Cool. Well, yeah." He glanced around—first at the Nereids, then at the fog bank in the distance, and then at the pale yellow ribbon of light that furled out into the darkness from the lighthouse on Roosevelt Island. "Listen . . . can you take us back to the hospital? There's someone there I want you to meet." He looked at Mason. "Someone who might help make some sense out of everything that's happening."

Mason sat on the edge of the bed in the posh health-care facility, a blanket wrapped around her shoulders, staring back and forth between Cal and . . . an older, bearded version of Cal. The father-son resemblance was undeniable, almost shockingly so. Perhaps less shocking, though, than the news that Calum

Aristarchos, Mason's one-time crush and fellow student at Gosforth Academy, was a demigod.

"More like a *semi*-god, really," Cal murmured, staring absently down at the glass of water he held in his hand.

Mason watched as the surface of the liquid began to ripple and splash and a tiny, silvery figure—a water sculpture in the shape of a slender female with long hair . . . holding a sword, rose up out of the glass and gave Cal a fencer's salute before losing cohesion in a splash back down into the glass.

"Um. Wow." Mason blinked at Cal, who only just seemed to have realized what he'd actually done—his face reddening under her gaze.

Mason looked away, glancing over to Rafe, who stood silently leaning against the door frame. She could tell, just from the way he reacted to Cal's father, that everything Douglas Muir (not Aristarchos—she'd discovered that was Cal's mom's maiden name) had said was true.

"C'mon, Mase," Cal said, looking at her from underneath the fringe of hair that swept over his forehead, "is it really that hard to believe? I mean . . . you were just in *Asgard* a couple of hours ago."

"Yeah . . . hell of a week, right?" Fennrys said.

Mason shifted her glance to where Fenn was pulling a plain white T-shirt on over his head. There was a fresh bandage on his forehead, just beneath his hairline, covering the shallow gash he'd received banging his head on the boat bench. Cal's dad had procured both bandage and shirt from the hospital staff and then sent the orderly who'd brought them on his way with instructions that Cal and his friends were not to be disturbed.

"I don't want to interrupt," Toby said, pretty obviously not giving a crap about interrupting, "but we really have to be getting back to Manhattan now."

"Good luck with that," Douglas said.

Toby raised an eyebrow at Cal's father. "I'm listening," he said.

"The fog," Cal's father said. "It's not natural."

"Told ya." Rafe shot Mason a look.

Douglas looked over at his son. "Your mother's been busy. Don't ask me how, but she's called up a Miasma curse."

It was the first time that Mason had ever heard Toby Fortier swear in a language that she didn't know. She raised a weary hand. "What's a Miasma curse?"

"It's a kind of blood magick." Toby looked as if he wanted to kick a wall in. "Brutal blood magick."

"Care to elaborate?" Fennrys asked.

Mason found it faintly comforting that Fennrys didn't know what they were talking about either as Toby and Douglas exchanged a laden glance. Douglas reached for a television remote and hit the on button. "These news reports started coming in when you were out in the river."

A harried-looking news reporter from a station in New Jersey was sitting behind a desk commenting on a sudden, widespread affliction that had swept through Manhattan in a matter of minutes, accompanied by a thick fog, that had caused virtually all the city's inhabitants to fall into a kind of torpor. Traffic cams and ATM surveillance footage showed people lying crumpled on the sidewalks or slumped over tables in restaurants. Some still shuffled erratically down the streets, like sleepwalkers. Wrecked cars from drivers who'd gone catatonic at the wheel were scattered all over the road, along with pools of blood and broken glass.

The news anchor spoke of repeated attempts to contact their affiliates in the Manhattan stations, to no avail. The National Guard and terrorist response teams had been called in. No one had any idea what was happening. But it seemed that anyone who made it inside the fog barrier—even lowered from helicopters in full protective hazmat gear and respirators—succumbed almost instantly. New York, it seemed, was under siege. Authorities had offered varying opinions as to whether it was natural, biochemical, or something else entirely. None of them had so far speculated that the attack was of a mystical origin.

Mason couldn't tear her eyes away from the screen.

Eventually, Fennrys cleared his throat and said, "So what you're saying is that we're not getting into Manhattan anytime soon."

"That's pretty much what I'm saying, yes." Toby ran a hand over his face. "It would seem that, somehow, Daria Aristarchos has managed to procure herself a kin killer. A powerful one. And she's found an even more powerful conduit to draw on all the stray magick that's been pouring into the river from the rift between the realms. She's using both to focus that power and channel it into casting a curse."

"Her conduit is probably that haruspex she's been keeping on the payroll," Douglas said.

Toby nodded. "Most likely."

Mason raised her hand again. "What's a haruspex?"

Douglas grimaced in distaste. "A diviner. Normally someone who reads the entrails of slaughtered animals to see the future."

"And yeah," Rafe added. "That *is* as disgusting as it sounds."

"*This* one," Douglas continued, "if it's the girl I think it is, can also tap into deeper magick. Much deeper. She's sort of like a supercharged sorceress . . . the kind that only comes along once in a thousand years. Like Semiramis, or Merlin, or Medea. Only in this case, this girl has never been in control of the magick, or even her ability to access it. Anything beyond reading the future in the guts of a goat, and she needs someone else to pull the strings and channel the magick into a working enchantment." He spun his chair in a half circle and wheeled over to the tall window, yanking the pale curtain aside and peering out, even though the view was mostly just darkness and trees. "That someone, in this case," he said, "would be my beloved ex-wife. The harpy."

"She is?" Rafe asked.

"Oh. Ah, no." Douglas grinned sourly. "I only meant that as an insult. She's not an *actual* harpy."

"There was one of those outside her window, though. Last week. I saw it . . . with this guy." Cal pointed at Rafe. "You were there with Mason's brother. You work with my mom."

"Not exactly." Rafe shrugged. "I maintain alliances with several factions. Mostly, I'm just trying to work at keeping the status quo. And Roth was secretly meeting with Daria because he doesn't want Ragnarok any more than the rest of us. No matter what his father thinks."

"Can somebody please cut to the chase here?" Mason stood

up and paced restlessly. "I mean, I get it. There is very suddenly a whole lot more to the world—the *worlds*—than I ever thought. I understand that Gosforth is some kind of . . . link. Hub. Whatever. I get that we're all caught up in this. What I want to know is what *this* really is." She gestured in the general direction of the city. "This Miasma. Blood curse. Whatever. I mean, okay, my dad—who is clearly a lunatic—wants to end the world. But . . . aside from stopping *him*, what does your mom want?"

"Well . . . ," Douglas answered for Cal. "Daria *does* want to avert the end of the world. But only because she wants to reshape the world in her own, particular way. And she can't do that if Gunnar Starling wipes the slate clean. Now that he's ready to pull the trigger on Ragnarok, Daria is desperate. But the same set of circumstances that give Gunnar his chance also give Daria her own window of opportunity."

"The rift between the realms," Rafe said.

Douglas nodded. "All that arcane energy leaking out into the East River. Exactly. With Manhattan completely surrounded by water, the flow of magick is circling the island like a castle moat."

"So that's why she's used the Miasma—she's drawing it up out of the water in order to isolate the island. She's turning Manhattan into an arena." Toby grunted. "Her own personal coliseum."

"A fit stage for a fight to the death," Douglas said, "between her forces and Gunnar Starling's for what is, in her mind, the noblest of causes."

"And a whole shit-ton of collateral damage means nothing

to her," Fennrys said, the words laced with disgust.

Douglas sighed. "No. It doesn't. We used to argue bitterly about it. In her dearest-held dreams, she wants to turn the mortal realm back into a place that the gods—*her* gods, the Greek gods—would once again feel welcome in. The role of humanity would simply be to serve those gods."

"All of which sounds pretty much like ending the world, too," Cal murmured. "At least, the world as we know it."

Douglas nodded. "And most people's existence in it. That is, unless they have a fondness for toiling in the service of a bunch of spoiled-rotten superior beings. No offense." He nodded at Rafe.

"None taken." The god nodded graciously. "I am rather superior. And I naturally assume the 'spoiled-rotten' was directed at others."

"I can't believe Mom would do this," Cal murmured.

"Gunnar's forced her hand. But really, his Ragnarok ambitions are just a convenient excuse for her, son," Douglas said. "A way to get her biggest competition and, to date, her strongest deterrent out of the way once and for all."

"She's using the threat of Ragnarok to convince the other Eleusinians that what *she's* doing is to protect them," Toby explained. "And all of humanity."

"If only she were that noble of spirit," Douglas said. "The reality of it is, she's always wanted this kind of power for herself. Power and revenge."

"Revenge?" Mason asked.

"Yelena Starling was Daria's best and dearest friend," Douglas said. "From the time they were kids, those two were inseparable—closer than sisters—and Daria was the one who introduced Yelena to Gunnar way back in the day. She'd never admit it, but I think she holds herself partially responsible for Mason's mother's death because of that. Of course, nowhere *near* as responsible as she holds Gunnar. And I hate to say it, you, Mason . . ."

There was compassion in Douglas's green eyes. But Mason wanted none of it just then. She knew perfectly well what she was responsible for. And what she wasn't. And most of all, she knew what she would *never* be responsible for—and *that* was the end of the world.

No way.

Her hand tightened reflexively on the grip of her sword.

"Look," she said, the crackle of barely leashed anger suffusing her words. "The Odin spear is back in Asgard. I'm *not*. Even if I was, knowing what I know now, do you think I'd actually go within a mile of that thing? So if there's no chance of me becoming a Valkyrie, then there's no reason for your crazy ex-wife to keep up with this blood magick Miasma crap. I say we find a way to get that message across to her. In the most forceful way possible. And then . . . we do the same with my dad."

"She's got a point," Douglas said to the others. He smoothed his beard, thoughtful, and turned to his son. "Mason might also be the only person who can stop her father. And I think that *you* are definitely the only one who can stop your mother."

"That's ridiculous." Cal frowned. "Even if we could somehow get to her, she's not going to listen to me—"

"Cal . . . you're the *reason* she's doing this." Douglas leaned forward in his wheelchair. "Don't you get that? The reason she's finally gone to this extreme. There have been other times in the past when she could have made a move against Gunnar—broken the Gosforth pact—but she held the peace. Now she thinks she's got nothing to lose because she thinks you're *dead*."

Cal snorted, but there was a moment of genuine pain that flashed across his face as he said, "Like she cares."

Douglas shook his head and looked away. "More than you know. Clearly. I wish . . ." He trailed away into a silence that stretched out between father and son. "Look. I know Daria. It's only when she's lost something that matters to her that she goes off the rails. And you're the thing that matters to her most. But if you can get to her . . . If she actually sees with her own eyes that you're all right . . . you might be able to talk some sense into her."

"Except that we're out here, she's in there," Toby pointed out.

Mason frowned, thinking for a moment of everything that had just been discussed. It was a lot to take in, and she still wasn't entirely certain that she understood half of it. But the thing she knew was that she needed to get into the city to stop Daria, and she needed to see her father. Even if she didn't have the faintest idea what she was going to happen when she saw him.

"Okay," she said to Cal's father. "Explain to me this whole Miasma thing. What, *exactly*, does it do?"

"The Miasma is also called the Death Sleep," he said. "In the Middle Ages, a watered-down version of the concept found its way into fairy tales like 'Sleeping Beauty,' where a whole kingdom is isolated by an impenetrable barrier and cast into a magickal slumber. In more modern times, the word 'miasma' came to mean an airborne sickness or plague. Again—something that would require isolation." Douglas had a storyteller's voice, and it was easy to think that the tale he was telling was just that. A story. A fairy tale. "In reality, it's an ancient magick that was traditionally dished out by the gods, through their mortal agents—their priestesses and priests: a punishment that would afflict an entire tribe or a kingdom—turn them into sleepers—most often as a consequence of the wrongdoings of its kings and queens, when one of them had committed an unforgivable crime. A blood crime usually. The murder of a relative was one thing that drew down the Miasma."

"Okay . . . so that would be the whole 'kin killer' thing you mentioned," Mason said, holding up a hand, concentrating hard on following the logic of the magick. "Are you saying that Cal's mom killed a family member?"

Cal was frowning deeply, and Mason knew he was probably wondering the exact same thing.

What a horrible thing to think about someone that you love, she thought.

But Douglas shook his head. "No," he said. "Daria isn't the one *being* cursed—she's *doing* the cursing—using some poor wretch who has murdered kin as the engine of her curse. New York City is a big place full of a lot of people, and some of them, I'm sure, have done some very bad things. She'd found one who's done the *worst* thing."

"What do you mean 'poor wretch'?" Mason scoffed. "Someone murders a family member, I say they deserve whatever's coming to them."

"Maybe." Douglas shrugged. "Maybe not. I prefer not to judge unless I know all the facts."

Mason felt her cheeks grow warm at the subtle rebuke. Okay, sure. That *had* been pretty judgmental. Still, she wondered if she could be forgiving under circumstances like that. . . .

"Whatever the circumstances, as Toby said, this is blood magick, and blood magick is the most powerful there is. What Daria is doing is using a kin killer as a focus for the curse, her haruspex as the instrument to implement it, and the raging magick spill in the waters around Manhattan to fuel it," Rafe explained.

Mason shuddered. "That's horrible."

"That's Mom."

Mason looked over at Cal. The water from the glass now hovered in front of him like a crystal globe, rotating slowly.

"The circumstances are stacked up pretty overwhelmingly in Daria's favor at the moment—it's like a mystical 'perfect storm'—and I don't doubt she'll be able to keep the damned thing going as long as she keeps her kin killer alive. She'll have Gunnar trapped like a rat on the island for as long as she needs to find him and take him down. And you can bet he'll put up a hell of a fight, especially now that he's had the means to bring about Ragnarok just beyond the tips of his fingers. Whatever forces he has mustered and hers will tear the city to shreds before they're done if we don't stop them."

"So, all we have to do is keep your mom from wrecking the city, and my dad from wrecking . . . everything else," Mason said. "We have some truly screwed-up parents." She rolled an eye at Douglas. "Present company excluded. I guess."

Cal's father nodded graciously in reply.

"What would happen to us?" she asked him, waving a hand in the general direction of the fog-shrouded city on the island. "In there? Would we be just as useless as all the rest of those . . . sleepers?"

Douglas smiled at her. "Well . . . as I said. It's called the Death Sleep. But together in this room, we have a god of *death*, a couple of kids who've already proven they can walk beyond the walls of *death*, my son—whose blood makes him an immortal, so no *death* there—and . . . well, and then there's Toby. Who can handle himself better than most, even under conditions such as these, I would think."

Mason turned and stared at Toby, who avoided making eye contact. He just shrugged and muttered something about "Yeah . . . perfectly able to take care of myself in a Miasma . . . been there, done that," and Mason decided that, when time allowed, she was going to have to make a point of sitting down and having a long, informative chat with her fencing instructor. Whoever—or *whatever*—he really was.

"The Miasma was created by gods, and they're not stupid," Douglas continued. "The Death Sleep was designed to act on human physiology, human weakness. It doesn't affect the divine, or the semidivine. But the real problem would be getting past the Miasma's outer wall. Passing through the barrier, even for you lot, would still be like walking through your worst nightmare. It would probably render you all temporarily psychotic, which is why I didn't recommend it." He shrugged. "But . . . if you could somehow get past that, then no, I don't think you'd have too much of a problem with the Miasma itself. The only things still sentient in Manhattan will be anything with magickal protection . . . or magickal blood."

"So at least we'd have a bit of backup with my jackals," Rafe said.

"Jackals? You mean those *wolves* you were hanging around with in the park?" Mason asked.

"A jackal *is* a wolf," Rafe said drily. "My pack have the added benefit of also being *werewolves*, thanks to me. They come in pretty handy in a fight."

"And the Miasma doesn't affect them, either?" Fennrys asked Rafe.

"Werewolf physiology is supernaturally enhanced." The god shrugged. "My magick makes those kids the next best thing to unkillable—you know . . . like werewolves."

"What's the downside?" Mason asked warily.

"They're *werewolves*, Mason." Rafe turned a flat glare on her. "Monsters."

"But . . . you *made* them that way."

"I did."

"Why?"

"Different reasons." The ancient god's face remained impassive, but his gaze clouded. "Some had debts, some made bargains. . . ."

"And you turn people into creatures of nightmare for those reasons? Because they *owed* you something?" Mason could hear the judgmental anger in her voice. She was too stressed out by everything to even try and hide it.

The clouds in Rafe's gaze grew darker. "Not anymore. Not in a very long time. And not for just those reasons. Also? I am a *god*, Mason Starling. And you'd do well to remember what I told you about gods and bargains."

His voice took on an ominous, rumble-of-thunder quality and for a moment, Mason was afraid that she'd way over-stepped a boundary. But then Rafe took a deep breath and seemed to shake off the surge of emotion.

"And that's really all I'm going to say on the subject, all right?" He grinned wanly at her. "As a god—even one in exile—it's in my job description to be occasionally inscru-table."

Mason nodded and looked away. "Okay," she said, won-dering what any of them in that room might wind up owing the ancient deity when all was said and done. Not that it mat-tered in that moment. They were running short on options.

Mason crossed her arms over her chest and looked from face to face in the room, trying her best to convey a cool-headedness and a calm rationality that she really didn't feel. She turned to the television again and the pictures that kept flashing up on the news report.

"If we can't go *through* the fog wall," she said, "can we go *over* it?"

Toby's gaze sharpened as he looked at her. He was big on strategy, and Mason had a plan.

"What are you thinking, Mase?" Fennrys asked quietly.

"The Roosevelt Island Tram," she said, pointing to the TV,

where it sat in the corner of the room, scrolling pictures of the terrifying phenomenon plaguing the city of Manhattan. In one video feed, it appeared that one of the tram cars running from Roosevelt Island directly into the heart of Manhattan was still running, even though no one was on it. "Look. No one's bothered to shut it down. The cable cars might be empty . . . but they're still running into the city."

Toby's mouth curled into a wry smile. "The elevated tram. Ha. A hit, kiddo," he said, just like he did when she scored a point in a fencing match. "That's the thing about the ancient curses. . . . They were designed to afflict *ancient* man. Used to be, all you needed was a wall high enough to keep the average human out. The cable cars ride high enough to clear the top edge of the barrier. Brilliant."

Douglas nodded in agreement, a steady, satisfied look on his face.

Two fans of the plan, Mason thought, and looked over at Fennrys.

She sensed that he was torn between supporting her idea—which would mean following her into the heart of the danger—and just plain getting her the absolute hell away from there. She understood the impulse. He'd come to Asgard for her, found her, saved her . . . and now? Now she was about to ask him to risk losing her again.

Just like you're about to risk losing him.

Even the thought of that was unbearable, and Mason shoved it brutally from her mind. "Fenn?" she said. "What do you think?"

Fennrys held Mason's gaze—a calm, unwavering faith in

her shining from his pale-blue eyes. "I think we do it. I'm in."

Mason felt the tension in her neck loosen a bit. Until she looked over at where Cal was standing rigid beside the table that held the water jug. His reaction was the exact opposite of Fenn's.

"Am I the only one here who thinks this is a supremely stupid idea?" Cal asked, his expression stiff with stubborn opposition.

A small, angry voice hissed in the back of Mason's head. How dare he? Who did he think he was? Hell—who did he think *she* was? *Weak? Small? A coward?* Well, yes. He'd already told her as much, hadn't he?

You hesitated, he'd said. He'd blamed her. Made her feel less than the warrior that she was—

Whoa. Okay . . . let's just get a grip there, Starling, she thought, suddenly aware that in her anger, she'd started to frame her participation in this . . . this whatever, this weirdness, in the kind of language that her father might have used. Warrior . . . ? No. *You're not a Valkyrie, Mason,* she chastised herself silently. *You didn't take the spear. And you're not like Cal. You're human. And you're going to stay that way.*

"Well? Am I?" Cal asked again, looking to Rafe for support.

"Yes," Mason snapped. "You are."

Fennrys put a hand up over his mouth, hiding a grin.

"Look what is happening to the city, Cal." Mason pointed again to the television. "Our school is in there—our friends. . . ."

"So what?" Cal snorted. "Bunch of stuck-up rich kids?

Don't pretend you care about any of them any more than I do, Mase—"

"Heather's in there," Toby said quietly, his gaze fixed pointedly on Cal.

Mason felt herself grow cold. "What? But I thought . . . I mean, Heather was with me on the train. Didn't she just cross over the bridge into Queens? Like you did, Toby? I thought she'd be safe. I thought . . ."

In truth, Mason hadn't had much time to think about Heather at all. Heather, who'd come to warn her at the gymnasium. Who'd proven to be a better friend to Mason than she ever would have imagined before everything that had happened. She felt a stab of guilt.

"Yeah, Mase," Toby said. "She was on the train. After the crossing, your dad wanted me to . . ." The fencing coach scowled at the memory. "Well, suffice it to say, he didn't exactly want me to let Heather go." He put up a hand to forestall Mason's outrage. "But I *did* let her go, and I sent her back to Gosforth, because I actually thought she'd be safe there. So yeah. She's in Manhattan."

"Cal?" Mason turned to where he stood, shifting his weight from foot to foot, a look of conflicted reluctance on his face. "Don't you care about her?"

"Of course I do. I just . . ."

His hands flexed at his sides as if he wanted to reach out and grab something. Mason noticed the water in the pitcher on the table near him turned suddenly cloudy and cracked as it froze solid. Cal didn't seem to notice.

"It's *dangerous,* Mason," he said in a voice as icy as the water.

"I don't want anything to happen to you."

"You don't have to worry about me," she said. "I can take care of myself."

A twist of anguish skewed Cal's handsome features and made the scars on his face pull deeper at the corner of his mouth. Mason remembered what Heather had told her about Cal's feelings for her, remembered how he'd acted toward her in the last few days . . . but all she could manage to feel for *him* was a deep pity that she wouldn't ever let him see. She could do that much for him, at least. But no more. She glanced over and saw that Fennrys's calm, blue gaze was fixed on her. His expression was placid. Trusting. He would go with her to the ends of the earth. And if it came to that, she would ask him to. Because *that* was what love was.

She turned back to Cal. "Fine. You do what you want, Calum. I'm going into the city. I'll just have to convince your mom that you really are okay."

"Right." Fennrys took a step forward and cracked his knuckles as he flexed the hand that gripped the blade sheathed at his waist. "Ready when you are, Mase."

The blood sang in her ears at the prospect of a fight, and Mason realized that she might just be developing a taste, not just for fighting—but for war. "I'm ready now."

XXI

I n the end, Cal decided to go along—which hardly surprised Fennrys—and twenty minutes later, they left the town car Douglas Muir had appropriated for them from the hospital behind at the tram station. They were also leaving Douglas behind, at his insistence. It was better not to risk putting him in a situation that could prove, under the circumstances, impassable. Fenn wasn't sure it was the best idea—Cal's father seemed to have a wealth of knowledge that might have proved something of an asset.

Then again, he thought, *Toby seems pretty up-to-the-minute on his ancient curses and the insane cults who use them. . . .*

He also recognized the possibility that should they fail, there would be a need for someone outside the city to try to find help from other sources. And if the curse spread outward from the city, Douglas had his boat and could get away. If it came to that.

"I'm worried about him."

Mason's voice nudged Fennrys from his grim contemplation. He followed her gaze back to where Cal was saying good-bye and knew it wasn't Douglas she was talking about. Like Mason, he, too, had his reservations about Calum, and about bringing him along into the city. Fennrys would've cheerfully left the kid behind to catch up on old times with his pop if he'd thought there was even half a chance Cal would agree to it. But even with his earlier protestations, it was apparent that Cal wasn't about to let Mason out of his sight. She turned to see Fennrys frowning and reached up to smooth the crease between his eyebrows. Her fingertips were cool, and he leaned into the caress.

"I'm *just* worried," she said. "Nothing more. Fenn . . . remember what I said to you back on North Brother Island? I *don't* feel that way about Cal."

"Mase . . ." He smiled and reached up to cup her face in his hands. "I *do* remember. And I'm not bothered by what you feel about Cal. I'm not bothered about how you feel about *me*. It's okay. And you sure as hell don't have to worry about how I feel about you. That isn't going to change. Whatever else happens."

Truthfully, the only thing Fennrys was worried about was what Cal was feeling in that moment. Fenn knew that Mason had been overjoyed when she'd first seen him alive, and he couldn't blame her. Her reaction was perfectly normal for anyone who'd just experienced the return of a dear friend she'd thought was dead. But that spontaneous expression of joy had translated very differently for Cal. In that moment, Fennrys had seen something spark back to life in the other boy's eyes. Something frightening. Covetous. Ruthless.

Mason, Fennrys knew, *hadn't* seen it. Not the way he had.

She was still staring up at him, and he knew he'd been silent too long. Her eyes gleamed in the darkness, sapphire blue and brimming with emotion.

"Fennrys," she said quietly, "I—"

"Shh."

He pressed a finger gently to her lips and smiled when she kissed it in response. He could tell, by the look in her eyes and by the tone of her voice, exactly what she was about to say to him. He could *feel* it. And his heart longed to hear her say the words. But instead, he just traced his finger over her lips, memorizing their shape, reveling in their softness, the smooth warmth of her mouth. . . .

"Tell me when this is over," he said. "I want you to tell me when it's just you and me. No monsters and no gods . . . No peril. Nothing but us. Okay?"

"Okay," she whispered. "No monsters, no gods. Nothing but us. I like the sound of that, Fennrys Wolf."

So did he.

But for the moment, they were headed straight into the heart of peril.

Following Toby's lead, they made their way unchallenged into the tram station and onto one of the cable cars. Pretty much everyone else on Roosevelt Island was somewhere indoors, glued to a TV and the news broadcasts, or was already making plans to get farther away from Manhattan. Crouched down on the floor of one of the Roosevelt Island tram cars, they bided their time silently as it swung through the night sky on its way into the city that lay under a spell.

When the tram car was almost over the west bank of the river, Mason pulled herself up onto her knees so that she could peek through the window. Fennrys joined her, and together they looked down onto the Queensboro Bridge, where the cars were jammed almost all the way back to Queens, and police and soldiers in heavy gear with very large guns were swarming between the vehicles. They milled about, only a few yards away from the wispy leading edge of the barrier, looking helpless and frustrated.

Fennrys held his breath as the underside of the tram carriage only *just* cleared the upper reaches of the fog battlement. Down below, inside the swirling, shimmering whiteness, he caught a glimpse of a handful of shadowy figures moving erratically within—probably some of the National Guard who'd tried to rush through and been caught in the throes of a waking nightmare, trapped inside the Miasma's outer wall. Over the grinding of the cable car's gears, the occupants of the tram heard the tortured screams that issued from more than one throat. And then sporadic bursts of gunfire.

The men and women standing around on the Queensboro all hit the deck. Pulling Mason with him, Fennrys ducked back down onto the floor of the tram. A few more moments and they were past the barrier, and the Tramway Plaza station port yawned like a gaping mouth before them.

"We did it," Mason said, with a whispered sigh of relief. "We're in."

★ ★ ★

Down on the street, Mason almost turned and climbed the stairs back up to the station to take the next cable car back to Roosevelt Island. As she stepped out of the station doors along-side Fennrys, with Cal and Toby close behind, she felt like she'd suddenly been thrust into a horror movie. The clouds over-head were a thick, oppressive ceiling, blotting out the moon and the stars, leaving the streetlights and neon signs to illumi-nate the weird landscape of a city under a spell. Inside the fog barrier's enclosure, only a thin haze of mist hung in the streets between the buildings. It sparkled and danced, swirling in eddies, obscuring and then revealing the limp, sprawled shapes of Manhattanites that lay strewn everywhere. "Nightmare" was really the only word that even came close to describing the scene that stretched out in front of them.

Mason was familiar enough with New York to be able to find her way around just about anywhere without a prob-lem. But as she stood at the corner of Second Avenue and East Sixtieth Street, the relative silence and the stillness turned the streets into unfamiliar, forbidding canyons. Suddenly she felt as if she was back in Helheim.

She glanced around at Fennrys and Cal, and Toby and Rafe. None of them spoke. They just turned down Second Avenue and headed south. Before they'd left Roosevelt Island, Douglas had suggested that the first place they look for Daria should be Rockefeller Plaza. That was where she had her offices, and where she'd been known to stage lavish "parties" that Douglas said were actually ceremonies—gath-erings of her Eleusinian followers, where they would perform their strange and mysterious rites.

They walked a few blocks before they found an SUV that was idling at the side of the road with the window down and the driver sitting, head back and mouth open, in the driver's seat. Toby opened the door and eased the man out onto the sidewalk, then got back into the SUV behind the wheel, motioning for the others to pile in.

As they drove, Fennrys and Cal had to jump out a couple of times and clear the way of sleepers who had dropped in their tracks in the middle of intersections. Toby took side streets and alleyways to avoid log jams and more than once drove through a parkette or up onto the sidewalk, but thanks to his creative navigation, they made surprisingly swift progress. Mason saw more than a few cars that had run up on the sidewalk or smashed into bus stop shelters or other cars. Most were just stopped at odd angles in the street, drivers draped over steering wheels or slumped in their seats in dull slumber, like the people on the sidewalks who lay crumpled every few feet, senseless.

Not everyone was completely unconscious. There were those who were still awake, but they were hardly alert. Mason saw one woman dressed in head-to-toe Chanel who had obviously been hit with the stupor while reapplying a bright-red lipstick—only half of her top lip was filled in, and there was a bright streak of color in a line down her chin—but she still wandered, shuffling from shop window to shop window, pausing to gaze vacantly at the displays. It was like watching a shadow play of people's lives.

It was creepy as hell.

They also passed no less than four fires, burning out of control with no fire department there to douse the blazes. And Mason knew that among the unconscious, there were bodies. People who had hit their heads, or been struck by cars, or fallen down stairs . . . There was blood in the streets. And they couldn't stop for any of it.

But there was one thing they *did* stop for. Rafe's wolves.

A few blocks away from Rockefeller Plaza, Rafe instructed Toby to turn left. They drove until they arrived in front of the main branch of the New York Public Library, where Mason recognized the sleek black shapes of Rafe's pack, sitting and standing, a few of them pacing back and forth, on the steps of the terrace. Slumped in their midst, elbows braced on his knees and head hanging, sat a young man.

"Maddox!" Fennrys shouted.

He was out of the SUV before Toby had rolled to a stop. Mason watched as the young man rose to his feet and he and Fennrys embraced. Curious, she hopped out of the SUV and followed after him. She wasn't used to seeing Fennrys with . . . well, with *anyone*, and the sight of him sharing a moment with a friend brought a smile to her face in the midst of all the grimness.

"Seven hells, Madd!" Fennrys cried. "You made it."

"Told you I would." Maddox shrugged, grinning. "What's a couple of flame-throwing monkeys to a fully equipped Janus Guard?" He turned when he noticed Mason standing there, and his eyebrows lifted. He looked from her to Fennrys and back again. "Hello," he said, and Mason got the sense that he already knew something about her.

"Mason Starling, this is Maddox. He's a Janus Guard—the same as I used to be. We spent Halloweens together killing monsters."

"Good times!" Maddox said brightly.

"He's also a bit of an idiot, but he's damn useful in a scrap." Fennrys punched him on the shoulder. "He helped me and Rafe run a bit of a gauntlet so we could get to you in Asgard. I owe him."

Mason smiled up at Maddox's handsome, boyish face, and held out her hand. "Sounds like I might owe him one too," she said, even though she remembered what Rafe had said about owing those who might one day come to collect. If Maddox had helped Fenn rescue her, she was willing to risk it. "Thank you, Maddox."

Maddox took her hand and bowed like a courtier over it. "Anything for a lovely lass," he said. "Especially one who can hold her own against this great lout. We need more of your kind in the world—"

"That's enough of that." Fennrys elbowed him sharply in the ribs. "What happened after I last saw you?"

Maddox straightened up and waved a hand in the direction of the library. He looked, Mason thought, a bit like he'd been through a flaming wood chipper. His shirt and jeans were ripped in some places and scorched in others. There was a swatch of sandy hair on one side of his head that looked crispy, and there were smudges of soot on his forehead and one cheek.

"Walk in the park," he said. "By which I mean a walk in Central Park, and you know how those walks always turned out." He turned to Mason and explained. "That's to say, I almost died."

"Okay, hero." Fennrys rolled his eyes. "Sure you did."

"Nah. Not really." He grinned.

Mason couldn't help but appreciate his casual approach to epic danger. She felt her heartbeat quicken with excitement at the thought and grinned back.

"So. All of this"—Maddox circled one finger in the air, indicating the state of the city—"some kind of curse, yeah?"

"Yeah." Fennrys nodded. "We're gonna go stop it. You in?"

Maddox gave him a look. "You have to ask?"

They turned to head back to the SUV, just in time to see a pair of centaurs, flourishing crossbows, leap over a taxi with all the grace of a couple of thoroughbred show jumpers.

"Oh, not *these* guys again . . ." Fennrys groaned.

"Okay," Maddox said. "That's not something you see every day. Even in Manhattan."

Mason felt herself staring, mouth open, in astonishment. One of the muscle-bound, bare-chested half-man horse monsters kicked a Smart Car out of the way with a casual flick of one hind leg, and the other one punched through the hood—and the engine block—of the SUV with its front hooves. The vehicle vented a cloud of steam from its shattered radiator, and Toby and Cal dove out the doors and headed up the library steps at a run.

Rafe was running too.

Mason and Fennrys and Maddox joined the sprint across the terrace. They pounded down the shallow steps onto the lower level and, one by one, vaulted the broad stone balustrade, landing on the sidewalk on Forty-Second Street.

"Keep running," Rafe shouted. "Those boys are Daria's hired muscle, and this is just a distraction. Something to keep us from getting to her. Obviously, we're getting close—"

A crossbow bolt sang past his ear and he snarled viciously, barking what sounded like an order to his pack in a language Mason didn't know. She didn't dare turn around, but heard a cacophony of yelps and growling from behind them. And then angry shouts and curses.

"Things like centaurs are the reason I wanted to pick up the pack," Rafe told her, grabbing her by the wrist and yanking her out of the way of a rogue clothing rack that was rolling down the street, a chorus line of cocktail dresses swaying limply as they passed. "They're good at this kind of business. Let them do their work."

"Hey, Rafe," Mason panted as they crouched behind a still-steaming pretzel cart while crossbow bolts flew overhead. "Your pack . . . Are they ever, y'know, *not* wolves? Jackals? Whatever you call them?"

"Sure. See that one there—with the white blaze on her forehead?" He pointed at one of the dangerously graceful animals slinking along the sidewalk in a move to flank the centaur who had stopped to reload. "She's an investment banker down on Wall Street. But we don't *need* an investment banker at the moment. We need a hundred and eighty pounds of muscle with big, sharp teeth. So that is what Honora there has so generously provided us."

Mason tried to picture the wolf in a pinstripe skirt suit.

Having seen Rafe enough times in his transitional man-wolf state, she could almost do it.

"Now," Rafe said, "*your* job is to just keep running. Get to the Rockefeller Center. Go!"

Mason shot to her feet and started running again. She risked a glance over her shoulder and saw the wolves surge toward where the centaurs were weaving through the stalled cars. The pack attacked as if with one mind, dodging the massive hooves as they came within range of the horse-men and their deadly kicks.

As a second pair of centaurs came thundering out from between two buildings, Cal made a belated half lunge for Mason. But Fennrys had already grabbed her, and he pulled her out of the way, narrowly avoiding a crossbow bolt— which would have punched straight through her sternum if she'd still been standing in that spot. For a split second, he held her against his chest. She could feel his heart beating, and she could see the sparkle dancing deep in his blue eyes as he gazed into hers and said, "I've got you."

He thrives on this, she thought. *Danger. It's like caffeine to him.*

But she also felt herself grinning in response. Her heart was pounding, too, and her skin tingled where he touched her. She could get used to this—to the danger, the rush. . . . Especially if he was there beside her to share it with.

Maddox sprinted out from between two parked cars, swinging a length of chain around his head like a lasso. He snared the arm of one of the centaurs, jerking the bow out of the creature's hand. On the other side of the street, Mason saw Toby, crouched and running, dart out behind their other attacker with a black-bladed knife in his hand. With scarily exacting precision, he hamstrung the centaur, who screamed in pain and fell crashing to the ground.

"That way." Rafe pointed to a clear bit of road.

"Come on!" Fennrys took Mason by the hand. "Toby and Maddox will cover us."

"Come on, Cal!" Mason called.

And then the three of them were off running again. She could sense, without even turning around, the frosted hostility coming off Cal as he pounded down the street beside her, but there wasn't much she could do about it. The wolves and the others kept the centaurs off their tails. All Mason and Cal had to do was make it to the Plaza. So they ran. Past Bryant Park and turning up a car-snarled Avenue of the Americas, dodging the strafing runs the centaurs would make every time they managed to evade the others. At the next corner, though, the avenue became completely impassable, with stalled cars and a crashed tour bus.

Cal turned and shouted, "This way!" and took the lead.

He led them up West Forty-Ninth Street and through the promenade in front of the Plaza's Channel Gardens, with its statues of sea gods perched on the backs of dolphins, fountaining water into the long step-pools that flowed prettily through the narrow urban park. They pounded past the statue of Prometheus and kept running until they made it back out onto Fiftieth Street, heading toward 30 Rockefeller Plaza.

Once inside, Cal led them through the halls and down to the entrance of the Top of the Rock attraction—a circular lobby that showcased a hanging art installation made up of hundreds of suspended Swarovski crystals that shattered the light into thousands of tiny rainbows and reminded Mason uncomfortably of the bridge to Asgard. Her footsteps faltered as she stared up at it, and suddenly, the crystals began to sway and bounce, tinkling against one another in a musical protest as the floor beneath Mason's feet shuddered and rumbled.

She exchanged a glance with Fennrys and Cal.

"Tremors? Like we weren't having enough fun already?" she said.

"Sure. What's a Ragnarok without a few good old-fashioned earthquakes?" Fennrys muttered.

"No. *No* Ragnarok."

Mason stomped a foot on the floor, only half jokingly. The shuddering stopped, and she shot Fennrys a look. Then she turned and headed toward the security checkpoint. There were several uniformed guides slumped over the ticket desk or collapsed in heaps on the floor. One guy was pacing in a slow circle, a look of dull confusion on his face.

"We'll need a key card to operate the elevators," Cal called after her. "He's probably got one on him."

Mason walked up to him and reached out gingerly, pulling an elevator key card out of the pocket of his jacket. He didn't seem to notice.

"Thanks, uh"—Mason read his name tag—"Paulo. I'll bring this right back."

I hope.

Paulo murmured and twitched a bit, and a thin line of drool threaded from the corner of his mouth as he mumbled something about "enjoy the ride." Mason and the others stepped past him and hurried on through the attraction toward the elevators.

She hesitated as the doors slid open. "Should we wait for the others?"

"I don't think we have the luxury of time," Cal said quietly. "The sooner my mom knows I'm alive, maybe the faster we can stop this madness."

Mason looked up at him. The coldness was gone from his gaze, and he just looked sad and resolved. She almost couldn't imagine what it must feel like for him to know his mother was behind all the chaos and hurt. But then she remembered that her father was equally to blame, and she realized she knew *exactly* how he felt. She reached out a hand and squeezed his arm, and he flashed her a brief smile before stepping through the doors. Mason and Fennrys followed.

Just as the doors were closing, Rafe's manicured hand stopped them, and the Egyptian god squeezed through the gap.

"Room for one more?" he asked, panting a little from exertion.

"Sure," Cal said. "Never know when a god might come in handy."

"The others?" Fennrys asked.

"Fine," Rafe said. "Fighting. They'll follow us up when they can."

Mason's stomach lurched as the Top of the Rock light show began in the elevator shaft, shimmering and flashing above the transparent ceiling of the cab as it began its swift ascent up to the sixty-seventh floor. She knew it wasn't just the motion or the swirling colors that were making her queasy. What they were about to face wasn't something that she had ever thought was even possible. But then, a few weeks ago, *none* of the things she had experienced recently had, to her mind, been possible. She felt Fennrys's hand rest lightly on her back for a moment, between her shoulder blades. Heat radiated out from his palm and seemed to sink through her skin to wrap her heart with comforting warmth. Whatever they were about to face, she could handle it. With Fenn at her side, she could face anything.

"Or maybe not . . . ," she murmured when the elevator doors opened and they stepped out into the dim-lit corridor to peer carefully around the corner of the marble wall. The reception area that led to the soaring hall of the Weather Room beyond looked as if it had been set-dressed to resemble an ancient Greek temple.

Rafe's nostrils flared, and he closed his eyes for a moment. When he opened them again, Mason shot him a questioning look and a corner of his mouth lifted in a slightly feral grin.

"I miss this kind of thing," he said in a whisper. "People once worshipped me the same way. It's not something you really forget."

No, Mason supposed, it probably wasn't. Still, something about the way he'd cast his gaze longingly around the elaborately decorated room with its drapes and couches and displays of putrefied fruit made her uneasy. It obviously made Fennrys nervous, too.

He took a step toward the god and said quietly, "Is this going to be a problem? Because if you think you're in any danger of . . . falling off the wagon or whatever the godly equivalent of that is, then maybe you should wait downstairs."

Rafe locked eyes with Fennrys for a long moment.

"We're here to try and stop the end of the world you've become so fond of, remember?" Fenn said with an edge of steel in his voice. "The club, the clothes, the redheaded jazz flute player?"

Rafe blinked rapidly and seemed to shake off the effects of Daria's temple. His gaze cleared and the sharp, sardonic sparkle returned to his eyes. He nodded. "A moment of nostalgia. Followed by the clarity of our immediate situation. Indulge an old god for that moment."

"By all means. You good to go now?"

"Hell yes. Let's put an end to this silliness, shall we?"

In an instant, Rafe's form blurred, shifted, and transformed into his man-god shape. And that was something Mason was beginning to find surprisingly reassuring—they had a god on their side. *Two* gods, if you counted Cal's semidivinity. What did Daria Aristarchos have?

Some kind of lame-ass gut-reading sorceress and a murderer.

The reception room, dimly illuminated by hidden spotlights, was empty, but they heard the murmur of voices, chanting, coming from beyond. Mason carefully drew back the edge of one of the drapes and saw a small sea of white-robed Eleusinian devotees. They all stood with their backs to her, absorbed in whatever was taking place outside on a glass-enclosed terrace at the far end of the room. The hoods on the robes of the celebrants were down, and Mason caught glimpses of the sides of faces. Some of them were familiar.

With a shock, she realized that these were just normal people. She looked over at Cal and saw that he had gone a bit pale. Some of the celebrants were the parents of their schoolmates at Gosforth. Mason vaguely recognized one or two faces from event nights and academy open houses. These weren't draugr. They weren't monsters. Mason couldn't hurt them. She certainly couldn't kill them. Even though somewhere in that room, if Douglas Muir was to be believed, there *was* a killer. Someone who'd not just killed, but killed family. A murderer . . . a kin slayer. The ultimate taboo. The root of the most horrific blood curses.

Who? she wondered.

She knew that Fennrys had expected that there would be violence involved in what they had to do. He'd warned her about it before they'd left the island, and she'd readily accepted that fact. She remembered, at the time, that she'd even felt a sharp, electric thrill at the thought of an actual fight. . . .

She'd felt it again a moment ago.

But then she'd recognized faces, and that thrill was doused like a snuffed candle flame. She took her hand from her rapier hilt and left the sword hanging, sheathed at her side. *Words first, Mason.*

Talking and running always trumped fighting.

The blade was a last resort.

She looked around for a way to get to the head of the ritual without having to actually fight her way through anyone and saw that, where the long white panels of silky fabric hung from the ceiling to give the room its exotic, tentlike feel, there were colored spotlights placed on the floor behind the panels.

The lights pointed upward, drenching the shimmering cloth in cycling swaths of purple and red and blue. Blood colors. Bruise colors. The decorative arrangement left a narrow gap between the Weather Room's walls and the cloth, and it provided an unobstructed causeway, bypassing the crowd of Eleusinians and ending right at the doors that led out onto the terrace at the far end of the reception space.

Mason tugged on Fennrys's arm and pointed at the passage. He nodded and turned to Rafe, who indicated he would circle around and do the same thing on the other side of the room. And then Mason looked at Cal. Their eyes locked. She gestured for him to follow her. But he just smiled grimly, and then turned and headed straight for the crowd of his mother's devotees.

XXII

Calum ignored the shocked look on Mason's face as he turned and stalked purposefully through the curtains and down toward the end of the room. As the white-clad people turned to see who had disrupted the proceedings, they all recognized him and stepped back out of his way, clearing a path to the main event. In his peripheral vision he could see shadows moving behind the cloth walls and knew it was his companions racing to flank him. That was fine. They could do an end run if they wanted. Cal was tired of avoiding. He was tired of negotiating.

"Mother!" he shouted, and his voice rang off the marble columns and high ceiling of the room. "You have to stop this. Now!"

Out on the terrace, Cal saw the tall, elegant figure of his mother stiffen and turn. Her high, sculpted cheekbones were suffused with a hectic flush of color, and her eyes were dilated to black, glittering pits. She looked as if she was caught in the throes of stark madness, and she held a bloody, sickle-shaped blade in her hand. Cal shuddered inwardly, and his steps faltered.

Then he saw where the blood on the blade had come from. Mason's brother.

Roth Starling lay sprawled on top of a black stone altar. There were long, shallow gashes on both his arms and chest, and his face was covered in a sheen of sweat and—more likely than not—tears, fallen from the eyes of the thin, pale, purple-haired girl who stood hovering over him. It took a moment for Cal to recognize Gwen Littlefield, her face distorted in a horrifying, silent scream, and tears ran in rivers down her face as she stood frozen between two marble fountains, carved in the shapes of goddesses, that wept along with her. Indeed, the only sound on the terrace in the silence after Cal's cry was the musical splashing of the fountains . . . and the ragged weeping of the girl.

Then he heard a gasp.

Cal scanned the terrace and saw Heather Palmerston on her knees in the corner of the terrace, hands tied together with a torn strip of white cloth, her pretty eyes wide and staring at him. He saw disbelief in them and realized that Heather had probably spent the last few days thinking he was dead. He saw the spark of hope flaring in the depths of her gaze and felt a searing stab of guilt in his chest. He had felt so damned sorry for Heather ever since she'd broken up with him. But none of this was his fault. . . . He shoved all thoughts of the reason *why* Heather had left him from his mind. He knew what he had to do, and he knew who he was doing it for.

"Mother!" Cal shouted again, turning back to where Daria Aristarchos stood frozen.

"What kind of trick is this?" she hissed, her eyes wide and rolling.

"It's not a trick. I'm not *dead*. I know you thought I was, but I'm not. Mom . . . please. Listen to me." He took a step forward, and his mother's fingers tightened on the hilt of the knife. "You have to stop what you're doing. I'm okay. I'm alive and everything's going to be okay. There's not going to be any Ragnarok. The world's *not* going to end. All right? I promise. But you have to—"

"*Roth!*"

The sudden cry tore from Mason's throat as she reached the terrace. Cal turned to see her staring, aghast, at her beloved older brother, and then saw her gaze ricochet from Roth to his mother. He thought he saw Mason's eyes flash red.

"What have you *done* to him?" she cried.

Mason sucked in a breath as a cold grin appeared on Daria Aristarchos's face. The answer to her question became suddenly, horrifyingly obvious. Daria wanted to take down Gunnar Starling. She'd wanted to do that for a very long time. And she wanted to use his son to do it.

But how . . .

The muscles on either side of Roth's neck stood out, taut, like steel cables as he lay on the altar, limbs thrashing heavily, and his head lolling from side to side. His booted feet kicked at the stone beneath them and his T-shirt was soaked with sweat. Crimson flowed from long, shallow cuts on the insides of both his arms, seeping down into channels cut in the black stone altar, which seemed as if it was generating the sickly gray, shimmering mist that drift out from the terrace, flowing like a ghost waterfall down the sides of the building and into the streets of the unsuspecting city, far below. The Miasma.

I don't understand. . . .

A slender, pale girl, her eyes red and weeping beneath a shock of purple hair, stood above Mason's brother, her face frozen in a mask of horror and the palms of her hands pressed flat into the blood that pooled on the altar surface.

Roth's blood.

"Roth . . . ?" Mason whispered, aghast.

His head rolled on the granite slab, and his gaze met hers. His pupils were so dilated that there was no color to his eyes. They looked as black as the polished stone beneath him. "Mase . . ." His voice broke on her name. "I'm so *sorry.* . . ."

And in that moment, Mason felt herself falling into the abyss of that gaze.

She saw what had happened, so long ago, that led to this moment.

She saw *everything.*

Caught in the circle of Roth's black, unblinking stare, Mason went instantly numb, head to foot. His gaze bored into her, and it was as if a floodgate opened from his mind to hers. The vision crashed over her, a memory of the past. Mason suddenly saw young Roth Starling—very young, ten or eleven years old maybe—the Roth she remembered from her childhood, standing in dappled sunlight beneath an old oak tree.

He'd been her big, strong, handsome brother, and she had loved him.

And so had the awkward, shy little girl who had sometimes joined them when they'd played in the quad at Gosforth. The daughter of a cook, one of Daria Aristarchos's household staff. Not a privileged, super-rich kid like all the others at Gos. Just a regular girl . . .

A girl named Gwen.

Mason had liked Gwen. So had Roth, she remembered.

In the vision, Mason saw him wearing a gift Gwen had given him—a childish, homemade charm—made out of a carved wolf's tooth strung on a braided piece of ratty purple yarn. Mason remembered the day Gwen had shyly tied it around his neck. She'd been given it, Gwen had told Roth, by the nice lady her mom worked for. The one who'd taken care of Gwen when she'd been so sick with seizures and fevered hallucinations. . . . The lady who'd gotten her a scholarship at Gosforth. Daria Aristarchos.

In the vision, the scene shifted, but Mason could still clearly make out the cross-hatched pattern carved on the wolf tooth charm—it looked like the braided seed heads of the barley stalks hanging all around her on the Weather Room's marble pillars. The markings on the tooth were glowing faintly, flickering with the same silvery-gray light that filled young Roth's gaze as he stepped through a cramped, darkened doorway . . . into a shadowed and cobwebby old garden shed, where a tiny, dark-haired figure lay curled up on a bench.

Roth had been tall for his age, serious, with dark eyes and long-fingered hands. Hands that, in Mason's vision, he pressed tightly over his baby sister's face, sealing up her mouth and nose so that she couldn't breathe. Mason couldn't see her own young face. She didn't know if the little girl with the long, dark braids had ever even awoken from the exhausted and hungry sleep she'd fallen into after being trapped for days in the abandoned shed. She couldn't remember.

She couldn't stop it. She couldn't change the past.

Roth . . . No . . .

In the vision, her brother's eyes were dark, empty. Lightless, except for the flickering threads of silvery-gray light twisting in their depths. He had no idea what he was doing in that moment—that much was clear—and Mason understood suddenly that somehow, the wolf tooth Gwen had made a present of had given Daria power over Roth. And she had used that power to make him murder his own sister.

Mason Starling had died that day.

That Roth hadn't been acting under his own power— hadn't even known he'd *done* the horrid deed—did not alter that reality. Neither did the fact that Mason had somehow come back from the dead. From that moment on, Roth was blood cursed.

And now all of Manhattan would feel the effects of that curse.

Daria Aristarchos would see to that.

Mason heard herself howl with rage, and the vision shattered.

*   *   *

Cal stood there, shocked and unsure of what was going on. One moment, Mason had gone rigid and still—almost as if she was being electrocuted—and the next she was screaming with anguish. Behind Mason, Cal saw Fennrys lunge forward to get to her, loosening the long dagger he carried in a sheath at his hip. Cal knew perfectly well that Fennrys would use it without hesitation if the situation went any further south than it already had. Fenn gripped Mason around her upper arm, but she shrugged him off violently and advanced on Daria.

Cal's mother had kicked one hell of a hornet's nest.

Oh god . . . What has she done?

"How *could* you?" The sound of Mason's voice was the sound of a heart tearing to pieces. Her face was pale and twisted with anguish, and her hand had dropped to the sword hilt at her side.

Cal's blood turned to ice as he suddenly remembered something Rafe had said on the night they crossed the Hell Gate. *Roth . . . your sister died,* the ancient god had said. But Roth had been just as shocked as any of them. Only, if Mason's brother was the one on the altar, then—

"You . . . vicious . . . *bitch!*"

Mason took another lurching step toward Cal's mother.

"We were *children.*"

Cal felt those words like a punch in the stomach. He'd always understood that his mother had a cold, calculating streak. That she could be ruthless when it came to getting what she wanted. But he'd never imagined that she could have done something like what Mason was clearly accusing her of. And yet he knew, in that instant, that she had.

Mason yanked the swept-hilt rapier half out its sheath, and the air of the terrace suddenly blazed with crimson light. Mason's face, contorted with rage, seemed lit from within.

"Mase!" Fennrys cried out.

Cal realized that the angry, deep crimson glow surrounding Mason didn't seem to be shining *on* her, but emanating *from* her.

"Mase—no!"

She drew her sword the rest of the way, and suddenly bloodred light flared on the terrace like the blaze of a funeral pyre. Forks of lightning arced overhead, and in that flash of stark illumination, Cal saw Fennrys surge forward, drawing the long dagger from its sheath and slashing the blade through the air. Slashing at *Mason*.

Before he could think, Cal reacted instinctively to protect her.

The water from the nearest fountain suddenly leaped through the air into his outstretched hand. He felt the water hit his skin as if it was electrified, and the power that had coursed, untapped, through his blood since the day he was born shaped it to his will. A sea god's will. The formless liquid solidified in his hand, turning hard and shining as forged steel. And as sharp.

In front of him Fennrys's blade flashed in the red light.

Cal reacted.

And it was only after, when the moment of confusion passed, that Cal understood exactly what had happened. That Fennrys wasn't trying to hurt Mason. He wasn't trying to kill her.

He was trying to save her.

* * *

Fennrys would have let her do it.

He saw what had been done to Mason's brother, and he understood in that moment exactly what Daria Aristarchos was responsible for. And he simply couldn't bring himself to intervene on her behalf. What would happen next would be Mason's call. It was her right.

But something . . . the *light* . . . it was terribly wrong.

"Mase!" he cried out, alarm bells going off in his head.

As she drew the blade of her sword, Fennrys caught a sudden, clear glimpse of the jewel at the center of the baldric she wore. The one he'd had custom made, set with a blue stone that he'd chosen specifically to match the color of her eyes . . .

The stone was bloodred.

It glowed violently as if it was on fire . . . an angry shade of crimson *exactly* the same color as the iron head of the spear of Odin had glowed. Fennrys cursed himself a *thousand* times for being so fatally stupid. No *wonder* Heimdall had been so quick to let them leave Valhalla without the Odin spear. No wonder he'd waited outside the hall of Asgard—where Mason had left her sword in the weapons pile at the doors of the feast hall. Whether she'd taken the spear from inside the hall or not, the *real* spear—cast with a shape-shifting glamour to look like Mason's rapier—would go home with her as well when she retrieved it from the pile. And the first time she drew the weapon, it would transform her into a Valkyrie.

Heimdall had planned the whole thing from the beginning.

How could Fennrys have been so blind?

"Mase—no!"

His brain screaming denial, Fenn lunged and drew his own blade, sweeping it in a downward arc, aiming to shatter the rapier while it was still in its sheath. Before Mason sealed her fate, and the fate of the world. Before she became a chooser of the slain.

But the weapon flew from his hand in a wild, off-kilter trajectory.

His entire body arced backward in sudden, shocked rigidity. Immobile . . .

The Fennrys Wolf looked down to see two elegantly tapered razor-sharp points of a trident protruding from the muscles of his chest and shoulder. It was the same shoulder he'd already been both stabbed and shot in.

I guess third time's the charm, he thought, with shocked detachment.

The third tine of Cal's trident had missed piercing his flesh and just sliced along the outside of his rib cage, but two was enough. Especially when Fennrys knew—could feel—that one prong had pierced his lung, and maybe, just maybe, the other had grazed his heart. The heart that belonged to the girl who stood before him clothed suddenly, head to toe, in shimmering silver armor. A winged helmet shadowed her brow above her sapphire-blue eyes. And there was a coal-black raven perched upon the blade of the Odin spear held tightly in her hand.

Fennrys felt his legs give out beneath him and suddenly Rafe was there, catching him, easing him down onto the cool, hard surface of the terrace. Mason watched from above, her expression detached, remote. Goddesslike. But then a tiny shadow of a frown ticked between her brows.

"This is not right," she murmured softly as she sank to her knees beside him.

The breath bubbling in his lungs was warm and wet with blood.

"I am the chooser of the slain. . . ."

She was the most beautiful thing he'd ever seen.

"I did *not* choose this."

"Neither did I, sweetheart," Fennrys whispered. "Not this time . . ."

He'd cheated death so many times. And now, when a Valkyrie knelt on one side of him, and a god of death knelt on the other side of him, and he felt his life truly leaving his body, he thought, *Okay. I'm content. If her face is the last thing I see . . . I'll go.*

But then, as his eyes began to drift shut, his head rolled to the side and he saw a white feather lying in a pool of his blood. The feather from the library. He'd tucked it away in his dagger sheath, and it must have slipped loose when he'd drawn the blade. The feather of his heart . . . slowly turning red with his blood.

Fennrys thought of how much he'd longed to hear Mason say the words "I love you" to him. As he slipped into darkness, he almost thought he heard her say just that. But then he realized he was wrong.

She hadn't said "love you."

She'd said "*owe* you."

And she'd said it to Anubis. God of the dead.

XXIII

The sky was on fire.

Rory stood on the balcony of his father's penthouse apartment, gazing out over a city that, far below, writhed in the grip of a twisted kind of chaos. In the room behind him, the frenzied monotony of the news reports droned on. He'd stopped watching an hour ago and had come out into the chill night air to see—to *feel*—for himself what was happening. He'd been about to go back inside when the fiery red glow had suddenly erupted from the Rockefeller Plaza's observation deck, half a dozen blocks to the north, painting the low-hanging clouds in hues of blood and flame.

Roth hadn't returned, and Rory hadn't seen his father since he'd regained consciousness. His hands flexed on the balcony railing, one warm—flesh and bone and skin—and one cool. Silver and alien. Magickal. Terrifying . . .

Powerful.

The whole night was full of power. Saturated with it, soaked to the marrow.

Rory could sense it. He closed his eyes and pictured his father's diary.

> *One tree. A rainbow. Bird wings among the branches.*
> *Three seeds of the apple tree grown tall.*
> *As Odin's spear is gripped in the hand of the Valkyrie,*
> *they shall awaken Odin Sons.*
> *When the Devourer returns, the hammer will fall down on the*
> *earth, to be reborn.*

Rory could hear the words, thrumming in his head. And he wasn't surprised when his father suddenly appeared at his side, a silent shadow in the darkness. Gunnar Starling leaned his elbows on the rail, and his gaze drifted down to Rory's gleaming fingers. He stared at them for a moment, and then he looked up and nodded to the crimson light emanating from the top of the Rockefeller Plaza tower, red as heart's blood. As father and son watched, a jagged fork of blue-white lightning stabbed down into the center of the redness. Then another . . . and a third. In the distance, they heard the rumble of thunder. Like the sound of a god waking from slumber.

"It begins," Gunnar said in a calm voice.

He turned to look at his youngest son, and Rory saw that strands of weird, golden light twisted and writhed in the depths of his father's left eye. Gunnar smiled, and it was the most terrifying expression Rory had ever seen on the face of another human being.

"The beginning of the end . . . ," Gunnar said, turning back to look out over the city. "And who was to know that all it would take was my daughter falling in love?"

ACKNOWLEDGMENTS

As this series continues rolling on down the road toward Ragnarok, I find myself in the joyous position of getting to say thank you, once again, to all the people who've helped drive this magick bus.

Jessica Regel, my wondrous agent who continues to have faith in me and my stories, is first in line for a suitcase full of gratitude. Keep on keepin' on! You and Jean Naggar and the whole staff of JVNLA rock seriously hard. Please continue.

Next, of course, is my terrific editor, Karen Chaplin, and all of the industrious, creative crew at HarperCollins: editorial directors Barbara Lalicki and Rosemary Brosnan; Maggie Herold, my production editor; Cara Petrus and Laura Lyn DiSiena, my designers; and Andrea Martin. Thanks, also, to Hadley Dyer and everyone at HarperCollinsCanada for continuing to take such good care of me up here.

My mom and my wonderful family deserve all of the love and gratitude I can give—and then some. So does my awesome collection of friends, both brilliant and bonkers (frequently both). But especially, this time around, Karl (and Nathaniel, Michelle, Mike, and Casey!) for rain-soaked, badass fighting trailer goodness.

And, once again, thank you is not enough for John. I'm running out of ways to say how much it means to have you not only on board the magick bus, but reading the maps, gassing the sucker up, squeegeeing the windshield, and frequently getting out to push when I get the wheels stuck in the ditch. So instead, I'll just give you the winky-face super-secret signal and hope that gets it all across.

As always, endless thank you to my readers, and to the fans and bloggers who get the word out about these books and make this whole crazy trip worth every mile. Keep those seatbelts fastened . . . the ride's not getting any less wild!